I0677080

VERMIN

Book One of the Stanley Cooper Chronicles

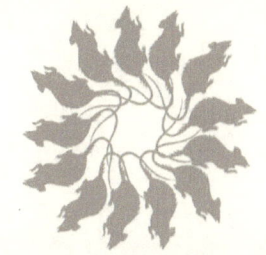

Scott A. Johnson

Copyright© 2018 Scott A. Johnson
All Rights Reserved

This book is a work of fiction. All names, places, events, organizations, businesses, characters, towns, and incidents are products of the author's imagination and used fictitiously. Any resemblance to persons living or dead is purely coincidental.

ISBN-10: 0692112472
ISBN-13: 978-0692112472

Edited by Lily K. Coy-Johnson

Printed in the USA

Second Edition

This book is dedicated to the person who gave me back my life and made me feel like me again. Thank you Katie. Without you, this book wouldn't exist.

The author would like to thank:

There is a long list of people without whom this book would never have been written. Therefore, it is from the bottom of my heart that I offer thanks: First and foremost, to my wife and children, my parents, my brother and the rest of my family for your support and love. To my friends at Evergreen, the people of Monroeville, and the Lifeless, a big heartfelt thank you is also in order. To Gary Braunbeck, Tim Waggoner and Mike Arnzen for all their wisdom, wit and friendship. To Dr. Pus, Kody Boye, and Heather McCrocklin, for putting this book together, and to all my friends, students, colleagues, and fans, without whom I wouldn't have a job. To the faculty, students, and alumni of Seton Hill University's WPF program. Also to Steve, Debi, Nomad, Buzz, and the rest of the Dread Central staff. And finally, to the great state of Pennsylvania, and more specifically, Pittsburgh, for making such a lasting impression on this Texas boy.

Addendum: In 2013, a chapter of my life closed, and it took another three years for a new chapter to start. Without the love and support of the people above, I wouldn't have made it. But there are still more. To Professor Emcee Squared, Pointy, Stiffy the Clown, Hellga, Rachel and Anton, and to everyone else in Monroeville, thank you. To Nikki, Ward, Wes, Jake, Kristin, Jarrod, Clint, Matt, Meg, Zoe, Anna, and especially my Katie, thank you, from the bottom of my black little heart. You are the family I've chosen.

The harness fit tight, and that was good. It meant the nylon straps had me by the legs and back, safe as a baby in his mother's arms. Below me, open air yawned to a backstop of concrete. My feet pressed against the glass, and I leaned into the comfort of my web cradle and raised my caulking gun. Seventy-five panes down, five hundred more to go. I heard a snap, a metallic ping, and my world went topsy-turvy. The wind whistled in my ears as my stomach tried to climb up my throat and out of my mouth. I didn't have time to think, didn't have time to react. There wasn't even time to breathe. I'm sure my heart stopped beating. I felt the first gulp from my pulse, then I swear there was nothing after that. The cable got smaller as I fell away, and all I could think was, *"Not now. Not like this. My birthday's next week, for Christ's sake. I can't..."*

My telephone woke me up from the nightmare. It was the same damned dream I'd had almost every night for five years. Falling from thirty feet up and coming down hard.

I've had the dream so often that I don't wake up screaming anymore. I wake up, wipe the sweat off my face, and go about my business. It's amazing what a person can get used to.

I cleared my throat, wiped my hand across my face, and pulled the receiver off my nightstand.

"Hello?"

"Is this Stanley Cooper?" The voice on the other end of the line was female, shaking and scared.

"Yeah, this is Cooper," I yawned. A call from some random stranger wasn't how I wanted to start my day.

"Mister Cooper, I... You..."

I get stammering phone calls a lot. For some reason, people feel embarrassed about calling for certain kinds of help. No one feels embarrassed about calling doctor or a priest, but for some reason people feel nervous about calling someone like me, like maybe the neighbors will hear and think they're crazy or something.

"Something I can do for you, Miss?"

My tone must've put her off, or let her know that I was tired of the stuttering bit. Lack of sleep makes it hard for me to mask the morning grumpies.

"I'm sorry," she said. "This was a mistake. I thought... Since you helped the McNeils..."

The name made my stomach roll and my eyes snap open. Memories of yellow eyes and a voice that didn't belong to a twelve-year-old girl flashed through my mind.

"Hold on," I said. "Don't hang up."

I cupped my hand over the receiver and sat up on the edge of my bed. I cleared my throat a couple of times as I picked up the pen and pad from beside the telephone.

"Ma'am? Are you still there?"

There was silence on the line while she debated hanging up.

"I'm here," she said.

"How can I help you?"

"I don't want to discuss this over the telephone." No one ever did. Everyone preferred to meet face to face.

"Can you meet me at the Carnegie Library in an hour?"

"Sure," I said. "You didn't tell me your name."

"Shannon," she said. "I'll be waiting by the main entrance." The line went dead.

Philosophers and songwriters often write about finding the silver lining in every cloud. The good in the bad, that sort of thing. I'm not talking about real philosophical geniuses like Plato or Ozzy Osbourne here, but pop-philosophers like Dr. Phil or people who write show tunes. Essentially, they're made up of the same type of Pollyanna people. On the other side of the coin are people who point out that there is a slight amount of tragedy in every good thing that happens. We found a cure for cancer, but think of all the poor test animals who died to find it, that sort of thing. Optimists on one side, pessimists on the other, which leaves people like me somewhere in the middle.

I died.

I got better.

That's really the only way I can describe my situation, and both good and bad came from my untimely passing. The good news came in the form of a check from the company that killed me. It was enough that I didn't really have to work again if I didn't want to. Not enough to live in luxury, but enough to buy an apartment in Pittsburgh, pay off my car, and afford cable and a few other creature comforts. For anything else, I needed a steady income. Not much, but enough to support my video game habit and keep me in imported horror movies.

I also see dead people.

I'm not sure if that's a good or bad point really, but it's a fact. It isn't as if I see cadavers everywhere. It's more like I walk into a place and every restless soul that's ever died there comes out to meet me. I'm pretty sure it has something to do with my own passing and returning from the other side, like they want to meet the guy who made it out. The trouble is, most of them look just like they did when they died. It doesn't make for very happy dinner conversation.

I don't advertise my abilities. I never hung a shingle out by the roadside or put an ad in the yellow pages. People pass me on the street all the time and never bat an eye, but people find me all the same. A friend of a friend, an acquaintance of a former client, somehow they all find me, and they all ask for my help. And when a person comes to me, quaking in fear and begging for my help, I can't turn them down. For the most part, they're looking for closure or they want someone to tell them that their house is haunted by more than banging pipes and faulty wiring. Still, every now and then, someone finds me who really needs help. People like the McNeils, or maybe this Shannon person.

The Carnegie Library is the second most popular place where people like to meet me. The first is a bar on Carson Street named "The Copper Tank." They usually choose the Tank because there are so many people that they're unlikely to be noticed. They choose the library for the same reason. I prefer the Tank because the library doesn't serve beer, but some folks are more comfortable surrounded by musty books than by hormonal college students. Go figure.

I came up from the parking garage into the cold February air and saw her straight away. A long black winter coat pulled tight around her shivering frame, hair coiffed just perfectly in a high golden mound, and a face full of thick makeup matched the quivering voice on the telephone. I could also tell that she hadn't clue one of what I looked like. Every time she saw a tall, muscular fellow pass by, she looked as if she wanted to introduce herself. The hero type was what she expected, with just the right mix of brawn and beauty. I'd be a serious disappointment.

Unlike the movie heroes who are built like college athletes and have charming smiles, I'm short and a little dumpy. I don't have chiseled features, but a round face with a pixie-nose that looks sharp enough cut glass. My hair isn't quite long enough to pull back yet, but is too long to be manageable, which gives me a crazed look even when the wind isn't blowing. A blustery day in February makes me look positively deranged.

I pulled my coat snug against the wind and made my way quickly to the woman.

"Are you Shannon?"

As the woman turned to face me, her face melted into a mask of horror.

"I don't have any money!" she shrieked. "Get away from me or I'll call the police!"

"Mister Cooper?"

I turned away from the recoiling woman to see a younger girl in fatigue pants and sneakers rise from the bench. Her sandy-blonde hair was pulled back from her face in a loose knot to reveal freckles and lines of worry. Over her Duquesne University sweatshirt, she wore a Navy surplus pea coat.

I turned back toward the other woman, who seemed to regard me with more disgust than fear. "Excuse me," I said.

"Mister Cooper?"

"You must be Shannon. Hi. Stan Cooper."

"Can we go inside, please?" The way her eyes darted around, it was as if she were afraid she was being watched. "It's freezing out here."

I shrugged and gestured for her to lead the way. Once inside, she made her way to a private study carrel and closed the door behind us.

"I don't really know where to begin," she said. "I don't really even believe in all this stuff myself."

"Why don't you just tell me what's going on?"

"I feel like I'm losing my mind is what's going on," she said, a mixed laugh and sob catching in her throat. "I think my house is haunted, but it's more than that. There's something weird going on there."

As I watched her face, I saw a strong woman driven down by something she couldn't understand. The color under her eyes showed she hadn't been sleeping well. Her hands shook with fatigue. Someone else might've thought she was a meth-head in detox, but I saw her for what she really was: out of her element and terrified.

"Hey." I took her hand in mine. "You don't have to worry about me not believing you. Okay? Just tell me what's happening."

It took an hour for her to spill the whole story. She was a student, which I could've figured out on my own. She and a group of classmates decided to get a house together to save on expenses. They pooled their resources and managed to buy a run-down house on the south side. There were five of them living together, sharing rooms. Things started disappearing, that was their first clue that something was wrong. Then there were noises, then other signs. She said that her roomies were starting to act strange, and she was beginning to feel ill. In fact, they all started skipping classes and just staying inside the house. I asked her why she didn't just leave.

"I have to stay," she said.

"Yeah, but why?"

"I have to stay."

Her tone was the same one an abused woman had when she refused to leave her lover. She knew it was bad, but there was something keeping her there, something unexplainable.

I agreed to follow her to the house to get a first impression of what was going on.

It takes a lot of guts to come forward when something weird or frightening happens to a person. Most people feel like no one will believe them, or that people will blame them and laugh behind their backs. And most people are right. It leaves people with a sense of hopelessness, that there is nowhere left to turn. When people begin to feel that way, those dark forces win. I don't mean that metaphorically, I mean it literally. They win a victory, a conquest over a soul when a person loses hope. Someone experiencing what Shannon claimed to experience has to be at wit's end to come and find someone like me. Most of the time, they dummy up and don't tell anyone. When it first happened to me, and I thought I was losing my mind, sure, I mentioned it to a few people. A shrink here and there, a few friends, a bartender or two... My friends stopped hanging around with me, the bartenders cut me off, and the shrinks told me I was suffering from some sort of post traumatic stress syndrome brought on by my "untimely passing."

They never say "death," always "passing." "Passing" sounds so much nicer, less final than "death." "Passing" sounds like something a person might do walking between two rooms. It doesn't sound like what happens when a piece of safety equipment fails due to production cutbacks, dropping a person thirty feet onto the back of their head. It doesn't bring to mind waking up on a gurney with a sheet over one's head and a paper tag on a person's toe. That's not "passing," that's "death" with a capital "D."

Good things came out of it, though. I developed a new respect for people I might have thought were crazy before. I also quit drinking and smoking. I've heard of so many people who've had near-death experiences who came away with the "live for the now" attitude and saying things like "I've been dead, so nothing scares me." Frankly, the thought of dying and not coming back scares the ever-loving Hell out of me. People talk about seeing the long corridor with light at the end or seeing dead relatives. When I died, I saw nothing. I saw darkness. I didn't even get to float up above my own body or relive my life in fast forward. Just black. Just cold.

2

We went west just before the Fort Pitt tunnel, which took us into what was widely considered the "bohemian" part of the 'Burg. Older houses shoehorned in next to each other made up the hillsides, with mom-and-pop shops dotting the neighborhoods. It was bohemian in that a large portion of those who lived there were like Shannon, groups who lived communally for the sake of cheaper rent. Most of the houses were small, though they all had cavernous basements, which the majority of the inhabitants turned into something interesting, usually a studio or extra living quarters. I once knew a guy who shot his own public-access television show from his basement showing public domain horror movies every Saturday night. He had a dead clown and a demon for sidekicks. It was a good show.

What I said before, about being able to see dead people, was true, to an extent. For the first few months, I would sometimes get glimpses of the netherworld. Sometimes I couldn't *not* see it. Other times, I saw the world just like any normal person, just through diffraction glasses. It depended on the day, how tired I was, whether the planets were in the right alignment, some such nonsense. But, thanks to lots of practice and guidance from a friend, I can pretty much turn it on and off at will, and most of the time I choose for it to be off. But I still have days, be it from lack of sleep or coffee, when it either doesn't work or kicks into overdrive. It doesn't just apply to dead people, either. I see what some people call auras, others call remnants. I can see energy patterns as they lay around people or objects... or houses.

The house Shannon and her four roomies lived in sat at the end of a cul-de-sac. It was a two-story matchbox with a huge front porch and strange art-deco angles to it. What used to be the garage was bricked off to make a third level. Shannon's VW Bug looked right at home parked on the street in front of the house. I put my Chrysler behind her Bug and watched as she got out and made a beeline to the front door. It might have been my imagination, but to me it seemed as if she were running to get inside, like something beyond the front door was pulling her in with a rope around her middle. I scanned the eaves of the house for something that would tip me off about a dark presence, but there was nothing.

Like I said, some days, it just doesn't work.

I watched Shannon's reaction as I took my time getting out of my car. It made her nervous. I could tell by the way she shifted her weight from foot to foot that she wanted to be inside the house. It was the same type of nervous shift that an addict gets while waiting for their supplier. She didn't *want* to get past the threshold; she *needed* to. She kept glancing from me to the door, hungry for whatever was inside.

"So this is it," I said as she let me in the front door.

She nodded.

The place was decorated in early American student. Framed art prints and long cloth tapestries of Celtic knotwork covered the putty-colored walls. What furniture there was bore the distinct signs of being either purchased second-hand or dug out of dumpsters. I half expected to see black lights and psychedelic posters on the walls, along with that famous picture of Einstein sticking his tongue out. The air smelled of a mixture of incense and mold, no doubt one used to cover the other. It looked typical of any such bohemian house, but there was something missing that I couldn't quite put my finger on.

Seated on one rumpled couch was an equally rumpled man who looked up when I walked in. He looked as if he'd been watching television, staring at a fixed point, except that there wasn't a television to be found.

"This is Todd," she said. "Pre-Med."

For some reason, college students feel compelled to introduce each other by their first names and majors. I think it hearkens back to the days when a person's last name denoted what they did. Bakers baked, Thatchers thatched, and so on. In those days, a person named Tailor was, in fact, a tailor. For some reason, it always struck me as a little odd that my name meant "barrel maker" or "coppersmith."

Todd Pre-Med shifted his gaze to meet my eyes. They were rimmed in red, glassy and almost without depth. Then he cut his glance toward Shannon.

"Hi," he said to me, his voice emotionless. "Friend?" he said to her.

"Friend," she said as she turned her eyes toward me. The expression on her face pleaded for me not to say anything, so I didn't. His eyes moved back onto me, then he gave a slight nod and went back to staring.

In the kitchen I met Jason English-Lit and Heather Pre-Med (possibly related to Todd Pre-Med, but I doubted it), staring at each other the same way Todd Pre-Med stared at nothing. Like Todd, they both gave me a cursory glance before glaring at Shannon. Then, like Todd, they went back to staring at each other.

The fourth roommate, Andrea (Andi Anthropology),

was nowhere to be found, though Shannon assured me that her absence was more or less normal.

She led me on a tour of the rest of the house, during which the three staring students did not so much as twitch. It was as if they were mannequins, which made me nervous. Each of the upstairs bedrooms looked typical of college students. Piles of dirty clothes dominated at least one room, the one occupied by Todd Pre-Med and Jason English-Lit, while a second that belonged to Shannon and Heather Pre-Med seemed at least a bit neater, though it smelled of stale perfume and feet. The fourth room, the master bedroom, belonged to Andi Anthropology. She'd won the room by cutting cards, said Shannon. Her room, unlike the other two, looked almost unlived in. The bed was made, a fact strange enough in itself, and the dirty clothes were packed in a hamper beside the bathroom door. In fact, the only thing that gave a hint about the room's owner was a small tray covered in crystals, carved stones, and a few other items that looked too rustic to be anything other than artifacts. The room almost looked like a model from a college pamphlet.

I said there was something wrong with the house, but I couldn't put my finger on it. During the tour, the feeling got stronger. By the time we were done, the unease at whatever was missing wasn't the only thing wrong. I felt sick. I didn't feel nauseous or have a headache, but my muscles felt drained of energy and my head felt heavy. I knew it wasn't healthy inside the house, but I didn't know why.

The feeling got stronger when Shannon opened the door to the basement and led the way down. Every step into the damp darkness made my stomach flip, my head feel heavier. But the basement looked like any other basement in the city. Cinderblock walls, piles of discarded boxes, dark corners. A pile of boxes and an empty shelf dominated one wall. It might have been messier than some I'd been in, but then again, I'd seen worse.

"Is there anything else?" I let go my breath as we emerged from the basement. Shannon pointed to her somnambulistic housemates and waved me into her room, and closed the door behind us. She pulled a chair from beneath a high-piled desk and I sat while she made herself comfortable on her bed. Maybe it was the way my stomach rolled, or the dizziness in my head, but to my eyes it wasn't so much like she *sat* as much as it was she *nested* in her blankets. When she was sufficiently comfortable, she seemed to calm down, like the tattered comforter she sat on might have been a security blanket.

"Is there anything else you can tell me?" I tried not to stare at the blanket.

"It's strange," she said. "I feel better now. I think it may have been in my imagination."

It wasn't true. There was genuine fear in her eyes, real need in her voice when she talked to me at the library. Something almost physically took hold of her and dragged her back into the house when we arrived. But, after only a few minutes in the house, she felt better, like a junkie after a fix.

"When you called me, where you in or out of the house?"

"I was out," she said. "I think."

"Maybe we should go somewhere else and talk about this," I said.

She shook her head, her expression serious.

"No," she said. "I'm fine now. Really, I think I just needed some air."

"But what about..?"

"I'm fine," she repeated. "I'm sorry I wasted your time."

It wasn't until I was driving away that it clicked: No scats.

13

There are things in the world that exist in the periphery. Whether people acknowledge them or not, they're there, just waiting to be noticed. Most people train themselves not to see them and write them off to being scatterbrained or imagination. Scats are among those things. Ever catch movement out of the corner of your eye, a darting dark shadow right near the floor? That's not imagination. They're real. They exist whether people want to acknowledge them or not and they're drawn to people or places where emotions run high. Once a person sees them, and recognizes them for what they are, he'll see them everywhere, but never straight on. They only exist out of the corner of a person's vision. It's like living in a house full of feral cats that can't be caught. Sure, they're there, a body can occasionally catch a glimpse of them, but move and they scatter. They look like little shadows, but they act like cats.

Shadow cats. Scats. Get it?

No matter where I go, houses, apartments, businesses, restaurants, I see them. Sometimes they interact with me, but most of the time they just go about their business. That's what struck me as wrong about Shannon's house. No scats. I couldn't remember seeing a single one. I was beginning to think there was something seriously wrong with that house.

3

When my friends stopped hanging around with me, I did what any normal person would do. I wallowed in self-pity for a while and retreated into my computer looking for information about what was wrong with me. One of the positives that came out of my abandonment was that I found new friends. As I drove out of Shannon's neighborhood, I made up my mind to go and see one of them.

Carson Street in Pittsburgh is a strange little strip with shops of every shape and size. There are three-story antique shops next door to a toy store that specializes in pop culture from the seventies and eighties. There are music shops and tattoo parlors and used book stores next to eateries where a body can get the best soup and gyros in the region. It's the kind of place where anything can be found, if one only knows where to look.

I pulled into a side street next to a cafe, parked and fed the meter, then walked a block to a storefront with no sign hanging over the door. Painted on the door was a symbol, two crescents with a circle between them. People that didn't know what it meant usually didn't ask, and people who did already knew what they were looking for.

The bell sounded as I pushed the door open.

"Hello?" I called.

"Just a moment!" her voice lilted through the air. A moment later, she came through the beaded curtain, pulling a robe over her naked flesh.

"Hi, Maggie," I grinned.

"*Don't* call me that," she snapped in a whisper.

Maggie looked like a plus-sized model. She had a bit of weight on her, but any less and she wouldn't have been nearly as pretty. Her long deep red hair fell down over her shoulders and blended in with the purple and black of her velvet robe. She wore a silver pentacle on a chain around her neck and crystal earrings, which completed the image of a modern witchcraft shopkeeper.

"It's your name, isn't it?"

"Here, I go by my *magickal* name. Electra."

I stifled a laugh. Maggie knew how much I hated that "magickal name" bullshit.

My opinion is that a person has to be comfortable with their own name. Stan Cooper isn't exactly a name that oozes sex appeal. I can't even get by going by my middle name, Irving, but I'm comfortable with who I am. What if I went around calling myself some obviously fake name like Jake Steele? Sure, Stan Cooper might not know what to do, but that wouldn't stop Jake Steele! I don't think using that name would make me seem any sexier. I'm pretty certain I'd look like some kind of goon.

"I'm not going to call you by that idiotic name," I said. "I've known you too long. I need some advice."

"I'm a little busy," she said. "Come back in an hour."

"What're you doing back there?" I pretended to crane my neck around to see behind her.

"I'm helping a couple of clients," she said.

Sex magick. It was Maggie's favorite form, though far from the only one she knew. The way she explained it to me once was that the energy created during the creation-act, sex, could be focused, channeled into any number of spells. She could also use various bodily fluids to create charms or potions, depending on what the situation needed. Maggie's opinion was that sex was nothing to be ashamed of, but something that was wholly positive and should be used as often as possible. I wasn't sure about the "magick" part of it, but Maggie knew how to make a man, or a woman for that matter, feel like no one else could.

"Sorry to interrupt," I said. "I'll head down the block for a sandwich. About an hour?"

She nodded.

"Unless you'd like to add your energies," she purred. "I know yours are strong. Want to help?"

"No, thanks," I said, as tempting as the offer was. "I'll be back in an hour." She disappeared through the curtain. As I let the door close behind me, the deadbolt clicked into place.

Pittsburgh may not have the market cornered on fine food, but it does have some damned fine sandwiches. Philadelphia may be home of the cheesesteak, but the 'Burg has some of the best delis in the world. I stopped at a shop just a couple of blocks up that advertised Greek wraps called "gyros." It came out piled high with lamb and cucumber sauce on pita bread.

I took out my notebook and started to write down thoughts about the case. No scats, drugged-up expressions, one immaculate room. Except for the scats, it seemed like a typical college house, complete with the token "good-girl" roomie.

"Excuse me." The voice came from inside my head. I looked up to see a thin balding man wearing a business suit. "Can you see me?"

I saw him when I came in, but he looked like any other customer at first glance. I didn't notice him asking everyone in the place for help, or everyone ignoring him. My eye must've twitched, because his expression changed from fear to joy.

"You can see me, can't you?" he practically shouted. "Oh, mister, you've gotta help me. I can't get anyone else to pay attention to me."

I kept my eyes down at my food and dragged my pencil over my notebook. People tend to stare when a guy with crazy hair starts talking to himself in the middle of his lamb gyro.

"Don't ignore me," he pleaded. "Come on, don't just sit there. I need help."

I pointed to the notebook with the pencil.

Outside

He nodded and sat fidgeting while I finished my lunch, then followed me when I got up and paid the bill. He was hot on my heels when I turned down the alley beside the deli.

"You have to help me," he said. "Please. I don't know what's going on."

I took a deep breath. I never enjoyed being the one to break the news, especially to someone who looked like he died on his way to a meeting. They never took it well.

"What's your name?"

"Dennis," he said, relief that someone acknowledged his existence etched on his face.

"Okay, Dennis," I said. "Think hard and tell me. What's the last thing you remember?"

"I was in the elevator," he said. "On my way up to my office. I had a board meeting to prepare for. It starts in like..." he glanced at his watch. "Christ! It's already started! You had to make me wait while you ate, didn't you? I'm gonna sue your ass..."

"You're kidding, right?" Business executives were the worst. "You want to tell me what happened?"

"I was on the elevator, going over my notes, and my arm started hurting."

Heart attack. He looked like the type that ate granola, snacked on tofu, and drank shakes made of wheatgrass and yogurt. He probably had a key to the executive gym and thought it helped him pick up women. Eat right, exercise, and die anyway.

"Look," I said, trying to be a gentle as possible with the guy. "Dennis, I'm sorry, but you're dead. That pain you felt was your heart giving out."

"That's not possible," he said. "I exercise! I eat right! I'm only forty-seven years old, for Christ's sake!"

"I'm sorry," I said again as I tried to keep my voice as even as possible. I could hear Dennis, but no one else could. That meant I either had to not attract attention, or appear to be a crazy street person. "You have to move on. Death doesn't care how old you are or how good a person you were. It's just your time."

"I don't want to go," he said. "I've got too much to do! My business is finalizing a shipping deal today and..."

"And they're going to have to do it without you," I said. "I'm sorry, but that's just how it is."

"I'm..." his eyes swiveled in his head like ball bearings. "I'm going to sue..!"

"Sue who?" I laughed. "Death? Good luck. You're dead. Deal with it."

"I could stay around, couldn't I?"

I knew this line of questioning. More often than people would think, the dead took a few moments to get used to the idea before moving on. Every now and again, however, one couldn't let go. For whatever reason, the life he lived wasn't enough, and he wanted more.

"You could," I said. "But it's not how you think it would be. Imagine walking around, unnoticed, no one being able to hear or see you. Watching your colleagues take over your business dealings, your business go on without you like you never existed, all of your friends move on, then die. Watching all your loved ones get on with their lives. It's not like living at all. It's much worse."

"I could stay with you, couldn't I? Don't you psychic-types need a spirit guide or something?"

"No. No way." It was an argument I did not want to get sucked into. It was worse than the commitment argument with an over-attached girlfriend.

"Come on!" he pleaded. "I'm the CEO of a major international company! I could help you out! I've got connections!"

"First off," I growled, "You've been dead for what? An hour? You couldn't guide a fly to shit and you certainly don't know anything about the spirit world. You didn't even know you were dead, remember?"

"But I could..."

"Second, you *had* connections. The only thing you're connected to now is the suit you died in."

I reached into my jacket pocket and pulled out a zipper bag full of business cards.

"You need closure, or guidance, or something I can't give you. But I know someone who can."

I fumbled with the packet until I came up with a card for a priest who worked at a church several blocks down. He wasn't the typical man of the cloth. Rather, he was like me. He saw dead people. Unlike me, however, he'd always had the sight. It wasn't something traumatic for him, but something he'd been born with. It led him to the priesthood, where he could help lost souls.

"Look here," I said. "This is the information for Father Deyer. He's at the Holy Cross Church. He can help you."

Dennis reached to take the card only to have his hand pass through it.

"You're dead," I said. "Remember? You can't do things

like hold business cards. Just read it and remember."

"But I'm not Catholic," he said.

"Doesn't matter," I said. "Just talk to the priest."

Dennis made a slow turn and made his way down the street. After a block, he even stopped looking back at me. I hated to be that way, but it was for the best. If I started taking in every stray soul that crossed my path, pretty soon I wouldn't be able to sleep at night or even live in my own place. I also wasn't stupid enough to play armchair psychologist and try to give them advice. More often than not, that kind of meddling made things worse. Deyer, though, was good at what he did, both with the living and the dead. He was never judgmental, always kind. Even to me.

I glanced down at my watch and saw that a sufficient amount of time had passed, so I headed back down the street to Maggie's shop.

I got to the door in time to see the couple she'd been working with exit. The woman was pretty, young and blonde with wide eyes and a nervous smile. The man was slightly taller, with long dark hair, and the relaxed expression of a man who's just had an intense three-way. The woman avoided looking at me as I passed them in the doorway. The man made sure I saw his smile.

"Maggie?"

"Just a minute," she called back.

Maggie's shop didn't really have a name. Some people called it "that witch shop," others just "the magick store." Most people just called it "the shop," like it was the only one in town. While some shops that catered to the Craft operated more toward dabblers and tourists, selling "Blessed Be" bumper stickers and statues of fairies, Maggie's was more for the true practitioner. One shelf held nothing but candles, which Maggie made herself in the back of the shop. Another held books, some as old as I was and older. An entire wall of the shop looked like a medieval apothecary, with herbs of every shape, size and color, some of which I knew to be poisonous and others I'd never heard of.

She also had quite a collection of ceremonial knives, swords, bells, and other things that no modern witch should be without. It was behind the curtain at the back of the shop, however, that she did her most interesting work.

She came through the curtain, this time wearing a broomstick skirt and tasteful blouse, still dabbing the sweat off her forehead.

"How'd it go?" I couldn't keep the smirk off my face.

"She's really improving," she said. "He's *really* interested in the sexual aspect of ritual, and he's got a lot of energy to draw on. Either way, it was an eye-opening experience for both of them."

"I bet," I said. "I came across something weird, and I don't quite know what to make of it."

She rested her elbows on the counter, her typical position to let me know she was listening.

I told her about the house, about the people, about how they acted when I came in. She nodded with every description.

"Sounds like psychedelic drugs to me," she said with a shrug. "I see it all the time with students. Someone gets a bunch of 'shrooms or some datura and you get a room full of naked people talking to lamps and playing poker without cards."

"I thought that too," I said. "But then I noticed something bizarre... no scats."

She sat a little straighter, her eyes widened.

"Can't be," she said. "No such place."

"I walked room to room," I said. "And I'm telling you, there were none. And the longer I stayed, the stranger I felt... like I was getting sick or something."

"Don't go back," she said. "It sounds unhealthy. What were you doing there in the first place?"

I told her about the girl.

"She asked for help," I said. "I can't turn her away."

"Sure you can," said Maggie. Then she read the expression on my face, "but you won't."

"C'mon Maggie. I don't know what I'm dealing with. If you know anything that can help me..."

"What you're describing sounds like a combination of a haunting and possession to me," she said. "Scats are produced and attracted to living things. They're made of the energy put off by the life force. The only places where there are none are places where there's no life. Not just vacant, but no life at all... dead places. But people live there, so it doesn't make sense."

"What can I do?"

"Get them out."

4

People say they don't believe in magick or monsters. They call people like me and Maggie delusional or say that we're living in a fantasy world. Magick isn't real, they say, and there's no such thing as ghosts. They go along their happy daily routines, safe and secure in the knowledge that the unexplainable or things that go bump in the night aren't real. These same people are the ones who avoid shops like Maggie's, who watch me as if I might do something spooky, and are the first ones to scream and run if so much as an odd noise is heard in the old dark and creepy house. They say they don't believe, but it's a lie. The trouble is they *do* believe, but they don't take the time to try to understand. They believe, but they'll never admit it to each other because that would let the possibility in that there are things in the world that don't fit in with their neat little model of what life is supposed to be. In the light of day, it's easy to say there are no such things as ghosts, or possession, or haunted houses. But in the dead of night, tucked in bed, hiding beneath the blankets while the sounds of footsteps cross the floor and the sounds of breathing come from under the bed, everyone believes.

My apartment isn't much. Two bedrooms, a kitchen, one bathroom. Still, the window in the main room looks out over the Monongahela River, and it's paid for. From the window of my bedroom I can see the lights of Steel City at night. From the other room's window, I can see the building I fell from. I use that room for storage, and I don't go in there much.

One of the things Maggie taught me early on was how to protect my space, and I don't mean from potential thieves. A good steel fire door and an electronic security system take care of that. She made sure I knew how to keep disembodied souls from following me home. Bad enough to see them walking down the street, but waking up to find some bus accident victim staring me in the face is a shock I've had one too many times, thank you very much.

The lock on my front door, for example: I had it installed upside down. Voodoo practitioners say it confuses the spirits and won't let them pass. I doubt that, but I'm covering all my bases. Just inside the door, under a black rubber strip, is a line of kosher sea salt mixed with red brick dust. On my side of the door and all around it, written in silver painted Latin, is the equivalent of "Keep Out." The same holds true for around the windows, the faucets, drains, even the electric and phone outlets... any possible way in. Anyone who visits, as if anyone ever did, would think it was just interesting decoration. I tried for a while protecting the whole building, but the super kept sweeping up the salt. Now I just have to be content to protect my own place, my own little corner of the 'Burg.

I felt out of sorts after talking with Maggie. What she said made sense, but something still nagged at me. I was missing something, and I couldn't figure out what. I walked into my apartment, tossed my keys on the kitchen counter, and headed to my bedroom. The telephone by the bed would still have Shannon's number saved. Even if I wasn't sure of what was going on, I was certain that staying in that house was a mistake. I pulled up her number and dialed.

A voice I didn't recognize answered the telephone.

"Hello?" It was a woman, probably the elusive Andi Anthropology who hadn't been home earlier.

"Hi," I said, and tried to sound as non-threatening as possible. "Is Shannon around?"

"She's out right now. Who can I say called?"

A roommate that actually took phone messages? That *was* weird.

"My name is Stan Cooper," I said. "I just wanted..."

"Shannon will be out for a while, Mister Cooper," she said. Her voice crystallized like ice. "I'll be sure to let her know you called." The line clicked and went dead.

I put the telephone back on the charger.

Odd. I'd gotten the brush-off before, but not like that. It wasn't just that she'd gotten cold at the mention of my name, because that happens on a regular basis from people who think I'm nuts. But when Andi Anthropology heard it, she got *angry*. As if my asking to talk to Shannon was a violation of some sort. Part of me wanted to get back in my car and drive over to the house. The more rational part of my brain won out, however, and I decided to wait and see if Shannon would contact me.

My days and nights got mixed up a while ago. It wasn't planned, but due to my unique condition, I spent less and less time out of my apartment during the daytime. Most of my new circle of friends were night-owls, and there were fewer chances of encounters with people during the day, so I just started staying up later and later. Eventually, my world went nocturnal.

There was a whole lot of daylight left, and despite my nightmares, I was still tired, so I went back to bed. But I couldn't sleep. I just laid there, eyes wide open and staring at the ceiling while I tried to figure out what was going on with Shannon and her house. It took only about twenty minutes for me to decide I wasn't going to get any sleep, so I got up, made a pot of coffee, and flipped on the television. For a while, I surfed the dismal wasteland of daytime programming. Between infomercials and celebrity endorsements were lurid shows in which everyone cheated on everyone, talk shows where mothers couldn't remember who fathered their babies, and of course, the most depressing thing on cable: the news. I sat for a few minutes and sipped my coffee while some perky bleach-blonde made her most serious face and talked about dead celebrities, plummeting economies, and the latest rash of missing teens in Pittsburgh. I clicked over to my DVD player and started a day-long marathon of bad movies. After hour number four, I started to relax, and Shannon finally drifted to the back of my mind. Whatever was going on at her house, she said she didn't need me anymore. It wasn't my problem. In fact, considering the brush-off from her roommate, I didn't expect to hear from Shannon again.

So when my telephone rang in the early morning hours, I didn't think much of it.

"Cooper," I said.

"Mister Cooper." The voice on the other end of the line was shaking, choked with tears and terrified.

"Shannon? What's wrong?"

"I... I don't know... I didn't know who..."

"Calm down," I said. "What's wrong? Where are you?"

"I'm in the park," she sobbed. "But I don't remember how

I got here."

"What, did you get mugged? Are you okay?"

"I don't know. Please... please can you come and get me?"

I didn't really know her, and part of me thought that I shouldn't get involved, but there was real fear in her voice. Between that and the strange situation in her house, there was no way I could say no.

"Where are you?"

I drove down Carson Street and turned right on 21st, the whole time wondering just what the hell she'd gotten herself into. First she wanted my help, then she didn't, then she called just as the sun came up begging for my help again. I couldn't help the feeling that maybe I was being played for a chump.

The thought died in the back of my skull when I pulled up at the payphones at the front of the park and saw her. Despite the frigid temperature, she wore only a t-shirt and pajama pants. No shoes, no jacket, just bare feet and arms against the snow and biting wind. I could see her shivering from the road.

I clicked on the seat-warmer, pulled a blanket from behind the seat and got out to meet her. Her hair whipped in the wind and her cheeks looked burnt by the cold. I wrapped the blanket around her shoulders and helped her into the warmth of my car.

She wanted to go home, but I convinced her that winding up in a strange place, freezing, and with no memory was cause enough for a trip to the emergency room. She protested a little, but I won out in the end.

The waiting room was busy for early morning, but then, I'd never seen one that wasn't jumping, no matter what time I visited. All the seats were taken, most of them by glassy-eyed kids that looked right around Shannon's age. College students were notorious for partying, and it didn't take much for me to figure that a party got out of control. I wondered how many of them couldn't figure out where they were either.

The receptionist took one look at Shannon and sent her directly to triage. The nurse took her vitals and sent her to a private stall in the Emergency Room where we sat and waited.

"Think," I said. "What happened? What the hell were you doing out there?"

"I don't remember," she said between shivers. "I remember you leaving, I remember my room, then I remember waking up in the middle of the park with no idea where I was."

"Did you do any drinking last night?" I checked her eyes for signs of substance abuse. "Maybe something else..?"

She shook her head without looking at me.

"I don't do drugs," she said. "And I only drink at parties. I swear, I don't know what happened to me."

Her body shook as she tried, and failed, to hold back a fresh tide of sobs.

"Okay," I said. I put my hand over hers. "I believe you. Try to think. What's the last thing you remember?"

"You left," she said. "I stayed in my room and read for a while, then I went out to the living room. My roommates were standing by the window, watching something, so I wanted to see what it was."

"What was it?" I asked.

"Sunset," she replied. "The sun was just going down and the sky was getting dark. It was pretty, but nothing worth staring at. I figured they were just being weird, so I started to go back to my room. Then I blinked and I was standing there in the snow with no shoes on."

"What about anyone else? Your roommates? Did you see them anywhere?"

"I was alone," she said. "I was so scared."

The curtain snapped as a hefty nurse in purple scrubs walked in. She looked at the chart, then from me to Shannon.

"Are you family?" she asked.

"Uh... no."

"Then I'm going to have to ask you to leave, sir."

"But I brought... I mean... she..."

"Can he stay?" asked Shannon. "Please?"

The nurse cocked an eyebrow and made a face that made her look like she'd eaten something very sour.

"Fine," she said. "Let's see what's what."

I stayed for as long as I was comfortable, but when the nurse suggested checking Shannon to see if she'd been sexually assaulted, I took it as my cue to step back into the waiting room. I stood near a window and tried not to look at all the blank faces that occupied every chair. None of them moved or stared at me. In fact, none of them even seemed aware of my existence, kind of like Shannon's roommates. It was like standing in the middle of a scene from a Romero movie.

After what seemed like an hour, the nurse came out and waved me back. Shannon gave a brave tiny smile as I walked through the curtain.

"They say I'm fine," she said. "They can't explain why I can't remember, but they said there was no sign of assault."

"Thank goodness for that," I said. "Are you released?"

"I think so," she said. "I just have to get my paperwork. Would you mind giving me a lift home?"

"I don't think that's such a good idea," I said. "I don't think it's a healthy environment for you. You said yourself you felt sick when you were there, and your roommates..."

"No," she said. "I need to go home."

"I could take you to a safe..."

"Home," she said. There was such determination in her eyes that I knew reasoning with her was pointless. "Please take me home."

"Okay," I said. "Let me get your release papers."

I got up and went to the receptionist station. The person behind the glass informed me that there was a problem with her insurance. Since, when I found her, she didn't have her purse, she didn't have an insurance card to give them. I made my way back into the Emergency Room to ask her for a number to call, but when I got to her stall, it was empty.

I grabbed a passing orderly and asked if he'd seen her, but he shrugged, muttered something about it being busy and how was he supposed to keep track of every slacker that came through, and went on his way. I ran out the door and scanned the parking lot, but she was nowhere to be found.

Back inside, I found the nurse who'd examined her.

"She's gone? I haven't discharged her yet!"

"Wasn't someone watching her?"

"Sir," she said. "My job is not to play babysitter to everyone who comes through that door. I have to take care of people who are really in need." She turned and went back into the emergency room.

My cynical side reminded me that she called for help, then said she didn't need it, then called again, and just walked out. By all rights, she wasn't my problem and I should've left well enough alone. But I couldn't. When she called the first time, she reached out to me for help. The second time, she was terrified. I couldn't just turn my back on her. Her house was where she wanted to go, so I figured that's where she was headed.

I kept my eyes open for her as I slowly drove the most direct route back to her house. That I didn't find her, in a way, made me feel better. At least she wasn't walking in the snow. Maybe she hailed a taxi.

I rounded the corner to her house and parked behind her bug. That the other driveways on the block were empty shouldn't have bothered me, but it gave the street an empty, lonely feeling, ominous somehow, as if I'd just walked into a cemetery. I pushed the thought aside as the result of not enough sleep and too much time in the emergency room as I walked to the door. I knocked and waited, but there was no answer. I rang the doorbell and waited a moment more. Nothing. No sounds from within the house, no approaching footsteps. Everyone was probably in their classes. It was a rational explanation, so that had to be it. I made my way back to my car and headed back to my apartment. I tried not to think about Shannon, half frozen in the snowy night, her teary eyes begging me for help, but no matter how I tried to occupy my mind, she kept jumping back into focus. She'd be fine, I was sure of it. I just hoped she'd call once she got home to let me know she was safe.

I got home and realized how much of the day was wasted in the emergency room. It was already well after noon, and I needed sleep. I pitched my shoes by the door and crawled into bed. My telephone rang before I'd even finished pulling the blankets up over my head. I snatched it up.

"Shannon?"

"Who's Shannon?" came a gruff voice on the other end of the line. "You been holding out on me?"

Doug Winter ran one of those strange little shops on Carson Street, about six stores down from Maggie's. In the front, his shop sold t-shirts, pre-torn jeans, and leather belts with the names of punk bands stamped on them. The back of his shop was a showroom of drug paraphernalia. Of course, he called them "water pipes," to keep his shop legal, and also placed large, hand-written signs which warned customers that the items in the case were to be used for tobacco only.

Wink wink, nudge nudge.

I met Doug through Maggie. In fact, I'd met most of my new friends through Maggie.

"Nevermind," I said. "What's up?"

"Probably nothing," he said, "But I was hoping to get your opinion on something."

"Sure," I said. "When?"

"How 'bout now?"

Doug was many things. Laid back, maybe. Hell, most of the time, he was downright slothful. I'd never known him to be impatient about anything. It just wasn't in his nature. For him to want me to come straight away struck an odd chord with me.

"Sure thing," I said.

By the time I made it back to Carson Street, several of the shops were starting to close up for the day. It was late, and February business was always slow, so it wasn't strange to see them pulling in their placards and sandwich boards before the sun went down. The good thing about arriving when I did was that I could park just about anywhere I pleased.

I pulled the car into a space right in front of Doug's shop, a shameless little place called "Rock Rags" with "Punk Clothes and Accessories" printed under the name on the sign. I noticed that "water pipes" was conspicuously absent from the list of goods and services offered.

Doug stood in the doorway outside the shop smoking, which also struck me as weird. He was the type that most people never saw from the waist down, because he hardly ever came out from behind the counters of his shop, particularly in the cold of February. In fact, most of the time, I had a hard time picturing him with legs, just a torso that kinda floated around.

"What's up?" I said as I got out of the car.

"You still driving that POS?" he said. The jibe did little to mask his nervousness.

"That's me," I said, patting the hood of my car. "Buy American. Good for the economy." I arched an eyebrow at him. "What's going on?"

"I got robbed," he said.

That he was so calm when he said it sent a chill through me. Anyone else would be panic-stricken, or at least show some sign of anger. But Doug just stood there, puffing a cigarette, in his t-shirt and jeans in the bitter cold.

"When?"

"Just now," he said.

"Did you see them?"

He shook his head.

"What'd they get?"

"Go inside," he said, his smile fading. "Do that thing you do. Tell me what you see."

I looked warily at his face. The laugh lines and permanent wrinkles caused by smiling were still there, but there were new lines on his face, unaccustomed to the smooth patches, that showed worry.

I nodded and opened the door.

The electronic chime sounded a happy ding as I walked into the warmer air of the shop. To one side was a glass case that usually held rings and necklaces and other jewelry with skulls, pentagrams, devils and boobies on them. The case was all but empty, save for a few gold-plated "Playa" necklaces and one that looked like a pacifier. The wall behind was usually a mess of tacked-up fliers for local bands, movie festivals, and poetry nights. Only tacks remained.

To the other side, just inside the door, the magazine rack was in shambles, with tiny bits of shredded glossy paper strewn about and what looked like teeth marks through the wood shelves. Further into the shop, the usually crowded racks of concert t-shirts and deliberately faded jeans stood all but empty, the few pieces remaining left in tatters.

I made my way to the back of the shop, careful not to touch anything. The back glass case, the one filled with bongs and pipes, wasn't touched.

It was then that I noticed a strong odor, pungent and heavy, coming from the direction of the changing room. "Room" was far too generous a word for the little closet with a folding slatted door over it. Inside, it was like a coffin, where a person any larger than me couldn't have even fit. Whatever was in the tiny alcove couldn't have been large, but it smelled terrible. I held my jacket over my nose and slid the door aside, and wished I hadn't.

The floor of the tiny alcove was broken upward, as if something had burst forth from the shop's basement. Small bits of concrete and plywood formed a messy circle that looked like a cartoon rabbit hole. Around the hole was the source of the smell. Piles of what appeared to be rat droppings, only much bigger, lay in small mounds. Also sitting around the outside were a few stray rings from the front case, no doubt dropped when whatever had robbed the shop made its escape.

I backed away as my stomach lurched from the stench and made my way back toward the entrance. Something, other than the big hole, piles of giant rat turds, and the fact that the store was mostly empty, didn't seem right. I stopped at the door and took another look around, then it hit me.

No scats.

I stepped out back into the frigid air to find Doug, his hands jammed into his pockets, smoking. He still wasn't wearing a jacket, but he didn't seem to notice the cold.

"Did you call the police?"

"Of course I did," he snorted. "They said they'd have someone out soon, which means they'll show up some time between now and next winter."

"When did this happen?"

"Right before I called," he said, throwing the cigarette on the ground and stomping it out. "But I can't figure out how. I went to the back of the shop to get someone a bong..."

"Water pipe," I corrected him. He stared for a moment, his face humorless.

"And then I heard this God-awful noise, smelled something really foul, and by the time I got back out, it looked just like you saw in there." The edge of his mouth twitched and his eyes darted up and down the street.

"There's something else, isn't there? Why'd you call me?"

"The shop just doesn't feel right now," he said.

"Has Maggie seen it?"

"I called her," he said, a tiny smile forming on his lips. "But she was... uh... busy. With clients."

I nodded. The woman was insatiable.

He lit another cigarette and blew smoke out his nose. "What do you think?"

"I don't know," I said. "But I know why the shop feels weird. No scats. Your shop used to be teeming with them, but now they're gone."

"How?"

"I don't know," I said, "but this is the second place I've seen like this today. Don't spend any more time in the shop than you have to for now. Let me see what I can find out."

He nodded toward the street and I followed his gaze to the flashing bubbles on top of the police car that was taking its own sweet time in arriving.

"Give your statement," I said. "Let the uniforms do some poking around, then go home. I'll call you as soon as I figure something out."

He gave a sullen nod.

It was hard for a fellow like Doug to just go home and wait. That shop was his lifeblood. He'd invested everything he had into it, not to mention the time. It, in turn, was his main source of income. Sitting at home and waiting, for Doug, was like counting the hours until his house was repossessed.

I got in my car and drove a block until I sat in front of Maggie's door. Sure, I could've walked it, but the cops would want to know whose vehicle it was and why it was there, and they'd probably move it themselves to block off the crime scene. I was being considerate and saving them a step. At least, that was what I told myself.

The lights in her shop were off, but the upstairs window glowed bright, which let me know she was home. I rang the bell. The little speaker beside it crackled and spit before something resembling Maggie's voice came through.

"Hello?"

"It's me," I said. It was always a gamble that the intercom wouldn't distort my voice so much she wouldn't know who "me" was. "Open up."

The door buzzed and I let myself in.

The stairs up to her apartment were dark wood and old,

worn from decades of stomping feet and little maintenance. I got to the top and rounded the corner.

When I see the energy of the world, it can be a beautiful or terrible experience. Watching the soul slip out of a dying person is not something anyone could forget, and seeing the throb of raw lusting energy when passing by a strip club is something I've marveled at time and again. But nothing quite compares with the doorways of peoples' homes. A door is a door is a door, I know. But to people like me, doors aren't the only things filling up that doorway. There's also a thin curtain of energy that that folks like Maggie call a "Threshold." It keeps out the majority of unwanted nuisances. The happier the home, the more powerful the Threshold.

Maggie's glittered gold and silver, rippled like an inch-thick shower curtain over her front door. As she explained it to me, unless the owner of a house actually invited someone in, the curtain kept out a good portion of their energies. Sort of like the whole vampire thing, but it worked with everyone.

Maggie opened the door before I could knock.

"Come on in," she said as she padded back inside her apartment. The curtain parted a bit, then fell back into place as I passed through.

Maggie's apartment wasn't what a person would expect from someone in her profession. There were no gargoyle candelabras, no massive crystal thrones, not even a bubbling cauldron with white smoke coming out of the top. In fact, the closest thing to the latter was a battered old green teakettle that sat whistling on the stove. Her apartment looked, for lack of a better word, normal. She had a giant papasan couch with a floral-print cushion sitting under the large window of her living room, a worn leather easy chair, a few throw rugs. Nothing that would scream "witch" to anyone who didn't already know her. One wall was dominated by a big-screen television with two large bookshelves stacked high with chick-flick DVDs. Another wall held another bookshelf covered in knickknacks. The only thing that seemed to belong to a witch was the small altar against the East corner of the room.

"I'm making some herbal tea," she called from the kitchen. "Want some?"

"What kind of herbs?"

"Hemlock and wormswart," she said with mock exasperation. "It's chamomile, jerk."

"In that case, I'd love some."

Something brushed against my legs. I looked down to see Bitsy, Maggie's cat, vying for attention. She, more than anything else, might have given a hint that her host (Maggie hated the term "owner") was something more than the average woman. The cat was about half the size of a normal cat and solid, shiny black, except for a single white crescent between her emerald eyes. She was the kind of cat that, when she looked at you, you could tell she was thinking, puzzling things out in her head. I sat down on the couch, followed by the cat who jumped up in my lap and stood pacing beneath my hand.

"Why is it I can't sit down in your apartment without your cat climbing into my lap?" I called out.

"She likes you," said Maggie, entering with two mugs of tea. "I think that's a positive thing. She's usually a pretty good judge of character."

She'd traded her skirt and cloak for sweatpants and an oversized t-shirt. Her feet were covered in fuzzy pink socks.

"Such an imposing figure of a witch," I snickered.

"I'm off work." She wrinkled her nose at me. "What's up? Is this a social call, or..."

"Have you talked to Doug?"

"No," she said as she sipped her tea. "Why?"

"His shop was... robbed."

"By who?" She sat up a little straighter.

"Or what," I took a sip. It was good, for tea.

She sat with wide eyes, holding her mug of tea without drinking it, as I told her what I'd seen.

"Do you think it's a coincidence?" I leaned back on the couch when I was done.

"Gods, I hope so," she said. "Otherwise something is really wrong. For something to just be able to suck the life force out of a place like that is..." She shivered.

"Did you find out anything? About why the scats might be missing?"

"No," she said. "I can't find any reference to any place without them unless that place is a dead cell."

"All the same," I said. "You might want to keep an eye on your shop."

"Mine's protected," she said. "I have wards around every entrance. Nothing gets in there that will do harm."

"Might want to reinforce them," I said. "And keep looking. Something's gotta turn up."

I finished my tea, gave Bitsy a scratch on the head, and headed out to my car. Up the street, Doug was still talking to the police. The officer took dutiful notes in her notebook while her partner looked on with disdain. I couldn't even begin to imagine what Doug was telling them, or what they were telling him in return.

5

It's true what they say about death altering a person's perception. Once a person has been through the great nap, he begins to notice things he might not have noticed before. Take trees, for example. Drive down any given street, even in the city, and there are bound to be trees lining at least a few of the parkways. Most people just drive past them without ever looking to see the birds nesting in their branches or the squirrels under them. Sunrises are another good one. People like I used to be drive in to work every morning just in time to catch the sun coming up over the city, and never really notice how beautiful Pittsburgh really is in the early morning light. I'm not saying I had some sort of Zen moment in which all of life became clear. I just started appreciating things I hadn't noticed before.

The first thing I noticed when I pulled up in front of my apartment building was a police car, its lights off, parked in front of the door.

Relax, I told myself. *Just because there's a cop car out in front of the building doesn't mean it's here for you.* There were at least nine other apartments in my building, any of which might need the police for something. I pulled into the parking garage and made my way to my apartment.

The two uniforms standing outside my door reminded me about the old phrase that it wasn't paranoia if they really are out to get you.

"Stanley Cooper?" The larger of the two regarded me with suspicious eyes.

"Can I help you officers?" I nodded and tried to appear as non-threatening as possible. I've had several bumps with the Pittsburgh police. I'd been called in the past on a couple of missing persons cases, and have figured out a few murders when the regular PPD was stumped. Officially, I was regarded as a psychic, which seemed to make them more comfortable than my telling them that the murder victims themselves told me whodunit. Most of them regarded me as a nut. A few of them thought of me as dangerous. To the latter group, I try really hard to appear as gentle as a lamb.

"Could we speak to you for a moment?" His name tag read "Menold," and he looked angry. "Inside?"

"Of course," I said. "Excuse the mess."

I unlocked the door and let them inside. Menold entered first, his eyes never leaving me, while his partner, whose name tag read "Appel," scoured my apartment with his eyes.

"Now," I said, hanging my coat in the closet. "What can I do for you?"

"Sir, you were identified as the man accompanying Shannon Richards to the hospital this morning. Is that correct?" He passed me a photograph. Richards. So that was her last name. The photo was taken in one of those fly-by-night studio set-ups, possibly for a yearbook.

"Yes," I said as I passed the photo back. "She called me to come pick her up at Southside Park."

"Do you know why she was at the park this morning?"

"No. She just called and said she needed me to come get

her. Why?"

"And you took her to the hospital, is that correct?"

"Yes."

"Did she seem to be in any trouble to you, sir?"

I didn't like where this line of questioning was going.

"Well, she was in the park with no shoes or a coat, and couldn't remember how she got there," I said. "Other than that, I have no idea."

"Good friends, are you?" Appel glanced around at the writing on the walls.

"Not really," I said. "I just met her yesterday."

"Just met, and she called you?" Menold stared at me as he jotted down notes. It made me nervous. "Not one of her friends? Any idea why?"

"No," I said. "She lives with four other people... I guess she could've called one of them, but she didn't."

"And you said you've known her how long?"

"The first time I heard from her was yesterday morning. We met at the library, then I followed her to her house."

Menold cast a glance at Appel who cocked an eyebrow.

"At her request," I added. "Then I left. That's the last time I saw her until I picked her up in the park. Why?"

"Could you please tell us of the nature of your visit?" Menold's face gave nothing away.

"She wanted to talk to me. That's all." I decided to leave out the part where she thought her house was haunted and her roommates were acting like zombies. "What's this all about?"

"Ms. Richards' body was found two hours ago a few blocks from here," said Appel.

I stopped breathing as the news struck me like a physical blow to the gut. My legs went rubbery. I sat down and looked from one stony face to the other. Menold's expression didn't change. Appel's eyes narrowed just a bit, his jaw set a little harder. I didn't need to see his aura to tell me what he was thinking. He had the same condemning look on his face that cops got on television just before they arrested someone.

"How?" was all I could manage to squeak out.

"We're not at liberty to discuss the details of the case at this time," said Menold. "At around what time did you leave Ms. Reynolds' house?"

"I don't know," I said. "Noon maybe? One? Some time around lunch, I guess. I went from there to a sandwich shop on Carson Street."

"Yessir," said Menold, pulling a notepad from his breast pocket. "We also have that she was admitted to the Emergency Room this morning around eight, is that correct?"

I nodded.

"And that she left without you. We have a statement from a nurse that you were very agitated when you discovered she'd left without you."

"I was worried about her!"

"But you didn't report it to the police," said Appel. He didn't say much, but when he did talk, he made it count for plenty.

"We also have that you were seen entering the 'Rock Rags' clothing store less than an hour ago. Is that also correct?"

"Yes," I said. "Doug Winter is a friend of mine. He asked me to come down." I wasn't sure where they were going with this, but I didn't like it. I'd done nothing wrong, but the looks on their faces made me feel like they were sure I was guilty of something.

"You are aware that Mr. Winter's shop was robbed and vandalized?"

"I am."

"Did you enter the crime scene?"

Gulp.

"Yes," I said. "Doug wanted me to look at it. He'd already called you guys."

"Why didn't you wait for the police?" Appel's voice was a little higher than I'd have expected from his thick Italian frame.

"I guess you guys were taking too long," I snapped. "He asked me to take a look, so I looked. Am I under suspicion of something?"

"No, sir," said Menold. "We're just checking a few facts. You were one of the last known people to see Ms. Reynolds alive, we have a statement from one of her roommates that you called soon after you left, it appears that she ran from you at the hospital, and a shop you were seen at was the site of a robbery and vandalism."

I nodded. Geez, I looked suspicious. Not necessarily guilty of anything other than being in the wrong place at the wrong time, but suspicious nonetheless. Story of my life.

I sat there, numb, while the officers asked a few more questions. I answered as best I could, but I still couldn't get over the thought of Shannon in the park, shoeless and coatless, her eyes full of fear. Somewhere in my mind, a tiny voice whispered.

You failed her, boy. She came to you for help, and you failed her.

The officers left. I didn't move from the couch, just sat there trying to figure where I could've done more. If I'd only warned her ahead of time. If I'd only told her my suspicions. If I'd just turned around and pulled her out of that house when I realized the scats were gone. If only... Optimists would say there was something to be learned from her death, but damned if I could find anything.

I pulled the shades up and watched as the sun flirted with the skyline. Another hour, maybe two, before sunset. I tried to shake the thought of Shannon lying in a coffin from my mind.

Vermin

It was time to go to work.

I said before that the only reason I needed a job in the first place was to afford a few luxuries. That's not entirely true, unless food counts as a luxury. I don't pay rent and my basic utilities are covered, but I do have this nagging desire to eat.

For that reason, I took a night job working at a wholesale warehouse running a forklift. Not one of the big monsters, just one of the little run-abouts. My shift started at seven in the evening, ended at three in the morning. My job was to pull pallets of merchandise off trucks, take them to their various departments, and put surplus stock up on high shelves. It was easy work that didn't require much lifting, and I never had to climb ladders. Besides, I only worked three days a week, which left me plenty of time for other activities, as if I had any.

I got to the warehouse about ten minutes early, which gave me a chance to sit down and drink a cup of coffee before becoming a slave to monotony. The others who worked the same shift were like me. Not psychic, just weird by the standards of the folks who worked in the daylight. Sure, some of them just had other things to do during the day, but others were playing a little too close to the train tracks.

Billie walked in, muttering to herself as usual. The woman held entire conversations with herself, and irritated almost everyone who came into contact with her. I caught a glimpse of her aura once, mostly shades of pinks and blues with a few brown blotches in it. She was a good person, but damaged somehow. Behind her came Seth, who worked the night shift so he could write during the day, away from the distractions of his wife and kids. Within a few minutes, Cal (Post-Traumatic-Stress-Disorder), David (conspiracy theorist), and Matt (asshole) all arrived, clocked in, and made their way to their respective territories. My co-workers were a rogue's gallery of interesting characters, which I figured was the real reason Seth chose the night shift. Day workers were just boring in comparison.

After four hours of moving pallets and avoiding contact with most everyone else, I still couldn't get Shannon off my mind. Worse, I couldn't help but think there was something else I should've done. Rather than run my lift into something, or somebody, I stopped for my lunch break.

The only drawback to working the late shift was that there were no places close by to grab a bite at 11:00 p.m. My lunch usually consisted of a sandwich brought from home or, on a good day, leftovers from a restaurant the night before. Today wasn't a good day. I sat with Seth, as usual, and tried to listen to the plot of his latest novel outline, but Shannon kept drifting back into my thoughts. He kept swearing he was going to base a character on me. I told him I wouldn't mind, so long as he remembered me when royalty checks came around, then went back to my lift.

I felt them before I saw them, eyes crawling across my back like a hunter's through a scope. Whoever it was, he wasn't in the warehouse, but outside, in the truck dock. The hatred was real, tangible, like needles in my neck. I turned toward the feeling, stared into the darkness of the parking lot. I couldn't see him, but I could still feel him breathing in the night as surely as if his breath were on my neck.

One of the first things Maggie taught me was how *not* to see. Most people who are interested in the occult spend their lives trying to develop the ability to see just a glimpse of the energy patterns that surround us. I, on the other hand, couldn't turn it off. It took her a while, working backward from her usual methods of opening doors, to show me how to erect barriers in my mind so I wouldn't be driven insane by the things I saw. She told me it was one of the most difficult things she ever had to do.

I pulled my focus inward and dropped those barriers and opened doors until the colors of the world began to swirl and grow. To anyone else, black is black. To me, there are hundreds of shades, thousands of hues. And there he was.

The dark may have camouflaged him from anyone else, but to me, he stood out as if he were on fire, his aura licking the blackness around him.

Everything living has an aura. They range in colors and hues at all ends of the spectrum, depending on whether the owner is a human, plant, animal or something else. It's pretty easy to tell a person's demeanor by the colors around them. Pinks and yellows, the person's generally happy. Greens and blues, that person's laid back. The colors people hope never to see are only two: black and red. Black is a cancer, a malignancy. Red is anger or passion. To date, I've seen quite a few with red, but no one with more than a speck or two of black. I have, however, seen a few with something else influencing them.

Around the man outside was a thin layer of blue, surrounded by great arcs of red and tendrils of black. He was possessed. The other colors had his own all but snuffed out, and I could see the crimson and ebony fingers reaching toward me, grasping for my own light. Even if I hadn't known what the colors meant, I'd have known bad intent.

I couldn't see his face, but I could still feel his stare. I thought about ignoring him. Let him watch me, see if I cared. But then came the prickle again, like centipede feet on my neck. And again. And again. I climbed off my forklift and walked toward the edge of the loading dock and stared out into the darkness. He wasn't alone.

One by one, a dozen red and black auras emerged from the green of the trees.

There's a moment in movies, when the hero suddenly realizes that, no matter what he does, he's in big trouble. It's that moment when his face sweats, when he licks his lips, and when he begins a slow backpedal away from whatever window he was standing by. I never understood that moment until I saw them begin to move, to *run*, toward me.

My mouth went dry as cold perspiration beaded upon my forehead and I lurched toward the bay door and pulled it closed. There was no slow backing away, however. I scrambled backward until I got enough room to turn and run, looking for anyone I could find to warn.

I didn't have time to get even the first syllable out before they slammed against the loading bay door. I skidded to a halt, my body transfixed by whatever was outside. The way they scrabbled on the metal, it sounded like animals pounding and scratching at the door. Then I heard an awful sound, screeching and groaning of metal being pierced and torn. The door wouldn't stop them. They were coming through, one way or another.

The other employees must've heard the noise, because one second I stood there alone, and the next there were six people around me, all wearing the same ugly blue smock and horrified expression as I did. When the first hand, the first very human hand, reached through the torn hole in the door, they scattered and left me standing frozen.

As the hole got wider, they started coming in, sniffing the air and letting out guttural shrieks. Though there were only a dozen or so, it seemed like an endless tide of crawling forms poured through the torn steel. Their eyes were wild and wide, their backs hunched. The black flames around their bodies reached out wherever they touched, wherever they drew breath, and infected everything around them like a plague. It was as if they were sucking the energy out of the air, out of the walls, out of the people. I watched as all but two scattered and darted through the shelves and around the corners. The two that remained locked eyes with me and hissed.

I've said before, I'm not in great athletic shape. However, when the need strikes me, I can run at amazing speeds for a person of my girth. One look into the blazing eyes of those possessed bastards and I felt my feet kicking backward before I was really aware that I was moving. A few stumbling steps and I managed to get turned around and took off in a dead run, hurling anything within arm's reach into my path behind me as I went. I heard screams as I ran, the sounds of terrified customers and employees mingled with the sounds of enormous shelves being tipped over.

I chanced a glance down one aisle and saw one of my co-workers, Billie, pounced upon by one of them while another stuffed bags of chips and crackers into a gunny-sack. Billie screamed from beneath him as his aura bit into hers, devouring it until there was nothing left. Another pair busied themselves by smashing through the jewelry counter while the attendant screamed in terror. I rounded the corner near the bakery, threw myself into the walk-in freezer, and pulled the heavy steel door shut behind me.

My knuckles screamed as the cold made its way through my skin and into my joints, but I didn't let go of the door handle. I'd rather freeze to death than get pulled apart by a pair of savage monsters, no matter whose bodies they were in. I have no idea how long I stayed holding that door closed. Five minutes, maybe ten? The howling and scratching sounds stopped and I chanced a look outside the door. They were gone.

The warm air made me shiver as my body fought to shake off the cold as I came out to survey the damage.

The warehouse was in shambles. More than a dozen of the high shelves lay on their sides. Employees helped raise those that had fallen on customers. Others tried to help the ones who got in the way of the beasts, their broken bodies testament to their fury. Billie lay on the ground gasping, her lips crimson and her leg at an unnatural angle. David and Matt stood by with helpless expressions on their faces as they tried to figure out what to do. I slumped to the floor. It wasn't my fault, a small part of me knew, but I still ran. I could've helped in some way, maybe pulled them off her. But I ran. I hid like a coward.

Across the warehouse, through the glass doors, I recognized the red and white lights of Pittsburgh police cars. The officers filed in, weapons drawn. Late again.

I was still sitting on the floor, telling myself that there was nothing I could've done, when a pair shoes stopped in front of me. I looked up to see Officer Menold with Officer Appel close at hand. They both looked at me, first with surprise, then with stony faces.

Oh boy.

There's an old saying: If something happens once, it's weird. Twice, it's a coincidence. Three times, and it a legitimate phenomenon.

Being linked to first one robbery, then a dead girl, and now another robbery, I could see why the police brought me in. I didn't exactly appreciate it, but I had a grudging understanding of their motives. Were our positions reversed, I'd have probably suspected me too.

The little interrogation room wasn't like the ones they show in movies. It wasn't a huge dark room with a single bare bulb in a lamp that shone into my eyes until I confessed. The room was tiny, about the size of the storage room of my apartment. The two-way mirror was also absent, replaced by safety glass, the kind with wires running through it. I sat in the little wooden chair and watched as other policemen brought in drunks and purse-snatchers. Some of them looked young enough to be Shannon's age, and sat staring at a blank wall while the officers processed them. At the counter, other citizens stood and complained about their shop being the one robbed, or their child being the one missing, and the cop behind the counter just nodded and took their names.

Menold and Appel talked to a man in a suit, probably a detective assigned to the case. I tried not to flinch every time they both glanced at me. When they finished, they both fixed me with a scowl before they stormed out of sight.

The detective, an older man with salt-and-pepper hair, turned, saw me, and smiled as he made his way to the door of the interrogation room. He walked in and closed the door behind himself without taking his eyes off me.

"I'm sorry to make you wait, Mr. Cooper," he began. "It's busy in here tonight."

"Am I being charged with something?"

"No, no," he said as he put a large file down on the table. "You're free to leave at any time. The officers who arrested you acted... hastily."

"I don't really blame them," I said. "That's the second time I've seen them today."

"Yes," said the detective. "I know. First at the scene of another break-in, now this one. And Officer Menold tells me that you're connected to the death of a young lady..."

"Shannon," I said.

"That's right. But you're not a suspect." His smile, I could tell, was practiced, a cop's version of a poker face, a mask to put people at ease while he was busy dissecting them with his eyes and intuition. I *was* a suspect, but he couldn't pin anything to me. Yet.

"You have to admit, it is strange that the only thing the three cases have in common is you."

"I work for the warehouse," I said. "Doug asked me to come by his shop, and I'd just met the girl. That's all there is to it."

"Maybe," said the detective. "I've been asking around. It seems you don't have a huge fan club here. Between you and me, half the guys here are scared of you, and the other half think you're a fraud."

"Which category do you fall in?"

"I'm undecided," he said. "I hear you can do some impressive stuff, but some of the other guys say it's all black magic and bullshit."

I'd guessed as much. People feared what they didn't understand, and for most people, that meant me.

"Why don't you come with me." He picked up his folder and motioned for me to accompany him. "I've got something I'd like to show you."

I nodded and followed, down the hall past more uniforms and street clothes. Some looked away when I approached, others didn't hide their opinions. He led me down a hallway to another room, one that looked straight out of one those T.V. cop shows. It was dim with a large pane of glass, which I guessed was a mirror on the other side. In the room beyond was a man, huddled in a corner.

"We caught him at the warehouse," said the detective. "The others got away, but this one got cornered. He fought like a lunatic when we caught him, but once we got him in here, he settled down."

"Why show me?" I'd been down here before, but only on a few occasions. Those times, I'd been brought in by families to work with the police, but never officially part of an investigation.

"I'd like to get your impression," he said.

He smiled, likely because of the expression of distrust on my face. I felt like a magickian asked to do a party trick. Still, I wasn't under arrest when, by all rights, I should've been, so what the hell? I closed my eyes and dropped the walls in my mind. In the cell, the man sat huddled in a corner, his back to us. Even in the harsh light of the holding room, his aura was clear. Again, there was the thin shell of blue with an overwhelming overcoat of black. He lifted his head and sniffed the air.

"Don't worry," said the detective. "He can't see us."

But he did. Whether he saw us or smelled us, he sensed our presence somehow. When he turned his feral eyes on us, the black around him swelled, roaring like ebony fire. He hissed, then darted to the window, slamming against it with his fist. His ferocity scared me, and I stepped back a few feet without realizing I'd done it.

"Maybe he can," muttered the detective. "So? What do you think?"

In my head, I went over the list of responses I could have given. I could tell him the truth, set myself square in the crackpot category. I could tell him the guy was on drugs. I was pretty sure his bullshit meter would start clanging about that one, but what else could I say? Something in his expression, in his stance, told me that it was a test. He wanted to know if he could trust me, and if I trusted him. "What'd the other cops say?"

"Crack or meth or some other drug," he said without expression. "They say he's higher than a kite and'll behave when he comes down. What do you say?"

I took a deep breath and prepared for the worst.

"They're wrong," I said. "He's possessed." No matter how many times I said it, the phrase still sounded stupid to my ears.

"He'll calm down when whatever's got him lets go." *If it doesn't kill him first*, I decided not to add.

He stood looking at my face for a moment, his narrow eyes appraising my features. I could almost see the pendulum swinging in his brain between "nut job" and "conman."

"Okay," he said. "I believe you."

The detective, whose name turned out to be Taylor, let me leave with the notion that he planned on calling on me again. Considering he didn't immediately throw me in a padded cell or tell me I was full of crap, the prospect of him calling didn't have as ominous a tone as it might have.

I took a cab back over to the warehouse, where my car sat waiting in the parking lot, and decided to see how much damage the possessed men had done. As I walked through the door, I was tipped off that something wasn't right by the way the other employees looked at me. Every one of them either hurried out of my path or avoided eye contact. I put it down to shock as I made my way back to the loading dock.

The hole in the steel door was smaller than I thought, only about three feet in diameter. Still, it was impressive that human beings could have torn the metal like tissue with only their bare hands. The area was still roped off with crime scene tape. Tiny flags marked wet shoe prints, things dropped, small droplets of blood on the concrete floor.

"Back already?" I turned to see the floor manager, Mike Millman, panting around the corner, his great bulk blocking most of the corridor.

"I wasn't charged with anything," I replied. "They just wanted to get a statement."

"They don't lead a person out in handcuffs just to get a statement," he snarled. "What were you doing while all this chaos was going on?"

"Hiding." I still felt a little sheepish, but glad to be alive. "In the freezer."

"I bet," he snorted. "Why weren't you out here trying to help our members?"

"It's against company policy to physically interfere," I snapped. "Even if I wasn't scared out of my mind, there was no way I was going to try to stop one of those things. My life's worth more than ten bucks an hour."

"I think it was because you were helping them."

The statement fell flat and left me speechless for a moment. When I got over the shock of his stupidity, my mind raced for a comeback.

"You're kidding," was all I managed. The soul of wit, that's me.

"I just bet you arranged this, and the police knew it, and that's why they took you in." The gleam in his eye told me he liked playing amateur detective. Even if someone proved him wrong, he'd never admit it.

"That's the biggest load of..."

"Go clean out your locker," he said, a note of haughty triumph in his voice.

"Oh come on..."

"You don't work here anymore! You're fired!" He turned and waddled away.

I stood there for a moment, fuming over his stupidity, then made my way to the break room. As I entered, half a dozen pairs of eyes glanced up, saw who it was, then snapped back down to their lunches or newspapers. The conversations stopped and left the room in eerie silence. I thought about making some kind of statement, telling them off or protesting my innocence, but de-cided against it. Better just to get my things and leave.

As I pulled my sweater out, I felt a hand on my shoulder.

"I'm sorry," said Greg, my direct supervisor. "I couldn't convince him you weren't involved."

"Don't worry about it," I said as I slammed the locker shut. "The fat old walrus probably would've fired you too for sticking up for me."

"I can try to get you your job back in a few weeks..."

"Forget it," I said. "I'll find something else. Hey, I was looking for a job when I found this one, right?"

He smiled.

"Don't stick your neck out on my account," I said. "I'll land on my feet."

He shook my hand and walked me to the door without another word. As we walked, I kept my barriers down, my mental doors open. As the front doors whooshed closed behind me, I'd found what I hoped I wouldn't. In a place like this warehouse, where people built their lives and more than a thousand custom-ers (members, Millman called them) a day wondered through, there should have been a pulse, a rhythm that teemed with life. Now, after the raid, the place felt like a dead cell. No matter where I looked, I couldn't find that heartbeat. There were no scats to be found.

6

I drove back to my apartment, fuming. My client was dead, my friend had been robbed, and now I was unemployed. And to top it off, I was a suspect in both robberies and the murder. It wasn't the best of days. The sun was already up when I passed through the Fort Pitt Tunnel, making Steel City sparkle in the early morning light. Most days, I love the sight of the Pittsburgh skyline in the morning. Today, it only made me feel tired.

I pulled up at my apartment, parked, and took the elevator up. Once inside, I pulled the shades on the window, threw my coat on the couch, and buried myself beneath the blankets on my bed. I tried my best to tell myself that I didn't care about what else was going on in the outside world. Maybe, if I went to sleep, the whole thing would solve itself. At least asleep, I couldn't get any further involved.

I'd just pulled the blankets over my head and closed my eyes when the telephone rang. I groaned and snatched the handset off the charger.

"Hello," I growled.

For a moment, there was nothing on the line, just a tiny bit of static and crackling. I thought about hanging up when a faint voice dropped the bottom out of my stomach.

"Mister Cooper..."

I knew the voice.

"Help me..."

Her voice was weak, choked with sobs. It didn't matter that she was already dead, I could tell she was suffering.

"Help me..."

"Shannon?"

"Don't let them take me..." she pleaded. "Don't let them..." I heard a shriek, the kind no person I've ever known could make, then the line went dead.

Telephone calls from the dead are not uncommon. In fact, the phenomenon is reported more often than most people think. I even received a few before I died, and many more since I came back. But this was the first one that made me feel sick, made me want to weep openly. She came to me for help. I'd failed her. And damn me for being so selfish as to think I could hide in my bed, under the blankets like a child.

I got up, splashed some water on my face, then went to find the business card tucked in the pocket of my coat. When I found it, I dialed the number.

"You realize I could lose my job over this, right?"

Detective Taylor piloted his brown four-door down the street. As cars went, his was a land-yacht, barely able to keep in one lane at a time and built in an era when gasoline prices weren't expected to reach much over a buck-fifty a gallon.

"I wouldn't ask if it weren't important," I said.

He chanced a glance from the busy road toward me then back again and shrugged. He took his right hand off the steering wheel and reached behind the seat, producing a manila folder which he dropped in my lap.

"You're sure you want to see this?" He didn't look at me, but kept a steady eye on the road. "There's some ugly stuff in there."

"Yeah," I said.

He wasn't kidding. If anything he was being mild. The photo of Shannon's body was gruesome. She lay on the concrete on her stomach, naked, her legs splayed wide. One arm was sitting a foot away from its stump, and it didn't take a psychic to see that the dark pool she lay in was blood. Her face was a crimson mask, all but the eyes. The lids were open, but there were nothing but empty sockets staring out at the world. The coroner's report also stated that her tongue was missing, as were several of her vital organs. The official cause of death was unknown, but most of the damage had been done to the body postmortem by rats.

I closed the folder and breathed deep while I waited for the nausea to pass.

"Told you," said Taylor.

The car came to a stop across the street from the alley where Shannon was found. As I stepped out into the street, I half-expected to see her standing at the mouth waiting for me.

"So why are we here?" Taylor got out of the car and stared into the alley.

"I don't really know," I said. "I'll know it if I see it."

"Anything I can help you look for?"

"No," I said. "I see things differently than you do."

I closed my eyes and concentrated, dropping the walls and opening the doors.

Places where violent death occurred always have a mark, a kind of scar. The violence of the act, the terror and pain of the victim, the joy and rage of the criminal, all leave impressions behind, the kind that replay over and over. To some people, it's a haunting. To those who recognize it for what it is, it's a reminder. To me, it's like watching a snuff film on a loop. I can't make it stop, and most of the time, what I see I'll never forget.

But in this case, I didn't want to forget. Part of me wanted to be reminded that I could have, should have, done more to help her. A big part of me felt like her death was my fault.

I opened my eyes and expected to see Shannon's death, her killer, the pink glow of her radiant life flowing out of her body and into the gutter… There should have been an aura, faint and iridescent, around the buildings whose walls made up the alcove. What I saw instead was eerie, diseased and wrong. I could tell where her body fell, but not for the remnant I thought would be there. Instead, it was marked by cold nothing, as if the site had been licked clean of all its energies. Even the life force from the buildings around it had been devoured. For a moment, I thought I'd left a wall standing, a door closed, but when I looked at Taylor, I could see swirls of brilliant green and yellow emanating from around him.

He must've noticed the look of confusion on my face.

"What's wrong?" he asked.

"Everything," I said. "She's not here."

"Um… She's downtown in the morgue."

"No. You know how forensics teams pick up little traces of evidence to help build a case? I'm trying to do the same thing here, only there's no evidence to collect."

"You mean, like someone swept the scene clean?"

I nodded, but it was more than that. It was more like someone had *sterilized* the scene, stripped it bare and left a patch of emptiness in their wake.

"So what now?"

"Take me back to my car," I said. "I need to think things through."

My father wasn't a particularly brilliant man. He had blue-collar sensibilities and a work ethic that would put a plow horse to shame, but his ambition stopped at wanting to be a good father and husband. His thoughts usually ran to the simplest solutions, matter-of-fact know-how about how things worked and where to find answers. "If you want to know about something," he often said, "ask someone whose job it is to know it. If you want to know about law, ask a cop. If you want to know about medicine, ask a doctor." Following that logic, if I wanted to know about something in the netherworld, I needed to ask a dead person. The trouble was, I didn't have a spirit guide, and I intended to keep it that way.

It's not like I'm against the concept of a guiding ghost, it's just that no one ever mentions the costs of such a relationship. I'm not talking about possession, but nothing in life, or death for that matter, is free. In the case of spirit guides, whom some would like to think are just benevolent and wise spirits, the price comes at a piece of the human's energy. A favor for favor. Usually, they use that energy to do something benign like visiting their loved ones or taking care of unfinished business. Others use it for other purposes, like spying on the women's shower of a college. Some, however, stockpile the energy until they can take over a body, throwing the owner's soul into limbo. I can't count the number of times I, or someone like me, has been called to evict a soul squatting in a body that's not his. Too often, that's for sure. To me, the whole thing is just too risky.

Instead, I have Maggie.

It was nearing noon. I hadn't slept in more than twenty-four hours, and I could feel it. It's funny the way lack of sleep can make the sun's rays feel a little too bright, car horns a little too loud. I drove to Maggie's shop in silence. Experience taught me that, without sleep, even the best music would just be annoying.

I parked on Carson Street, lucky to find another car pulling out about a block from Maggie's shop. The sidewalk was crowded with people on their lunch breaks. My stomach rumbled to remind me there was something else I hadn't done for quite some time: eaten. Maggie first, I chided my belly, lunch after.

The crowd grew thicker the closer I got to Maggie's shop. I don't know if it was the lack of sleep or just hunger that dulled my wits, but I didn't realize they weren't just the usual group of corporate hunters on their way to a meal until it had congealed so much that I couldn't get through. They were gawking, not feed-ing. I pushed my way to the front of the crowd to find Maggie's shop door was off the hinges, pushed out from the inside, yellow police tape the only barrier from the outside. My rumbling stom-ach did a somersault. I tore through the tape as I ran through the door.

"Maggie!"

The inside of the shop was in ruins. Far worse than what they'd done do Doug's, worse than the warehouse. Every canis-ter of precious herbs was shattered, every book shredded. The counter lay broken in fifty pieces around the room. Someone had smeared excrement on the walls.

I made my way to the back of the shop, where only a few beads of the curtain remained on their strands. The altar room was devastated, the candles scattered and broken, her statues of the god and goddess smeared with filth. In the center of the room, where Maggie's meditation symbol had been, was a large hole.

I ran from the shop to the side entrance, the door of which also was missing. Fear flooded my body as I ran up the stairs to Maggie's apartment. I didn't want to imagine her hurt, or worse, but I couldn't help it. Once the images started, I couldn't block them out. By the time I got to her door, panic had crept into my mind, sure of the worst.

"Maggie!" I pounded on the door. "Maggie, it's me!"

The door clicked and opened a breath, enough for me to see red, tear-stained eyes.

"Stan?" she whispered. She threw the door open and threw her arms around me, her body shuddering with every sob. Her tears were not of anger or sadness, but of child-in-the-dark, no-the-world-isn't-going-to-be-alright terror. I did the only thing I could think to do. I held her tight and let her cry.

It took me the better part of an hour and a cup of her own special blend of tea to calm her down enough to tell me what happened, during which time I just sat and held her hand and felt stupid and powerless.

"It happened last night," she said, her voice still shaking. "Late night or early morning, I don't know which. It was still dark outside. I was asleep when I heard..." She shuddered. "...*them* breaking in. My wards didn't hold. Oh gods, they didn't hold. They still got in."

"They came in through the basement," I said.

"It wasn't protected," she nodded, staring off. "I didn't think..."

"What else?" Every memory hurt, but I needed to know.

"I could hear them down there, screaming and destroying everything, and I was scared. Oh gods, I was so scared. And then..." Her voice trailed off.

"What?"

"They came after me. They came up the stairs, clawing

at my door, shrieking, but I didn't open it. My wards held on the door. But the noise. The noise was so terrible." Her voice gave way to a fresh batch of terrified sobs. I put my arms around her and she melted into them, no longer one of the strongest women I knew, now only a child begging for a night-light.

"Did you see any of them? Through the peephole maybe? Catch a glimpse? Anything that could help us identify them?"

"No," she sniffed. "I didn't get anywhere near the door."

"Okay," I cupped her cheek in my hand. "Listen, I'm going to find out what's going on. I'll figure it out, okay? This is going to be alright."

"Alright?" Her voice went from terrified to hostile in an instant. "Did you see what they did to my shop? I've got nothing left! They wiped me out, Stan!"

"Okay," I raised my hands in surrender to ease her back down. "What did the police say?"

"The police," she spat. "They think it was some religious group that doesn't take kindly to Pagans. Either that or I did it to commit insurance fraud."

"Did you have insurance?" It was an innocent question, but one I wished I could suck back in. Her eyes blazed.

"Yes, I had insurance. Do you think..?"

"Whoa, wait, slow down," I said. "I know you didn't. I'm talking about rebuilding the store."

"I don't know if I can," she said, shaking her head. "Everything's replaceable, but I don't know if I'll ever be able to re-sanctify the space."

"You will," I said, taking her hand in mine. "I'll help you. Whatever I can do, I'll help."

"Stan," she said, her eyes meeting mine. "I'm scared. They'll be back."

"Then you'll stay at my place."

I really should learn to think before I speak. At the time, all I saw was a friend in need. However, as my car approached my apartment, I began to wonder how wise it may have been. I wasn't afraid of whatever dark forces were at work coming after me. More, I wondered if I'd left dirty dishes in the sink, or underwear on the floor. I wondered if where I lived, the home of a nerdy bachelor, would be comfortable for Maggie, or anyone else for that matter.

"Don't expect too much," I said as I parked. I took one of her bags while she took the other and the pet carrier in which Bitsy patiently waited to be let out. Of the two of them, the cat looked like the less fragile.

"Remember," I said as I unlocked my door. "I live alone."

To me, my apartment looks fine. So what if I forget to clean up the dinner dishes every now and again, or if I leave the occasional errant sock laying on the back of my couch. My movies are in alphabetical order on the shelf, and I know roughly where everything is, and that's really all that matters to me. Besides, posters of imported horror movies on the walls, framed of course, are more my personality than dorm-room art prints.

I led Maggie in and closed the door behind us. Her eyes darted from window to door as she read the inscriptions around them, a hint of a smile on her lips.

"Wards," she said. "I taught you those."

"Yep," I said, pointing to the ceiling. "And there's another just like it under the carpet. Trust me, you're safe here."

"Thanks," she said. She put the pet carrier down and opened the door to let Bitsy take her first cautious steps to sniff the air. After a moment, the cat sauntered across the room, leapt onto my windowsill, and began cleaning herself.

"Where will I..."

"This way," I said. "I have an extra bedroom."

I led the way and opened the door. The room looked more cluttered than I remembered, with a few boxes growing into nearly a dozen, a pile of movies that seemed to be growing by the day, and a few items I had trouble recalling the last time I'd seen them. Or even why I had them in the first place.

"We'll put everything in the closet for now," I said. "And I'll get you something to sleep on. I hope this is okay."

She set her bag on the floor and put her arms around me, hugging me tight and kissing my cheek.

"Thank you," she said.

I told her to lie down in my bed while I pushed the debris into the closet. She was exhausted from a full night of fear, so she agreed. It took me half an hour to jam all of my things into the tiny space, but at least the closet door still closed. When I was done, I went to the living room and sat down to make a list of things I needed to make Maggie comfortable.

First, she'd need a mattress and a pillow. Toiletries might be good, maybe some perfumed bath-salts to help her relax. A litter box and some cat food. I was so tired that I didn't even notice when I fell asleep on the couch.

The wind whistled a familiar scream in my ears as my body fell. Gravity churned my stomach. I remembered strange things, insignificant things, like my high school locker combination and the color of my favorite pair of sneakers. The ground was coming up fast, impossibly fast, but my racing mind outran it with trivial bits of once-forgotten-now-remembered trash. And questions. What the hell just happened, and what'll happen to my apartment, and if I die, will anyone really miss me?

The dream was different somehow. I always fell alone, but not this time. Someone else, someone new, stood on the construction site, her sweatshirt bloodied, her hair matted. She looked up at me with eyeless sockets as I fell, and for a moment, I hung in midair, transfixed by her orbless gaze. She was watching me die, pleading with me to help her when I was helpless. I watched as her form shuddered and crumpled. From out of her clothes, rats streamed like a wriggling, twitching tide, until there was nothing left of Shannon but her bloodstained clothing. I screamed, and I fell.

My body jerked upright, leaving me gasping for breath on the couch.

"Gods, Stan," said Maggie from the door of my room. "Are you okay?"

"Bad dream," I said. "You?"

"Better, thanks."

"Good," I said. My head felt muddy, like it still wanted to sleep, but there were more important things on my mind.

"I cleared the boxes," I said. "The room is yours. I'm going to leave for a little while..." Her eyes widened. "But I'll be back soon. I'm going to get some supplies for you and some food, and then I'll be back. You'll be safe here. I promise. Okay?"

She nodded.

I turned to the windowsill where the cat still lay in a shrinking sunbeam.

"Watch her," I said to Bitsy. "Don't let anything happen to her."

As if in answer, the cat stretched and jumped to the floor, winding herself around Maggie's legs.

7

I dropped nearly three hundred dollars at Walmart, picking up things I hoped Maggie, or any other woman for that matter, might like. First was an air mattress and pump, then flannel sheets and the fluffiest pillow I could find. After that, I walked down the aisles and looked for things that I, being a bachelor, did not, nor would ever, have. Perfumed soaps, bubble bath, a fluffy new pair of pink socks. I figured, what the hell? I don't know anything about women other than that they completely befuddle me, but I wanted Maggie to be comfortable. I also grabbed a new towel/hand towel/washcloth set. There was no telling how old the ones in my bathroom were, much less the last time I'd seen fit to wash them.

On the way out, I picked up some orange juice and coffee and a loaf of bread. For me, breakfast is usually Pop Tarts and coffee, but I'm told that *normal* folks like breakfast. I tossed a bottle of raspberry preserves into the cart as well.

I paid for everything and got back in my car and headed home. On the way, I glanced back down Carson Street. Curiosity burned in the back of my mind. If the things that raided Maggie's shop were the same things that robbed Doug and the warehouse, I needed to know. I fought the urge to turn left and continued toward my apartment. Maggie needed the things in the bags, and in truth, I wanted her to have them. Maybe it was selfish, but I wanted to see her smile again, if just for a moment, if only for a clumsy gesture from a friend.

Carrying six fully-loaded shopping bags from Walmart was no easy task, but I didn't want to make two trips. With the lightest four in one hand and the heaviest two in the other, I hefted the bags into the building and onto the elevator, all the while expecting to feel something or someone watching me. I half expected some howling beast to come leaping horror-movie style out of the elevator as it opened. My good fortune won out, however, and I arrived at my door intact. I set the bags down as I fumbled with the keys and opened the door.

"Maggie?"

I needn't have shouted. She was sitting cross-legged in the middle of the living room floor. Naked.

"Holy..."

"I'm sorry," she said. "I thought meditating would calm me down a little. I didn't know when you'd be back." She got up and pulled a terrycloth bathrobe over her body.

"I... uh... got you some stuff," I said. That's me, the master of cool.

"Thanks," she smirked as she took some of the bags. Maggie wasn't modest, and never felt shame about her body. She also thought it was cute when someone got flustered at the sight of her nudity. That someone was usually me.

"It's nothing much," I said. "Just a few girly things. I got you a mattress, some bath stuff."

"Thank you," she said. "I'm feeling a little lost. Thanks for being here for me."

I dropped the mattress and pump off in her room, then came back to the living room to find her looking through the other bags, an expression of amusement on her face. It hovered just over the worry.

"I'll leave you to get settled," I said.

"You're leaving again?" The alarm in her voice made me want to hold her and promise to never leave her side, but I had to know.

"I'll be back soon," I said. "I just need to check something out."

"You're going back to the shop, aren't you?" It wasn't a question so much as an accusation.

"Yes," I said. "Look, if they're the same things that robbed Doug..."

"So what if they are?" she cried. "They're dangerous! Did you miss the part where they killed people? Or how about where they tried to kill me?"

"That's why I have to go," I said. "Shannon... Those things killed her. She came to me for help, and I have to see if there's something I can do."

"Would it do any good if I begged you not to go?" She sounded miserable.

"No."

She put her arms around me and pulled me close. The warmth of her breasts pushed against my body as she kissed me on the lips. It was a passionate kiss, but not the kind lovers share. It was almost like she was telling me goodbye.

"Then promise me you'll be careful," she said. "And come back to me."

"Hey," I said as I forced a smile. "You know me."

There's a little voice that everyone hears in the back of

their minds. Most of the time, that voice tries to tell us what to do, or if something we're about to do will embarrass us. Sometimes, however, that little voice is all that stands between a person and painful learning experiences, humiliation, or even death. In cases where a person has to overcome stage-fright, for example, that little voice is the nagging fear that everyone in the audience is going to hate them, throw rotten food, and generally laugh them out of the building. In that case, the little voice, whom I liken to a tiny, grumpy version of myself, isn't to be trusted. I usually tell him to go eat a plate of Oreos and shut the Hell up. Other times, that voice has good reason to be scared.

I've done a lot of stupid things in my life, most of them when I was a kid. Like every other boy, I got into my share of scrapes that would have been avoidable if I'd just thought about what I was about to do before I did it, or listened to the little voice in my head that told me to think about the consequences. In fact, as I was leaving my apartment, I could hear that little voice again. This time, I pictured him as a red-devil version of myself with a lolling tongue and an enormous bulge in his pants. He told me that it was stupid to leave a vulnerable, naked (under her robe) woman in my apartment alone instead of offering her "comfort." I blew that voice off and headed out anyway, secure in my knowledge that taking advantage of anyone, whether she was my best friend or not, in such a situation wasn't in my nature.

As I pulled the car back onto Carson Street, there was another little voice, this one coming with all the presence of a frightened child who wouldn't come out from behind his mother's apron, asking me if I was sure it was a good idea to go back to the shop alone, at night, to see where that hole led.

I probably should've listened to that last one.

The side street beside Maggie's shop was all but deserted, so I parked far enough away that I thought my car wouldn't attract attention, but close enough to make a quick get-away, should the need arise. Then I took a few deep breaths, grabbed the flashlight from my glove box, and headed into the shop.

The little voice in my head wanted to know if I was really certain about going in. What if whoever, or whatever it was, came back? Worse, what if the police came and found me poking around at a crime scene, connecting me with a third break-in? I should probably have gone home, given Maggie her frillies, and let the police handle it. Of course, that wasn't an option.

The police had been back, as evidenced by the repaired tape over the doorway. This time, I ducked under to get inside.

It wasn't that big of a stretch for me to believe that the break-in at the warehouse was related to the two on Carson Street. Sure, it was difficult, scary even, to picture a bunch of crazed human men clawing their way through the floor to get to the shops. But then again, seeing them rip through that metal door at the warehouse was enough to give me nightmares anyway. Maggie's was different though. They'd come after *her*, not just her shop. People in the warehouse were injured too, but they were in the way, incidental. In Maggie's case, it seemed like she was a target, just like Shannon… just like I would be, if I wasn't careful.

I stood in the doorway just out of street view for a moment and dropped the walls in my mind to let the energy patterns of the world back into my vision. When I opened my eyes, I felt a chill. Like the alley where Shannon was found, there was nothing left, no trace of energy, good or bad.

The only light in the room was the dying sunlight from outside, and with the room scoured clean of energy tracings, I would be stumbling in the dark like a blind man before too long. I picked my way through the debris, hoping to find some shred of Maggie's power, a spark, a residue, on anything. But the front room was clear, an empty cell.

The back room was darker still, without any light from the doorway reaching. I made my way through the door, crunching broken beads as I went. There had to be something left. When I first met Maggie, before I could close off my own strange sight, her shop glowed. A star that landed in the middle of Pittsburgh, that's how it seemed to me. For every scrap of that energy to be gone was just too horrifying a thought.

There, just in the corner of my periphery, I caught a glimpse of blue, faint and weak. I stepped around the great hole in the floor, also covered by police tape, and dug into the debris. Beneath a fallen shelf and several broken candles I found the source. It was a seashell, no larger than a quarter. I tucked the shell into my pocket and continued toward the basement stairs.

The back room was darker than I remembered, as if the absence of light left behind a thick mass of oppressive matter that wanted to push me back out into the street. The flashlight beam did little to hold the dark away. It swirled and closed behind wherever the pool of light moved.

I stepped around the debris and went down the stairs. My eyes strained against the feeble beam of my flashlight, my ears sensitive to every whisper, every scuff of my sneakers. With every step, my mind played a dozen horrific scenes from movies I'd spent too many late nights watching. It also gave me a chance to wonder what I hoped I would find. Sewer pipes were too small for anyone to wriggle through, even tiny people, otherwise they wouldn't clog so often. This basement didn't have another door, which meant the only way the attackers could have gotten in was if they'd dug their way in.

As the thought crossed my mind, I came off the steps and saw a large hole in the street-side wall. Sometimes I love being right. This wasn't one of those times.

The ragged edge of the hole was maybe three feet across,

large enough that I could get through without too much trouble. I shone the light on the concrete and wondered what tools they'd used to get through the wall so quickly. Embedded in the crevices, I found strings of hair, a few torn fragments of cloth, a fingernail, a tooth. It made me shiver. As dark as the basement was, inside the tunnel seemed darker still, but if I was going to find out what was going on, I knew I had to look. I shone the light through the opening and, seeing nothing, I climbed through.

The tunnel continued on for a few feet, then opened up into a space large enough for me to stand in, hunched over a bit. I shone the light around until I found a metal access ladder against a wall leading to an iron disc in the ceiling. We were under the street. Whether we were in a storm drain or an access tunnel, I didn't know, but the sight of something man-made gave me a strange sense of comfort. In the flashlight beam I could see three passages, one in front of me, two on either side. I took a deep breath, closed my eyes, and turned off the flashlight. When I opened my eyes again, the tunnel lit up with the life and energy of the city.

Whatever this gift of perception that I possess is, it works better than night-vision in some cases.

In others, like in the under-street tunnels, it allowed me to track the intruders by looking for the tell-tale absence of light, the tracks of darkness they left behind. Though I couldn't see far down any tunnel, the one in which the darkness was thick as tar lay right in front of me.

Creeping through the darkness without my flashlight, using only the lack of energy trail to guide me, didn't give me much in the way of seeing where I was going or what was around me, but I didn't want to chance the beam being seen by anyone, or anything, ahead in the tunnel. If I was lucky, I might be able to find what I was looking for before I was noticed.

In the dark, a person's senses play tricks on them. What seems like a great distance could only be a few feet, a tiny shifting of a pebble sounds like a cannon shot, and what seems like hours could only be a few minutes or even seconds.

I couldn't tell how far I'd walked, or even the direction, when I came to a wall. Thick cinderblock and concrete, damp and cold to the touch, rose up in front of me. I felt the texture, searching with my fingertips until I found another rough patch that gave way to a hole at my waist level. I reached into my pocket for my flashlight.

A hissing noise cut through the darkness, bouncing off the tunnel walls and reaching my ears in an eerie din. The hairs on my neck and arms danced as the pit of my stomach dropped out. I snapped the light on to see a face, twisted and full of hate, protruding from the hole. I yelped and jerked backward, sending myself down to the wet floor of the tunnel. In the dim light of the flashlight, the shadowy figure dove from the mouth of the wall and at me. He landed on me, and tore at my jacket with his clawed fingers, his teeth snapping inches from my face. I drove the flashlight into the side of his head and knocked him sideways just long enough for me to scramble to my feet and run back down the tunnel.

His howl echoed in the concrete tunnel behind me, a guttural screech that called more hissing forms to the opening. I didn't look back, but I could hear them following me, nails against the concrete, echoing screams in my ears.

The flashlight beam jumped in spastic jerks across the walls which left me alternating between painful brightness and near-blind darkness as I ran. When I reached the manhole cover, I darted for the chewed hole in the wall that led back to Maggie's basement. If I could make it back to my car, I thought, I might be able to get away from them. When I reached the spot where the tunnel narrowed, I felt fingers close in around my shoes and teeth tearing at my ankles. I kicked and screamed, pushing them back with strength that only pure terror could've given me.

When I fell through to the basement, I hit the floor hard, my bloodied legs screaming in pain. They followed, their squealing driving my kicking legs until I was upright again and limping up the stairs and through the door. I made it out of the back room when I felt the wind knocked out of me and a powerful shoulder drove me to the floor.

"Don't move!" said the second officer, his gun leveled where I lay struggling with his partner.

"Run!" I screamed. "They're coming!"

In answer, piercing screams cut through the air as the intruders came rushing through the hole in the floor.

"What the..?" The second officer had his gun trained on the doorway to the back room, the first stood up, forgetting about me, his face slack in bewilderment.

"Run!" I cried again, as I scrambled to my feet and staggered out the door. I heard shots, five, maybe six, before the officers started screaming themselves, though theirs were not screams of rage, but of agony, choked off with sick gurgling sounds. I slammed the door to my car without looking back, put the key in the ignition, and sped off for the only safe place I could think of.

My hands shook so badly that I couldn't get the key into the lock on my apartment door. The gunshots still echoed in my ears as did the officers' screams. I didn't see the names on their badges, didn't even take the time to look at their faces, and now they were dead. Because of me. Because I didn't listen to that little voice in my head. I fumbled with the key for a second or two more before my body began to shut down in a series of agonizing sobs. I flailed against the door.

"Maggie! It's me!"

She opened the door and I fell inside, curling up where I landed in a fit of labored breathing and tears.

"Stan!"

"Coming..." I panted. "They're coming. Door..."

She slammed the door hard and locked it, then she knelt beside me and cradled my head against her.

"You're okay," she said, though her voice shook. "You're safe now."

She said the words, and to her credit, she meant them. Then the lights went out.

"Oh, gods."

The metal door thundered as something heavy rammed against it, followed by the screech of nails as they tried to dig their way through. First one set of hands, then another, and another, until it seemed like our world was nothing but darkness and the metallic squeal of claws trying to pierce steel. Maggie sat and rocked me, held me close, but now it wasn't me she was comforting. She squeezed me tighter with every second that passed, her eyes growing wider, her expression more desperate, as moans of fear welled up from deep inside her most primal self.

Then it was quiet. The scratching stopped and we both dared to hope they'd given up.

In my building, there were ten apartments, all occupied. Mine held only myself and Maggie. The other nine held families. The screams started with the splintering of wood and plaster. Across the hall, the woman begged for the lives of her children. I heard them scream, then I heard their silence. Above me, two more families suffered the same fate. One went out fighting, with a few rounds from a pistol cutting through the din, but in the end, that family was quiet too. Below, the screams seemed fainter, farther away, as the sounds of splintering wood gave way angry shouts, and then the sounds of abject terror, all the while underscored by the shrill cries of the intruders.

Then there was silence. Awful silence.

I sat there, unable to move, numb, counting the dead in my mind. Two more, the officers from the shop, come to investigate because my car was there. Thirty more, dead because I'd led those infernal things here. They couldn't get to me, I'd seen to that. So while I hid in my hole, they cut short the lives of everyone around me. Shannon. Dead, because of me.

I felt something inside me give, crack or break, I didn't care which, and the fresh tears flowed out of me in a tide. I wept like a child on Maggie's lap, thankful for her comforting warmth, but feeling deep down that somehow, even her presence here was my fault. I don't know how long I lay there before exhaustion overcame me and I lapsed into unconsciousness.

I jerked awake, sure the pounding I heard was the intruders, back to finish the job. Then I heard angry voices from the other side of the door. I was in my room, though how Maggie managed to drag me to my bed I couldn't imagine. My ankles hurt, but Maggie had also cleaned and bandaged my wounds sometime in the night. She bolted up from a chair in the corner when the pounding started.

"Stanley Cooper! Pittsburgh P.D.! Open up!"

I crawled out of bed to Maggie, who stood shaking, a lost expression on her face. I took her hand and limped to the door. When I turned the lock, the door burst open as Officers Menold and Appel rushed inside, their sidearms drawn.

I didn't hear what they said as they put me and Maggie in handcuffs. I didn't care whether I had the right to an attorney or to remain silent. It didn't matter anymore. All those dead people, all those ruined lives, and all I could do was run and hide like a terrified child.

They led us out through the building. The doorway to the apartment across from mine swarmed with photographers, policemen, detectives, and men wearing black slickers identifying them as working for the coroner's office. Some of them turned to look at me as we passed, their jaws tight and eyes dripping with disgust. I didn't blame them.

Outside, I saw a man sitting on a bench, his head in his hands, his body heaving, as an officer tried to console him. I recognized him. He worked the night shift at one of the computer fabrication plants, leaving his wife and two children, a son and a daughter, alone in the darkness. He saw me as we passed, and his expression changed from sorrow to hatred in a flash. He made to run at me, but the officer held him back. Some might have said he was lucky he wasn't at home, but I knew different. He'd have been better off dead alongside his family than to have to endure life without them.

Maggie didn't speak during the ride to the police station. When they took us into the holding area, she chanced a brief, sad smile, before being led off in another direction. I was processed, searched, and put in a room with only a table, two chairs and a large mirror across one wall. I could feel the officers watching me from behind the glass. It didn't matter. I wasn't going to try to run or to hurt anyone. I was too tired, too drained. Too many people had been hurt because of me already. Better they just lock me away.

The door opened, and Detective Taylor walked in, a

thick manila folder in his hand.

"What a clusterfuck," he said, slapping the folder down on the table. "We have a serious problem."

"I know."

"No, I don't think you do," he shouted. "I think you're sitting here, wallowing in self-pity, and don't have clue one the amount of shit you're in!"

I sat there wide-eyed, too stunned to speak.

"I have a dispatch report from two dead officers who saw *your* car in front of your friend's shop, just before they got killed, which puts you first entering an active crime scene, *and* makes you prime suspect in the deaths of two cops! Not to mention a building with thirty-two dead bodies in it, where your apartment was the only one not destroyed! Do you have any idea how long they want to put you away for?" His face was red with anger, his chest heaving as he struggled to contain his fury.

"I'm sorry," was all I could manage to say.

"You're sorry. You're *sorry*? Just what the fuck were you doing there, anyway?"

"I was trying to find out how they got in, where they came from, where they went."

"By yourself?"

I nodded.

"Let's assume everyone buys that, which they don't. But what were you planning on doing once you found them?"

"I didn't think that far ahead."

"You didn't think!" he spat.

He stood there glaring at me for a moment, then sank down in the chair across from me.

"Jesus, Stan. You could've called me."

I raised my head, my eyes meeting his.

"I told you I believed you, didn't I?" There was still anger in his voice, but it was tinted with disappointment. "I took you to the alley where that girl got killed, showed you the photos and the file. What's it going to take for you to trust me?"

Trust. Maybe trust was in short supply with me these days. My circle of friends was small by design, after everyone I knew abandoned me. After the accident, after I trusted my friends enough to tell them what I saw, they laughed. They talked about me behind my back and gave each other coded looks that were equal parts pity and mockery. It took me a while to trust people again, to open myself up again. Maggie did that, with her kind words and unflinching belief in me. It sounds corny, but in a way, she healed a lot of the injuries that never appeared on an X-ray or on my skin. Since then, lots of people trusted me with the problems that no one else could understand. People like Shannon. I'd made myself promise I'd do my best not to let them down, and here I'd let so many people down in the past two days.

"Let Maggie go," I said.

He blinked at me.

"You want me to trust you? Let Maggie go. Whatever I did, she hasn't done anything wrong." I let the challenge hang for a moment in the air as I tried to read his face. "Maggie's freedom, my trust."

Taylor shook his head and slowly rose from his chair. Without looking at me, he crossed the space between us and stood behind my chair. Images of police brutality flashed through my mind.

He took hold of my wrists and, after a moment, I felt the bands of the handcuffs release. He walked back toward his chair, tucking the cuffs in his pocket before sitting down.

"The Medical Examiner already turned in preliminary reports on both the officers," he said. "They know you didn't kill them. The time it would have taken you, or any other person, to do that kind of damage, it just isn't possible. Plus they found hair and tissue under their nails."

He waited for a moment to make sure what he said sunk in. I was off the hook.

"The door of your apartment was shredded almost through, but they stopped just short of the last layer of steel. We know from security feeds in the building that it wasn't you that killed all those people."

There were security cameras? Since when?

"Then why am I here?" It felt like any moment someone would jump out with a camera and tell me it was all a prank. A sick, vicious prank.

"Due process," he said. "You were a suspect until we reviewed that evidence. That's what this is," he said, waving the folder in the air. "Your release papers."

"You couldn't have told me that before?" My blood pressure rose as I rose from my chair.

"Not before I said my piece," he said. "Now sit down. I'm not finished."

The tone of his voice stopped me, something like a mixture of fatherly disappointment and best-friend betrayal. Weird, considering I'd only just met the man yesterday. Even more strange was that I let it affect me like that.

"Look," he began. "You don't know me except that I'm a cop who said he believes you. Right? But I know a lot about you. More than you think.

"Pittsburgh P.D. doesn't have a 'weird crimes' division, no special task force to deal with unexplainable crimes. There are no X-Files here. Cases that don't have an easy solution get pigeon-holed, followed to their most logical end, and are never solved. People don't get closure. Those files are left in a drawer for cops to look at in their spare time, like pet projects. I came across one a while ago where your name was mentioned. Do you remember a boy named Eon?"

I felt a sudden rush of sadness. His was a name I'd never forget. It wasn't long after the accident. I was well on my way to recovery, basking in my victory over the company that killed me. I'd never really had a feeling of invincibility before, and I reveled in it. At the time, I couldn't move around very well, but was getting around, getting out of the apartment, and enjoying even limited mobility. That day, a boy followed me home.

He seemed sad, pale and wan, afraid of everything. I saw him at every corner I turned. He looked at me in a way that made me uneasy, the same look of desperation that many homeless people have when they first realize that they've lost everything. Every time I saw him, his eyes were fixed on me. When I got back to my apartment, he was there, at the end of the hall, not moving, not saying a word, just staring. I didn't know what to do, so I went inside and locked the door.

And he was there.

This was before I knew much about what I was seeing or how to protect my space, before I'd met Maggie. One moment he was standing outside in the hall, the next he was standing in the middle of my living room, that same plaintive look on his face. Then he spoke to me, asked me for help. His uncle had done something to him, he said. Something bad. Something that made his stomach ache and made him feel weak. It took me a few minutes to realize that he was dead, murdered with poison by his father's brother. I went to the police, told them what he told me, and they blew me off. They treated me like I was some mental case or a gold-digging eight-hundred number psychic who was trying to make a fast buck off a grieving family. But that wasn't it. I wasn't interested in money or fame. I just wanted the kid out of my home. But it was more than that. There was so much sadness in his eyes, so much pain in his stare, that I just wanted to help him in some way. I wanted to make the pain go away.

Three weeks later, they found his corpse. He was wearing the same shorts and striped shirt he'd been wearing when I spoke to him. They found rat poison in his body. Turned out, it was his uncle who killed him. The boy's name was Eon Lloyd. I've never forgotten him.

"You were right," said Taylor. "They didn't believe you, but you were right. I also found your name mentioned in a couple of other cases, usually brought in by the bereaved, but most of the time disregarded by the investigating officers. What I want to know is why? Why'd you keep coming back, even if you knew everyone here thought you were nuts?"

"I don't know," I said. It was a lie, the same one children told their parents when asked why they did something. I did know very well, and it wasn't just because the dead people kept showing up, or to just get them out of my apartment, or any of a dozen other selfish reasons I could've named. I did it because I needed to. I was so afraid, at the time, that I was losing my mind that I had to do something to validate myself. At least, that's how it was in the beginning.

Of course, a person can only scream unanswered for so long before they get the idea that no one's listening. Like so many of the restless spirits I'd encountered, that kind of hopelessness only breaks a person's will and wellbeing. And sanity. I've seen too many restless souls driven mad by the loneliness and pain that comes from realizing that, no matter how hard they try, no one notices them.

I didn't want to wind up like that. I kept coming back hoping someone would believe me. Then there was the other reason: Eon Lloyd.

I wanted so badly to do something, anything, to let this

kid find some kind of release, some sense of peace that would let him cross over to whatever's on the other side. The simple act of listening to him, then telling the police what he'd said, gave him enough peace. He stopped following me as much. The day they discovered his body, he stopped appearing at all. Even though the police thought I was loony-tunes, I felt like I'd done something good, like I'd helped him.

"Bullshit," said Taylor. "You know very well why you kept doing it. You wanted to help, didn't you? You're the kind of guy who wants to make a difference."

"Yeah," I said. "I guess I did."

"And you did," he continued. "You made a difference to those families and to the dead people you said you saw."

"Yeah," I said. "I made a big difference to those two cops and all those families. I went and stuck my nose in where it didn't belong, and now they're all dead."

"You were trying to help."

"Who're you kidding?" I seethed. "I can't help. You saw what those things did. All I did was make things worse. Better for me to stop before someone else gets killed."

"So that's it, huh? You're just going to roll over and quit?" I could tell he was angry by the tone of his voice. It was the same voice my father used when I told him I didn't want to play baseball anymore because I'd gotten hit with a wild pitch. That tone drove me to tears as a boy. It made me furious now.

"What do you want from me?" I demanded. "I'm not a superhero, I'm not a savior. Hell, I don't even have a clue what I'm doing. I'm just some guy who sees things."

"Yeah? Well I believe in what you do. Don't ask me why, but I do. And Maggie does too."

That stung. I didn't ask for this, any of it, and it cost me dearly. But at a point in my life when I was at my worst, Maggie saw me as worthwhile. I'd be a damned coward and a poor human being if I didn't at least try. Shannon came to me, both before and after her death because she believed in me. All the people I'd tried to help over the years, they believed in me. Hell, a cop I'd only met yesterday believed in me before he'd even met me. And here I was, thinking of throwing in the towel and hoping the big ugly from the dark didn't get me.

I looked up from the table at Taylor. He looked tired. His frustration showed on his face. If I was going to do this, I'd need his help, and Maggie's, if she'd give it.

"Alright," I said, meeting Taylor's eyes. "Where should we start?"

8

Taylor accompanied Maggie and me back to my apartment. Not for social reasons, but it seemed that, since the entire building was now considered a crime scene and the only way to access my little corner of the 'Burg was to walk *through* said crime scene, I was essentially homeless until the investigation was wrapped up. Just my luck for not having an outside entrance.

I didn't really want to go back just yet anyway. I didn't need any reminders of how close we came to being mutilated, or any of the families that weren't so lucky. Still, as I walked up the stairs and through the halls, I could see my former neighbors. Some were memories concocted by my own brain. Others stood there in shock, unable to come to terms with their sudden deaths. I pretended not to see them as we hurried through to my shredded door.

According to the police reports and the security cameras, the attackers, however many of them there were, were human, big men with animal ferocity. I didn't have to use my inner eye to know that the building, like all the others, was stripped of its energy. I could feel the difference. The place used to hum with life. Now it was cold, empty. They may have looked like men, but, looking at what remained of my door, I couldn't believe that human fingers had torn through the steel like tissue paper.

To my surprise, and relief, the energy hadn't been sucked out of my apartment. I opened the door and watched as more than a dozen scats zipped around the room. If Maggie noticed, she didn't say anything.

In fact, Maggie hadn't said much of anything since we were released. She hugged me when I came out of the questioning room, papers in hand, and asked me if I was alright, but after that she was silent. Her normally shining face didn't quite seem to have the will to smile. The whole ride from the police station to the building, her eyes never once met mine. She stared out the window with a blank expression, still in shock. It broke my heart to see her that way.

Her expression faltered a bit when Bitsy, the wonder cat, bounded off the windowsill and rubbed her back against her legs. She scooped her up and smiled a little, but there was no joy in it. We picked up her things, mostly still packed, and a change of clothes for me, then locked the door behind us. When we got out of the building, I could feel the windows looking down on me.

Taylor handed me a thick manila envelope and one that was letter-sized before he left. The smaller of the two contained a room reservation at a hotel, courtesy of the department. It seemed the law also stated that, since I couldn't go to my home, the city had to put me up for a few nights.

The other envelope contained a few details about Shannon, her room mates, the break-ins, and the destruction of my building. Nothing dealing with the crimes themselves, and nothing I couldn't have gotten myself by asking the right people, but Taylor shrugged and said he thought it might save me some time. We drove off in our separate directions and surrendered ourselves to the tender mercies of Best Western.

Hotels are horrible places for people like me. Stephen

King has written some classic horror stories about hotels, and I can't even count the number of horror flicks I've seen where restless spirits in a room go tormenting some unlucky traveler. In addition, there are the other types of horror stories, the ones in which the cleaning staff isn't as diligent as they'd like everyone to believe and the sheets are only washed for every *other* guest. To me, a hotel is the equivalent of using a port-o-potty at a three-day rock concert. You never know just how bad it can be. Still, I didn't like the thought of the two of us sleeping in my car. I mean, my car's comfortable, don't get me wrong. The seats are full and heated for the winter months, for which my posterior is thankful, but they're designed for driving, not sleeping. We pulled up in front of the hotel, and, with a silent prayer, we got our room key.

I went in with my walls lowered, and was surprised to see nothing out of the ordinary. The cups were wrapped in plastic, the sheets freshly laundered, and no traces of restless souls anywhere to be found.

And only one king-sized bed.

Maggie put her things down in the hotel-provided easy chair, put Bitsy on the floor, and set to work putting up defenses around the room. I couldn't blame her, as the first thought I had was how close we were to Carson street, and what would happen when night fell. Once finished, she put down a pan of litter and bowls of food and water for the cat and sat on the bed.

"Are you okay?" I took a spot beside her.

"No," she said. "You almost got killed. Why'd you have to go back to the shop?"

"I had to see. I had to find out if it was the same."

"Why? What does it matter to you?"

I told her how the last few days went for me. About the attack at the warehouse. About losing my job. When I told her about Shannon, I couldn't keep the quiver out of my voice, or tears from falling.

"Gods," she said. "I'm sorry. I didn't know..."

"Well, we have been a little busy," I sniffed. "This makes twice I've been to jail in the last thirty-six hours. I guess maybe we haven't had time to talk, eh?"

"You think the girl and the break-ins are related?"

"That's what I went to find out. Remember? Her house had no scats in it. Neither did Doug's place. Neither did the warehouse. Then they hit your place and came after you... I couldn't bear the thought of you in that alley like her. That's why I had to go. I had to see."

"And?"

"It's the same," I said. "There's nothing left. No scats, none of the energy you'd put into it. It was like walking into empty space."

She slumped down on the bed. Her eyes brimmed with tears and stared at nothing in particular, lost in thought of what she would do, how she would get her life back together again.

"I did find one thing," I said as I the shell from my pocket. "It isn't much, but it still has some of you in it."

I pressed it into her open hand, then curled her fingers around it.

"It's small, but it's something, right?"

She held the shell with both hands as though it were the most precious thing she'd ever seen.

"It represents the element of water," she said. "I found it on a trip to Florida when I was a teenager, while I was walking on the beach. It was the first piece I put into my altar."

"Well, I thought you might like to have it back."

She stood and put her arms around my neck, pulling herself in close.

"Thank you for this," she said.

"It's the least I could do," I said. "I know what it's like to lose everything."

She pulled away, holding the shell in her hand.

"This, at least, gives me hope," she said. "It's a good sign. Water moves around rocks, finds the holes in walls, and eventually works its way through. This shell makes me think maybe I can rebuild."

"I'll help, if you like."

She didn't answer, but looked up with me with a lost expression I'd seen too many times before. The only difference was, most of the people I'd seen wearing that expression were dead. But she had that same look in her eyes, as if the world overwhelmed her, and she didn't know how she would recover. She turned her back to me and laid down, then raised an arm to call me over. I laid behind her and put my arm over her. She pushed back into me, hugging me tighter for comfort. We lay like that, neither one of us speaking, until Maggie fell into an exhausted sleep. I hoped whatever gods were watching were merciful, and that she wouldn't dream.

When her breathing reached an easy rhythm, I climbed off the bed, pulled my half of the comforter over her, and sat down at the room's desk, the manila folder in front of me. I didn't want to open it because I knew what was inside, but I also knew it was something I needed to do. I took the thing in my hand almost like I was afraid it would burn me, then I squeezed the little brass brad together, lifted the flap, and poured out the contents onto the table.

The item on top was a photo of Shannon, paperclipped to a sheet that listed her name, her current address, roommates, occupations, and classes. It also listed the telephone number and address of her parents. Funny, that until that moment, I'd never even considered her family. Now, to put her death in perspective of a mother and father who were grieving the loss of their child, I felt a deeper sense of her tragedy. Parents should never outlive their own children.

The next paperclipped stack was information about the wheres and whens of her death. The hows and whys had been left out, which made it useful only to someone writing for the local paper. I didn't need to read the particulars, though. I knew damned well what happened to her. There was another small stack with information about the break-ins at Maggie's, Doug's, the warehouse, and my own building. There was more in the stack, though, than I'd bargained for. The reports didn't begin with Doug's place. There were three more listed, all the details vague, but there was something written in red ink beside a squiggle that bracketed the three robberies together.

Sounds familiar, eh? - Taylor

In every case but the warehouse, the robbers came up from the basement level, ransacked the establishment, and left through the same hole. The warehouse didn't have a basement, so they came through the loading dock. One of the places robbed was a bakery, another was a bead shop. The third was a printshop, where most of the paper, more than a ton of the stuff, had just disappeared.

I rubbed my eyes with the heels of my hands and groaned. None of it made sense. Other than the M.O., there was no rhyme or reason to the stuff they took, which meant there was no way to predict where they would hit next... which left me with damage control. I was the only one who knew for certain that Shannon's death was a direct result of these things. For all the police knew, it could've been anything that killed her in that alley.

I spread the papers out on the table like I was trying to put together a giant jigsaw puzzle and then just sat there staring at all the lines of text on forms. Nothing.

"Jesus Christ," I said to myself. "I don't even know where to start."

"Start with the girl," yawned Maggie. She pushed herself up to sitting and stretched. "She's where you and this thing started together, so start with her."

"Okay," I said. "You stay here, I'll..."

"Oh no you don't!" she said, her eyes snapping to full alert. "Last time you left me alone, you came back with your legs ripped up and a parcel of whatever those things were hot on your ass. You're not leaving me alone again."

I started to argue, but realized two things. First, I really wanted the company. I hated driving anywhere by myself, especially when I had things on my mind. Having Maggie in the car might make me feel less isolated, less vulnerable, and gave me a sounding board for ideas about the case.

The second thing I realized was a simple phrase that I used to see on a placard over Maggie's cash register: Never argue with a witch.

The closer we got to Shannon's house, the more nervous I got. When the old brain-bucket started ticking, weird thoughts flashed through my head. What if we knocked and no one answered? What if they did and threw us out? What if her roommates were dead, just like she was? Worse, what if the dead girl's parents were there? What would I say to them? What could I say?

I parked the car a block down from the house. It wasn't that I was scared of her roommates, but I didn't want to intrude, especially considering the icy reception from the elusive and as-of-yet-unmet Andi Anthropology. However she might greet us, if at all, my intention was just to ring the bell, offer condolences, ask if we could look around, and scoot.

As we got to the cracked section of sidewalk in front of the house, Maggie squeezed my hand.

"This is the place you told me about? The one without any scats?"

"Yup," I said.

"What does the outside look like to you?"

"Like a house," I said. I knew what she was driving at, but I'd already had a few too many ugly things burned into my memory by opening up my mind's eye to it. I didn't want to add a few more.

"Go on," she said, reading my expression. "Do it. You might find something."

"That's what I'm afraid of," I replied. "I'll do it on the way out. I don't want to chicken out of going in if I find something."

Maybe it was my own paranoia, or even the lack of sleep, but the neighborhood seemed quiet. Not the same kind of quiet that came with peaceful afternoons, but the kind that filled the room in an oppressive pillow when someone said the wrong thing at a dinner party. It was an anxious absence of sound as if waiting for the screaming to start. I felt Maggie's hand tighten in mine. She felt it too.

Maggie stood behind me a little so I could push the button for the doorbell. I heard it echo though the house, but seconds ticked into a full minute with no answer. I rang again, just to be sure.

"Hey." She gave my hand a gentle tug toward the window. "Look here."

She'd moved to the edge of the walkway where she could see through a gap in the front curtains. Sitting on the couch, just as he'd been the day I first saw him, was one of Shannon's roommates, Todd Pre-Med or Jason Lit, I couldn't remember which.

Just like the day I'd met him, he stared off into space, his jaw slack, his eyes glassy. Before I could move to stop her, Maggie tapped on the window. The boy didn't seem to notice.

"D'you think he's alright?" There was an uncomfortable tightness to her voice that suggested concern but masked fear.

"Probably not," I said. "That's how he was last time I saw him too."

Maggie shivered.

"See what I mean? He looks stoned."

"That's not stoned," she said. "Weed doesn't do that."

"What about that other stuff? Dat... uh..."

"No way," she said. "Datura's an hallucinogen, and 'shrooms don't do that either. If it's a drug, it's something I've never seen."

I led Maggie out of my way, then closed my eyes. When I opened them again, I knew she was right. Todd, it had to be Todd, had no aura of his own left. Most people in the throws of possession still keep a thin shell of themselves, something for the invading spirit to latch onto. Whatever had hold of Todd Pre-Med sucked him clean. There was no evidence of an invading spirit, or any other kind of energy for that matter. Todd Pre-Med was an empty shell, a husk. No wonder he wouldn't answer the bell, or even look up at Maggie. He was, for all intents and purposes, dead.

"Let's go," I heard myself whisper.

"But we can't just..."

"Now." I pulled her behind me as I hurried back down the path, pausing only when the cracked sidewalk gave way to smooth concrete. I turned to look at the house. What I saw made my stomach roll.

The house stood stark against the sky and trees, a black hole in the fabric of the world. Where life around it should have been vibrant, wisps of color darted away, sucked into the void left by the structure. Its darkness shifted. God, it *breathed.* From inside it reached out with fingers of darkness and took root all around it, diseased the land, the sidewalk, the neighboring hous-es. Whoever lived next door, across the street, behind or above, was prey to it. I could only imagine the people in those homes, their emotions growing less stable as the days passed until the houses would be mirror images of the cause. I glanced at Maggie. The greens and pinks of her aura still shone, but there were dark-ened pits in it, like something had taken a bite out of her life force.

"We have to leave now." I tugged her toward my car at just between a brisk jog and the panic-stricken run I felt the sit-uation warranted.

"Wait! What did you see?" she stammered as she tried to keep up.

I didn't answer. I couldn't. Somewhere in my mind, I felt as if to give the vision words, to try to articulate it, would make it more real, might give it power over me. One thing I did know. The longer we stayed, the more it would feed off us until we wound up like Todd Pre-Med.

We got to the car, got in, and I threw it into reverse rath-er than driving around the cul-de-sac. In my mind, it was still too close to the damned house for comfort. When we were several blocks away, I pulled over to the side of the road. My shaking hands wouldn't release the steering wheel without a fight. Maggie stared, her expression one of confusion and fear. I told her what I saw.

When I'd finished, she sat gaping.

"That's... not possible," she said.

"Believe it," I said.

We sat in silence for a few minutes while I got my hands to stop impersonating palsy. Whatever infected that house was spreading, and I had a feeling I hadn't seen the worst of it yet. Maggie knew more about this stuff than I ever would, and if she was stumped, we were all kinds of screwed. More important, by sticking my nose in its business the night before, I'd let it know I was interested. It came after me, so now it would be looking. I probably should've thought of that before trying to visit the house. If I wasn't careful, I'd wind up dead. Or worse, like Todd Pre-Med, an empty skin.

"So what do we do?"

"I was hoping you could tell me." I was out of my depth here, treading water in an ocean of metaphysics that I'd only just begun to explore. "We need to know what kind of entity can do this kind of damage."

"And how to stop it."

I blinked at her.

"Someone has to," she said. "It'll go on hurting people."

"Okay," I said. "But we don't know where to start."

"The girl," she said again. "I still think she's the key. Find out everything we can about her, we might find how she got mixed up in this mess."

I nodded, put the car in drive, and headed to the heart of downtown Pittsburgh and Duquesne University.

9

Parking in Steel City can be described with only one word that's repeatable in mixed company: nonexistent.

It took us about ten minutes to cross the bridge and catch sight of the old seminary-turned-institute of higher learning, but we circled the campus for more than an hour before luck smiled on us in the form of a haggard-looking student pulling his dented-to-hell-but-paid-for car out of a coveted parking place. It was on the far end of campus, but any port in a storm.

I fed the meter to its maximum appetite, two hours, and hiked toward the main campus in search of answers.

Shannon's schedule was unremarkable from any other list of courses. English, history, trigonometry, all marked Shannon as an average student, taking average classes. The electives, however, seemed to me to be where I might find some ideas as to what happened. Really, who ever heard of rampaging hordes of mathematicians?

One of her electives marked her as a volleyball player. Another, interested in public speaking. The third, noted in her schedule as "cult anthro," struck me as odd. Possession was at the root of the break-ins, and whatever killed her displayed the same overwhelming power, so a course on cults seemed the logical place to start.

As it turned out, the "cult" in the title stood for "cultur-al," with the second part being an abbreviated form of "anthro-pology." I checked my watch, and made my way to the admissions office to find the anthropology department. The bubbly girl behind the desk gave Maggie and me a nervous smile while she highlighted the building on a campus map. It didn't occur to me how we must've looked, but Maggie was the only one who'd really slept in two days, and I couldn't remember showering recently. With any luck, the campus police would mistake us for someone's backwoods, big-city-visiting parents. Or at least grad students.

The Department of Anthropology, as it turned out, was an offshoot of the Department of Sociology, and was staffed by one man in a large, dank office in the basement of the mother department's building. The door was open when we found it, with tribal drums and a strange instrument that sounded like a whooping howler monkey blaring from the back of the room.

I knocked on the door.

"Sociology is upstairs," sang out a voice from behind a pile of relics. "Back around to the first floor, toward the front of the building."

"Professor..." I read the placard on the door. "Jason Plumb?"

"I confess!" shrieked the voice again, this time accompanied by its owner, a small man in khaki pants, a flannel shirt, and a leather vest. His white hair stood up all around his head, except in the front where his scalp shone like a polished ostrich egg. He reminded me so much of a fluffy-headed John Hurt that I half expected him to speak with an English accent. "I did it! In the study with the candlestick!"

"I'm... sorry?"

"Y'know," he said. "Clue? Parker Brothers board game?

Do people even play board games anymore? Pity..." He stepped around the table, dropping one hand and extending the other. "I'm Doctor Plumb."

"Stanley Cooper," I said, shaking his hand. Despite the withered appearance, his fingers had real strength to them, no doubt gained from years digging up the trophies that cluttered his space.

"Delighted," he beamed. "Always glad to meet someone who actually came to see me. And you are?" he asked extending his hand to Maggie.

"Margarette Perry," she said. "But my friends call me Maggie."

"Then Maggie it shall be!" he boomed. "Charmed. Charmed! Now, what can I do for you?"

I've met people like Dr. Plumb before, flashy and theatrical. They take some getting used to, but after a while, their "flair," as they like to call it, just becomes part of their personalities. The problem with such exuberant people is, while their high points are extraordinarily high, the slightest thing can send them into the pits of despair. And they seem to be only comfortable when they're at the center of attention.

"We came to ask you about a student of yours," I said. "Shannon..."

"Oh," he said, crestfallen. "Miss Richards. That poor, dear girl."

"I'm sorry," said Maggie. "We don't mean to upset you..."

"What do you want of me?" said Dr. Plumb. "Are you with the police? I've already spoken to the police. Told them everything I know."

"No," I said. "We're... friends of Shannon's. We're trying to piece together what happened to her. She was in your cultural anthropology class, right?"

"Oh yes," he said, settling back into an oversized leather easy chair. The padded arms rose up on intricately carved pillars. Only after I took a good long look did I realize that the patterns and lattices were made up of hundreds of rats' tails, woven around each other in a squirming mess. The bodies of the rodents held up the arm rests.

"Did she have any... I don't know... enemies in the class that you know of?"

"Shannon? Preposterous. Shannon was very well liked. Good student, very polite. I can't think of anyone who ever said a cross word to her. Well, at least, not in my classroom. I'm afraid I don't know much about her outside life."

"Doctor," said Maggie.

"Please, you must call me Jason, my dear," he said with a sad smile.

"Jason," began Maggie again. "What was she learning in here before she..."

"Died," finished Plumb. "It's alright, you can say it. I'm not that feeble, you know. We were talking about cultures that embrace zootheism, different animals that represent different deities, demons, that kind of thing."

"Like what?"

"Well, many cultures worldwide embrace the spirits of animals as representatives of power. The American Natives, for example, thought of the coyote as a trickster. Some cultures worship cows as sacred." He turned to Maggie. "You, my dear, must know about snakes and spiders as symbols of power, owls as symbols of knowledge. It's very common among pagan religions."

"How did you know..?"

"You seem a little mature to be wearing that to annoy your parents." He pointed at her necklace, a silver pentacle.

"Anyway," he continued. "We were discussing various

myths and legends about calling up demons in the form of lo-
custs, fleas, and rats. The rat demons are particularly fascinating. Seems there was a South American village in which a group
of men went burgling every scrap of food or shiny object and
hoarded it all in what was later described as something of a large
burrow or nest. Claimed they were all possessed of this demon,
or some such thing."

Something he said struck a chord. It made sense. Not the
conventional, logical-world style sense, but it sounded awfully familiar to me. After all, what had they taken? Paper, jewelry, and
food. Nesting materials, shiny things, and feed.

"How dangerous were they?" asked Maggie. I could tell
by the look on her face that noticed the similarities too.

"Terribly," beamed Plumb. "According to published reports, they were damned hard to catch. Once they were caught,
keeping them in cages proved most difficult as well. They chewed
through wood and plaster walls, and even managed to burrow
through solid concrete. At least one was reported to dislocate his
shoulders to squeeze through a small opening and escape. Just
like real rats! Imagine!"

Maggie and I glanced at each other, and it seemed the
same shudder ran through us at the same time.

"What's more," said Plumb, obviously pleased to have an
opportunity to talk to an interested audience, "is that they managed to recruit more into their nests as they went. It was almost
like the madness was a pathogen. Many who came into contact
with them wound up either dead or joining them."

"How'd they wind up catching them?" I asked. The
thought of a mob of possessed rat-monsters roaming beneath
Pittsburgh was enough to turn my stomach to Jell-O.

"They managed to capture the leader, the 'king rat,' if you
will, and a shaman from a nearby village performed an exorcism

ritual on him."

"And everyone went back to normal?" asked Maggie.

"Sadly, no," said the professor. "Those invaded just... well... died. Purely psychological puffery, you know. But very common among primitive religions. Take Vodoun, for example. A voodoo priest can cause death simply by suggesting it to someone who believes strongly enough. The same thing applies here. When they believed the invading spirits had left their bodies, they truly believed that their souls were gone with them and they just quit living."

"Why didn't the ones who caught him become infected?" asked Maggie. "Were they wearing some type of protection or something? A rune, or a medicine pouch?"

"Or a big block of cheese?" I couldn't help myself.

Professor Plumb gave me a wry smile and shuffled over to a bookshelf behind his workbench and pulled a dusty worn volume down.

"When I visited the region, there were no reports of any such thing," he said. "None of police reports mentioned any kind of mark or charm, but when I visited the village where it all happened, I met one of the people involved in the capture. He was wearing this on a leather strap on his arm."

He opened the book to a photograph and held it out to us. The man in the photo appeared middle-aged, though it was hard to tell what passed for middle-aged in South American Native culture. He was rail-thin, bare-chested, with a dark mop of hair with a bowl-cut on top of his head. He held his arm up in front of him, displaying a thin leather strap around his wrist. On the strap was a piece of shell or bone, I couldn't tell which, carved with an intricate symbol.

"*That's* the guy who caught him?"

"Oh yes," Plumb nodded. "You should see him now! He's

considered a hero to his tribe. They sing songs about him! And the women, you just can't imagine!"

"Unbelievable," I said, shaking my head.

"Now, I'm afraid you'll have to excuse me," He said as he put the book away. "It's time for my Senior Thesis students. We're discussing various hallucinogenic plants, and they're all quite interested, I assure you."

"I'll bet," I grinned.

Plumb led us to the hall, slipped on a pair of hippie sandals by the door, and ambled toward the elevator.

"You're both welcome to audit the class, or course," he called out.

"That's very kind of you," said Maggie, "but we really should be going."

"Pity," he called back. "Can you imagine what the students would say if I walked into the room with you on my arm? At my age? My reputation on this campus would be legendary!" The elevator doors closed.

She'd never admit it, and I can't be sure, but I'd swear I saw Maggie blush and giggle.

"Well," I said after a moment. "What do you think?"

"First, I think we know what's going on here, but not why," she said. "Second, we need protection."

There are a lot of things a person like me fears, and I'm not ashamed to admit it. Heights, for example. That's a big one for me. My former shrink might say my acute acrophobia was a result of my untimely demise, and she'd be right on the money. Nothing like a high fall with a sudden stop to make a person think twice about going higher than a footstool. One of the other things that scares the ever-loving bejeezus out of me is needles. Any kind of needle, it doesn't really matter. The sight of one of the pointy little mini-skewers gives me the urge to scream like a ten-year-old girl and run.

So imagine my concern when Maggie's directions wound up leading us to a tattoo shop in the Pittsburgh suburb of Oakland. Before I had a chance to protest, Maggie got out of the car and walked toward the shop at a brisk pace, leaving me to feed the meter. I followed her in and found her talking to a young woman with full sleeve tattoos and large-gauge metal tubes in her earlobes.

"I can draw what I want," said Maggie. "It doesn't have to be very big, but it has to be precise."

The young woman nodded, then gave Maggie a pencil and a piece of paper.

"What are we doing here?" I tried to keep the anxiety out of my voice.

"It's the most efficient way to make sure we're protected," she said. "By putting a protective charm on our bodies, we can at least ward them off."

"Ever hear of necklaces? Rings?"

"Rings get lost," she said. "Necklaces can get snatched off. This is better. It's permanent. Besides, this works directly with the blood. It's a very powerful form of magick."

"Isn't there some other way?" In the background I could hear one of those needle-guns revving its tiny engine. "Something less... painful?"

Maggie looked up from her drawing, one eyebrow cocked and a smirk on her lips.

"Well," she said. "Any kind of bodily fluid that is associated with life is powerful." Her eyes drifted down. "We could always..."

"Tattooing will be fine," I said.

The young artist, whose name turned out to be Tina, led me to the back room.

"Where do you want it?" She held a razor in one hand and a damp cloth in the other.

"Wherever hurts the least," I replied.

"Forearm it is," she said. "Right or left?"

"Does it matter?"

"Of course it matters," said Maggie. "Which hand is your shield hand?"

The statement struck me as ridiculous. I lived in the modern world, and have never carried, much less used a shield. I've also never used swords, cannons, or slings. I have used a slingshot a few times, but that was as a kid shooting at squirrels in the back yard.

"I don't know," I said.

Without a word, Maggie's hand shot out and slapped me across the cheek.

"What the..?"

"Here it comes again," she said, cocking her arm back for another assault. When the blow came, I was ready for it this time, and raised my arm to cover my face. As it turned out, that instinctual block was with my left arm, which Maggie then dubbed my shield arm.

"Left," she said to Tina.

While the artist shaved a patch on my wrist, then traced the image onto the bald spot, Maggie removed a single white candle from her purse and lit it, then began a low chant to raise her energy and power.

Magick is an interesting phenomenon. While many believe it to be the power of positive thought or even all in the imagination of the witch, it's really more than that. I've watched

Maggie draw in her power, seen the energy course into her body from the earth and swell until she glowed like an arclight. I've also watched her release that focus of will into the world, seen it combine with other energies and change the way they interact with each other. Magick is real. I don't understand it, and I doubt I ever will, but it is real.

When Tina finished tracing the image on my arm, Maggie closed her eyes and touched a single finger to the lines and let her energy course into them. It burned its way into my arm, its path tingling through the flesh like electric shocks. When she was done, she turned to Tina and nodded.

I've talked to dozens of people with tattoos and almost all of them say things like, "It didn't hurt at all," or "Not too bad," or even "It just kinda tingles." It's all a lie. From the moment the first stroke of the needle-gun touched my arm, I knew what real pain was. It felt like the sadistic little bitch was trying to bore her way through my arm and out the other side. Maggie smirked at my expressions and hisses of pain until, after what seemed like hours, Tina was done. She wiped blood and ink away with a towel and only then did I chance a look at my freshly adorned arm.

The mark was a circle with crescents on either side. Within the ring were intersecting lines with a few other marks I didn't recognize. It didn't feel as much like a shield as it did an open wound.

"My turn," said Maggie as she plopped down in the chair.

I grinned at the thought of her going through the same torturous process. Sure, it was funny when I was in the chair grimacing and sucking air through my teeth, but let's see how funny it was when I was the one watching and she was on the business end of the needle.

It turned out Maggie was tougher than I was. Damn.

Far from showing any sign of discomfort, she smiled

through the whole process, even chatting with Tina as the needles ripped through her flesh. Maybe I'm just a wimp.

10

Slow lines on the road are a hazard of living in Steel City. Some people don't mind so much because it gives them time to think. I hate it for exactly the same reason.

Traffic was almost at a standstill as we made our way back toward the hotel. As the cars inched forward, the same thoughts kept circulating through my head. Whatever was possessing these people was sucking the life out of them, it was starting to get dark, and the damned tattoo on my arm itched like crazy. Maggie sat frowning, chewing on her lower lip in a sign of what I'd learned to be deep thought.

"We need more information," she said.

"Like what?" I beeped the horn and cursed under my breath as some kid in an old Yugo cut in front of me.

"We know what we're dealing with, I think," she said.

"What, a rat demon?"

"Why not? There're stranger things out there."

True. I'd seen a lot of them and I was pretty sure Maggie'd seen even more. And many cases of possession left the victim an empty, or at least near-empty, shell.

"Okay," I said. "So, rat demon. Now what?"

"I don't know," she said. "Demons aren't really my area

of expertise."

"Don't look at me," I said. Sure, I'd encountered more than my share, but not like this. Never on this viral a level. The demons I'd faced were cowardly, invading children, weak souls. This was more like a demonic plague.

"I wasn't thinking of you," she said. "Head toward Monroeville."

That was easier said than done. Getting off the surface streets in the middle of rush-hour proved to be a lesson in swearing, offensive driving and gestures, and a mental review of my insurance policy. Merging onto 376 was even more stressful. What should have taken us ten minutes took us almost an hour, and by the time we exited the highway, the sun was dipping below the skyline. As darkness fell, I felt eyes from both sides of the road watching us.

"Where are we going?"

"Bookstore," she said.

When I need information, the best place to look, I've found, isn't always a library. Sure, libraries are chock-full of books on many subjects, but there are some things you won't find in them. For example, most of them just don't have a great section on the occult. Most of them have entire sections devoted to the Salem witch trials or toward broadening a person's spirituality or even local ghost stories, but look for a book about witchcraft for beginners and you most likely won't find one. Plus, I've never seen a library with a café that serves great coffee, and when we walked inside, out of the frigid night air, and were greeted by warmth and the scent of fresh pastries and mocha, which made my stomach growl.

Food is one of my many great pleasures in life, as anyone who has seen me could guess. Missing a meal is a damned tragedy to me.

Most important, however, was that, once we walked inside, I didn't feel eyes on me. For the whole drive over, I pictured hordes of human rodents twitching in the darkness, scampering along the ice- and snow-covered road to keep pace, waiting for us to stop the car so they could tear us apart. But here, I felt none of it. Almost as if the place was warded.

Maggie took my hand and led me to the coffee bar where I ordered a large mocha and a huge slice of chocolate-chip banana bread for myself and a hot tea with a lemon scone for Maggie. I stood at the bar and waited for our order while she scanned the room. When her eyes came to rest on a table in the corner where seven people sat, her expression eased and she let go of my hand to join them.

"Stan!" she called after a round of hugs from the whole group. "Come over here. I want to introduce you."

I'm not much for meeting new people. I never know if they're going to think I'm crazy or maybe just the answer to their problems. It's sort of like finding out a mutual friend is a computer technician. He's either socially retarded or the answer to all their free tech support prayers. But Maggie had never steered me wrong before, so I picked up our coffees and made my way over.

"Everyone," she said as I reached the table, "This is Stanley Cooper."

It was a strange feeling, walking into a room, meeting a bunch of strangers, and being regarded like something of a celebrity. Or a boyfriend meeting the family for the first time. I wasn't sure which would make me more uncomfortable.

"This is the Evergreen Group," said Maggie.

The Evergreen Group. Maggie'd mentioned them before, but the group in front of me wasn't what I'd expected. When she spoke of them, Maggie made the Evergreen Group out to be some great mystery, part religious order, part secret society. If there were ever questions she had, or if she needed advice, the Evergreen Group had the answers. From the way she spoke about them, I expected them all to wear dark, peaked robes and meet in a secret cave on the side of some mountain. A wave of their hands would light burning torches around the room and they would dispense their wisdom amid a throng of hushed murmured chants. Nothing could've prepared me for the group that sat in front of me.

Far from what I pictured, there wasn't a hooded robe in sight. A few hooded sweat jackets, sure, but that was about as close as my mental image got. They looked, for lack of a better term, normal. A few wore khaki pants and sneakers, one wore a hockey jersey, others wore business-casual clothes, and one wore the loudest Hawaiian shirt I'd ever seen. Instead of sipping from goblets of bubbling potion, they sat with hot cappuccinos and biscotti. There wasn't a menacing, heebie-jeebie-inducing one among them.

"They meet here the first and third Thursday of every month. There's more metaphysical knowledge at this table than there is anywhere else in the state, I'd bet."

"Wow," I said, shaking the man in the loud shirt's hand. "You're not what I expected."

"Thought we met in a cave, eh?" he said with a smile.

"How'd you guess?"

"We get that a lot," he said. "I'm Bill. This is Brea, my wife. Over there is Kevin, Renau, Bob, Trevor, and Blossom."

I greeted them all with nods and smiles and handshakes all around. Brea was smaller than her husband, but her eyes crackled with energy. Kevin was a taller man, with a clean-shaven scalp and a close-cropped goatee, and eyes that looked like they could cut steel. Blossom seemed the most like Maggie, in a broomstick skirt and boots and a loose sweater. Bob ("neighbor Bob" I found out he was called) was a tall man with a polished dome instead of hair. He wore a Pittsburgh Penguins jersey and a warm smile that almost succeeded in putting me at ease. Renau's close-cropped hair and dress-slacks gave her the air of a person who just came from an office, and was likely the one managing it. When I shook her hand, I felt my palm tingle with the raw energy that zipped beneath her skin. Trevor was younger than the others, with a long dark ponytail and wire-rimmed glasses. Appearances aside, the Evergreen Group were everything Maggie'd made them out to be.

"So you're the mysterious Stanley," said Bill. "The clairvoyant. Maggie's told us all about you."

"Oh?" I turned and cocked an eyebrow at her.

"Yes," said Brea. "She says you're one of the few good men she's ever met."

I felt my cheeks flush hot, but I doubted I went as scarlet as Maggie.

"So," said Bill. "To what do we owe this visit?"

Maggie's smile faded as she scanned all of their eyes.

"We need your help," she said. "You know the robberies and killings that've been happing on Carson Street? Stanley... We're in pretty deep here and we need advice."

The seven looked at each other before turning their eyes back toward me.

"If there's any way we can help, of course we will," said Bill. "What's the problem?"

I sat down at the table and took a sip of my coffee. They sat around me and regarded me with rapt attention. It wasn't that they wanted to hear the story, or that they wanted to know just how crazy I was. They were genuine in their interest, and wanted nothing more than to help. Me. A stranger. And they believed me without question on Maggie's word.

I took a deep breath and another sip of my coffee, then told them the whole thing. From waking up to Shannon's strange telephone call, to the point where Maggie and I walked through the door. I didn't skimp on details either. I felt it was important for them know exactly what I'd seen, how the houses were devoid of scats, how the places where life should have hummed were wiped clean. When I finished, I looked around the table. A couple of them had tears in their eyes. A few looked horrified. Bill looked deep in thought. At least one of the group, Kevin, looked angry.

"This isn't a run-of-the-mill possession," said Bill after a moment. "It's more viral, more cancerous."

"Tell me about it," I said, leaning back in my chair. I wasn't aware until that moment that I'd been sitting forward and shaking. My hands were shaking. All this going on and to even tell it, my hands shook like I had palsy. "I've seen possessions before. I've chased ghosts out of buildings, helped guide lost spirits on their way. But this... I've never seen anything that just wipes life away like that. I didn't think it was even possible."

"It isn't," said Renau. "Not for a spirit or ghost. This is something different. Demonic even. Are you sure about what the professor told you?"

"Pretty sure," said Maggie. "It seems to follow the South American epidemic. I think what we're dealing with here is a rat demon, or rat spirit, or something like that. Until last night, they were only looting. The only people who got hurt were people in their way. But they murdered his client."

"Are you sure it was they," asked Brea.

"Yeah," I nodded. "The place she died was wiped clean of energies. And last night, they attacked us both, which I bet means they know who we are, and we're not safe as long as we're in Pittsburgh."

"Or even outside Pittsburgh," said Bob. I followed his gaze to the wide window on the wall. Outside, in the parking lot, I could see them, a dozen or more, standing near my car, doing their best to hide in the shadows of trees or bushes. They were waiting for us. A jolt of fear raced from my scalp to my heels and back again.

"You're safe here," said Bill with a smile. "You just might not get to leave for a while."

I crept to the window and stared.

"What're they waiting for?" I muttered. "They've busted apart bigger places than this."

"Open your inner eye and see for yourself," chuckled Bill.

I lowered the walls of my perception and gaped at the bookstore. Around every entrance, across the ceiling, covering the floor, was a gleaming sheathe of silvery light, all of it coming from the seven people seated around the café table.

"You're witches," I said.

"Some of us," Bill nodded.

"This is a metaphysical discussion group," said Brea. "We welcome any religion, any creed, so long as they have an open mind and want to have an honest discussion."

The rest of the group nodded, and I understood. In the grand scheme of things, a person's religion didn't matter a hill of beans against the darkness. What really mattered, what gave people strength, was faith. It didn't matter what or who that faith was in, so long as there was that anchor of the soul. The power pouring off the group was testament to their own individual faiths, and the room fairly crackled with the energy. I wished I had something like it.

Blind faith is an amazing thing because of the amount of power it can generate. My energies aren't as strong as the average person's because I don't have blind faith. I *know* what's going on. Believe me, there's a difference. *Believing* something is going to happen is stronger than knowing the outcome. Knowing that the power resides in the person and not in some benevolent God doesn't afford much in the way for disillusionment. It's not that I don't believe in a higher being. I do believe in a deity of some sort, though I don't know who or what he or she is. I do know, however, I never lost that belief. It just changed a bit from day to day. For a while, I believed in God with all my heart. And I believed he hated me.

The bookstore manager, a harried-looking woman with her hair falling out of a bun, noticed them outside and made for the front door, I supposed to tell them to leave.

"I wouldn't do that." I held up a hand and stepped in front of her. "They're not your average parking lot thugs."

She stared into my eyes for a moment, then moved behind the checkout counter, picked up a telephone, and dialed. As she spoke, she stared out the window, her face a mixture of fear and annoyance. When she hung up, she forced a smile at me, then went on about her duties.

A few minutes later, the parking lot was awash with red and blue lights as Monroeville's finest pulled up in front of the store. The pit of my stomach lurched in anticipation of what I thought would be a slaughter. Cops all swore an oath to defend the people, even up to their deaths, but I was pretty sure that rat-demon-possessed people weren't part of academy training. I held my breath and watched, as my mind replayed the images of the torn bodies of the two cops on Carson. Then the most astonishing thing happened.

They left. They saw the lights, lifted their noses to the air, and scurried off into deeper shadows of the night.

One of the police officers came in and spoke for a moment with the manager. As he turned to leave, he smiled and nodded to Bill and Brea, then went out the door, climbed in his cruiser, and left. A second police car stayed parked at the far end of the lot.

"Better go now, while you have the chance," said Bill. "And if you need us, Maggie knows how to reach us."

I nodded. Maggie got up and went around the table and hugged each of them, then we hurried out to my car.

"Not much information there," I said as I dug my keys out of my pocket.

"More than you think," she said. "They confirmed what we're dealing with is demonic, and that it's pretty powerful."

"Yeah, but we knew that," I said. "I'm sorry, but this seems like a wasted trip."

"Not quite," she said. "They're obsessive about things like this. They like puzzles. They'll research until they come up with an answer. With any luck, they'll have something that'll help us before..."

"It's too late," I finished, although I wondered what too late would be. People were already dead, and they were getting stronger. There were more of them, and I had a hunch their numbers would continue to grow. Just like rats.

"And what're we supposed to do until then? I know what you can do, but do you think you could protect us?"

"I don't know," she said. "Just me, I doubt it. I don't think I'm strong enough. But they each gave me a little bit of their energy when they hugged me. Magick is finite, and I know it won't last forever, but it might give me just enough of a boost to fight this thing."

The pig in me raised its ugly snout.

"No way," I oinked. "I don't want you getting hurt."

It was true, but not because I feared for Maggie. More, I

was afraid of what I would do without her. Maggie was more than just a friend to me. In my tiny circle of acquaintances, Maggie was the only *real* friend I had. Without her, I'd be alone again, and I couldn't bear the thought.

"You're so cute when you're being all Cro-Magnon," she said. "Remember who you're talking to?"

I nodded and started the car. We drove out of the parking lot in silence while I continued trying to puzzle things out in my head. Why did they leave? Why didn't they attack? There were enough of them to have shredded the police cars, torn the cops to tiny pieces, and ripped the store apart like as much newspaper. So why didn't they?

"Where to now?" said Maggie. "I'm out of ideas."

"Back to the hotel," I said. "I need to sleep."

"We have to protect the other guests," she said.

I nodded.

"Any idea how?"

I shook my head. I couldn't protect the others in my own warded building, so what made me think that the hotel would be any different?

"Maybe we ought to stay away," I said, "until we figure out what else to do."

"And do what? Drive all night long?"

"Maybe," I said. "All the attacks happened at night, right?"

Maggie nodded.

"Rats are mostly nocturnal, aren't they?"

"I think so."

"Then that's what we'll do. We'll keep moving during the night, and sleep all day."

"Just like high school," said Maggie with a sigh.

ii

The drive to Monroeville from Pittsburgh was easy enough, nothing that a seasoned driver couldn't handle. The drive back wasn't so easy, due to the fact that the entire highway was closed down to just one lane inbound. I wasn't really sure where we were going, and in my mind that was just fine. It meant that wherever we wound up would most likely be random, and harder for the demon-possessed hordes to follow.

Maggie sat beside me, her eyes closed, hands folded across her lap, her lips moving in a slight prayer. It was dark outside, but in the glare from the headlights of the other cars I could still see her. In profile, she looked so serene, so sure of herself. Again, the faith thing.

Maggie had several types of faith, all of which burned in her like torches. Her faith in the God and Goddess of her religion was fierce. Her faith in the magick, the energy she manipulated, was very strong. But stronger still, and a thing that made her even more beautiful, was her faith in herself. She wasn't arrogant or cocksure, but simply at peace with who and what she was, and confident in her abilities. Together the three made an impressive source of energy.

Her eyes snapped open just as I felt the eyes on me like

pin-pricks all over my skin.

"We have to get off this road," she said, her voice wavering. "Now."

Any other time, staying on the highway with lots of other cars would be a good idea, but now, with the traffic crawling, the only thing staying on the road would accomplish would be getting us killed faster and getting other drivers hurt in the process.

I made a sharp turn of the wheel and drove up the shoulder to the first off-ramp, kicking gravel and bits of asphalt behind me. The feeling of being watched grew stronger, but at least, down here, we had a better chance of gaining some room to maneuver. I followed the road as it curved to the left, moving under the highway. As we passed under the concrete, I heard Maggie let out a gasp. Crawling across the support beams and down the concrete legs of the overpass were dozens of them, each one with the same feral look on their faces, each one sniffing the air and screeching, each one with murder in his eyes.

"Get us out of here!" she screamed. I jammed my foot down on the gas pedal and sent my car lurching through the night. All around us, human rats dropped from their perches under the overpass and ran after us on all fours.

The road took us into an area I didn't know, and for good reason. It was one of the dozen or so little towns that went bust when the coal mines shut down. On either side, boarded up storefronts and gutted houses stared at the cracked streets like hollow skulls, their stoops and roofs fallen in long ago. Most of the towns like this one had a few, maybe a hundred, who still lived there because of pride or lack of options. This one seemed deserted, until I noticed shadows in the empty buildings pulling away and hunching down on all fours. Too big to be animals, I knew there were more vermin in every building in sight.

The car rocked as something slammed into the door.

Then another shockwave hit, and I watched as shadows darted toward us and used their bodies to try to stop the car. More of them came, each one hitting the car just a little bit harder, but I kept driving until my headlight shone on a group of what looked to be thirty of them in the road, all frozen in a defiant snarl, all staring at us. Possessed or not, hollow cores or not, I just couldn't make myself run them down to escape, so I turned again down a side road and realized too late that they'd been herding us. The road bottlenecked to a narrow pass with a blank wall blocking the way. We were trapped. If we waited, they'd get in. If we tried to back out, they'd tear us apart. Either way, we were screwed.

More howls came from behind us, moving fast up the road, closing in.

"Come on!" I yelled, as I pulled the handle and pushed the door, but the narrow alley wouldn't let the doors open. I spat a curse and hit the button on the roof to slide the sunroof open.

"Up!" I wriggled out of my seat and through the opening. Maggie followed and we scrambled down the windshield and off the hood. We both took off at a dead run toward piece of rotted plywood that covered a narrow opening at the end of the alley, and I prayed to whatever might be listening that there weren't any more surprises through its dark threshold. I kicked the board until the nails came loose, then shoved Maggie through and pulled the board back into place behind me. Then we ran. I couldn't tell what kind of building we were in, it was so dark, but we followed the hallway until it crossed with another and turned without slowing down. Through the echoing halls, the sounds of wood splintering and the shrieks of the possessed creatures created an eerie din.

"Oh, gods," said Maggie, every trace of the serene beauty gone from her face. Instead, her eyes were wide with fear, her lips trembling. "We've got to hide."

"I can't see," I hissed back. "Too dark." I lowered the walls of my perception to see if I could navigate the building by the energy that lived within it, but there was none. Like all the other places the human rats infested, there was nothing left, only darkness. The place was an empty shell.

"*Candere!*"

The space around us brightened in a soft glow that came from a ring on Maggie's finger. Around us were innumerable doors and steel lockers on both sides. The tile floor was littered with crumpled paper and fragments of the fiber-board ceiling tiles that sagged above us. We were in an old school.

"Just like high school," I muttered.

"I can't keep this up for long," whispered Maggie. "We've got to get out of here."

I looked around until I found a set of heavy doors at the end of another corridor, and froze the image in my mind.

"Douse it," I said. "Save your energy. We might need it."

Maggie nodded and took my hand, then the glow faded away. Guided by the image in my head, I led Maggie to the heavy doors, pulled them open, and pushed her through. I followed and pulled them shut behind us. Beside the door I found a heavy wood-and-steel bench, which Maggie helped me wedge as a makeshift door-stop, then we moved further into the room.

Pale light filtered in through broken windows above, letting us see at least part of the room. Four rows of lockers that stretched to the back wall gave way to another room beyond, with another door further down.

"Gym lockers," I said.

"That bench won't keep them out," said Maggie.

"I know."

With Maggie close behind, I ran to the other doors and pushed. Rattling on the other side let me know they were chained.

"Damn it," I spat. "Just a little help, God. That's all I'm asking for."

Wood splintered across the room, accompanied by in-human shrieks from the other side of the door. In the half-light Maggie's face crinkled, her eyes widened in fear. She had a scream stuck somewhere in her throat, and I felt one rising in mine.

"I don't think She's listening right now," said Maggie. She grabbed me by the arm and half ran toward the opening on the other wall, only to find it was the women's shower. No other exit, only one bank of frosted windows high overhead, and a few stalls.

The doors cracked and fell, echoing through the chamber like thunder. I stood there and hoped for some miracle, some sign of intervention from a higher being, but in the most closed-off spaces in my heart, the part that always told the ugliest of truths, I knew there was nothing left for me to look forward to but that awful black, the terrible silence, and a whole lot of pain.

Maggie grabbed my collar and dragged me into one of the shower stalls.

"Sit," she said.

"What're you doing? They're…"

"I think I can protect us," she whispered. "Now *sit!*"

I did as I was told.

"I need your energy. I don't know if this'll work, but I need you to take my hands and do what I tell you."

I nodded. I could hear them coming down the rows, slow and methodical in their search for us. My heart slammed a punk beat inside my chest. Right now, I was willing to try anything to save our skins, to save myself, from that awful black.

"Open your perception," she said.

Her body erupted in a fountain of white and blue fire.

"Now I need you to push your energy into me while I chant. Just visualize it going, and it'll follow your will."

She closed her eyes and I started pushing. Tendrils of blue and green light snaked down my arms and joined with her glow, making it stronger. I could feel it pouring out of me and into her, infusing her life with mine. While I watched, she pulled one hand free and traced a circle around us, then Maggie started a low chant.

"Please protect us with your might, Lady Athena, help us fight. Thrice around the circle's bound, evil sink into the ground."

At her word, the circle she traced in the dust and dirt on the floor glowed blue, and Maggie became blinding to look at. I only had a second to glimpse the raw energy pouring out of her, and then they were on us.

There seemed to be at least fifty of them, maybe more, all tearing at each other to get to us. Their dark shapes collided with Maggie's energy sphere, and were repelled. Every time they touched it, they tore out a piece of the brilliant light, only to have it replaced by more that came from within her body. She'd made a wall of energy, and they were feeding on it. No matter how much of it they stripped away, she threw more between them and us. So long as she kept expending her energy, they couldn't get to us.

I don't know how long we stayed there like that, Maggie chanting, me scared out of my mind and flinching when each twisted face appeared. But before long, they stopped attacking. They lifted their noses to the air and sniffed, then with a last guttural howl, they scurried back through the opening. I listened until I was sure they were out of the building then turned to Maggie.

Her chant was now barely more than moving her exhausted lips in time with the words, her voice raw and no longer able to even whisper. Her face dripped with sweat and her breaths came in labored rasps.

"They're gone now," I said.

Maggie slumped into my arms, her lips still moving in

the prayer.

"I got you," I said, as I cradled her close. "It's okay now."

My legs ached from kneeling for so long on the floor, but I pushed myself to standing and guided Maggie up as I did. I looked up to the frosted glass and saw the reason why they'd left. It was daybreak.

"Let's get out of here," I said, draping one of Maggie's arms around my shoulders and guiding her toward the door.

My car had seen better days. They'd bashed out the back window and left long scratches down both sides and across the top. The front windshield had a long spidering crack that ran from the top of one side to the bottom of the other. I just prayed it was still drivable.

We climbed to the sunroof and I poured Maggie in. Then I began the awkward process of putting myself into the driver's seat. As I slumped into place, I smelled something foul and felt a squish, and realized that the monstrous bastards had marked my car with piss and shit.

"Need… sleep…" she said.

"I'll get you back to the hotel," I said as I pulled the sunroof closed. As I fit my key into the ignition, I wondered if there were any prayers a witch might say to get a car to start. When it roared to life, I almost shouted with joy, but I didn't want to disturb Maggie.

She dozed the whole drive back to the hotel, her glassy eyes opening only twice. Once was to assure me she was still alive, the other when someone passed too close and I hit the brakes a little too hard.

We crossed the 10th Street bridge and pulled into the

hotel parking lot, where a familiar car sat waiting for us. I pulled in next to Taylor and got out.

"Jesus Christ," said Taylor. "What the hell happened to your car?"

"We had a run-in," I said. "Those things might've killed us if Maggie hadn't…"

"She doesn't look good."

"Help me," I said. "She doesn't have enough energy left to walk."

Taylor grabbed one side and I the other and we made our way past the reception desk to our room. We moved by fast, but not fast enough to miss the startled and derisive looks from the clerks. Part of me wanted to snap at them, but then I figured that if I worked in a hotel and saw two guys carrying a young woman, who looked like she might be drugged, I'd have thought the worst too.

We got her to the room and laid her down on the bed. Bitsy jumped up beside her and gave me an accusing glare before nuzzling Maggie's hand.

"What?" I actually felt defensive to the cat. "It's not my fault! I didn't do this!"

The cat, as if in answer, huffed and turned her back to me and thrashed her tail.

"Get me a cold, wet hand towel," I said. Taylor hurried to the bathroom.

"Maggie," I said. Her eyes flickered open. "You're safe now. You're okay."

"Sleep," she mumbled. "Need sleep."

Taylor returned with the compress, which I laid over her forehead before covering her with a blanket. I scrawled a quick note on the hotel-provided stationery and put it on the night-stand beside her, then I motioned for Taylor to follow me outside.

"Keep her safe, Bitsy," I said as I closed the door. The cat snuggled in beside her.

12

So far, I'd lost my client, gotten the residents of my apartment building killed, been responsible for the deaths of two cops, been attacked by rat-demon-infested people several times, got my car wrecked, and lost my job, all in a span of three days. In addition, I was going on two days without sleep, I hadn't eaten since noon the day before, and what little energy I had left, I could feel fading fast. Oh, and I got my first tattoo, which itched like crazy. As Taylor followed me to the parking lot, I stumbled as my legs went rubbery. My stomach cramped and my head swam. I wasn't aware I was falling until Taylor caught me.

"Whoa!" he said. "Maybe you need some rest too."

"No time. It'll be dark in just over ten hours. They'll come back, and we need to be moving by then."

"So get some sleep before dark," he replied as he propped me up against a wall.

"Need more information," I said. "I need to go back to Duquesne to talk to Professor Plumb."

"Fine," he said. "Have you eaten anything?"

I was too tired to lie, and damned hungry.

"Come on," he said. "I'll get you some breakfast. Don't make me put the cuffs on you."

He led me out to his car and put me in the passenger's seat, then drove to an Eat 'N Park down the road. When we went inside, the waitress smiled and nodded. Taylor took what I supposed was his usual place in a far corner, his back to the wall. I slumped into the seat across from him.

"Two of the same, Trish," he called to the waitress. I didn't even care what she brought out. It could've been roasted monkey, and I still would've eaten it and been grateful. She brought over two mugs of coffee with a boat full of sugar packets. Taylor grabbed four and dumped them in his mug. He gave it a slow stir, his eyes never leaving me.

"You want to tell me about last night?"

I took a sip of my coffee. It burned my mouth but felt good and warm going down my throat.

"We figured out that they come out at night," I said. "Because rats are mostly nocturnal. And we knew they'd tear the hotel apart looking for us, so we left. We drove around, hoping to keep the hotel safe. But then they found us. There were so many of them. We just ran. We wound up in some ghost town off the parkway. They chased us into an old school, where Maggie saved our asses."

The waitress brought two plates of Eggs Benedict, hash browns, and a short-stack of pancakes. I didn't wait for her to walk away before I tore into my food like a hungry dog.

To truly appreciate something, a person usually has to be without it for some time. Simple things like lights, people take for granted, but stick them in a dark room for a few days and sunlight will reaffirm their faith in a higher power. The same thing goes for food. Most people eat on a set schedule of three squares a day with snacks in between, but when a person goes without for a while and gets a serious case of *hungry*, food becomes more than simple nourishment and borders on a religious experience.

While I know there are people out there who have gone without far longer that I, it wouldn't have surprised me at all to see the face of baby Jesus on at least one of those pancakes.

Halfway through the meal, Taylor cleared his throat.

"So, Plumb, huh?"

"Yeah."

"Like the guy from 'Clue?'"

"That's what he said."

"I'll give you a lift," said Taylor.

"Aren't you supposed to be at work or something?" I leveled my eyes at him between bites.

"I am at work," he replied. "I'm keeping my eyes on a 'person of interest' to the department. Besides, I want to hear more about what happened to you two last night. If there were that many of them, we might have a bigger problem on our hands than we realized."

I nodded as I slowed my chewing to a more normal pace.

"Also, if Maggie was able to save you two, maybe we could..."

"Won't work," I said.

"Why? How'd she save you?"

I finished chewing and swallowed before fixing his eyes with mine.

"Witchcraft," I said.

"Oh."

Taylor swung back by the hotel before we went to the college, explaining in his most tactful way that I stank to high heaven and looked like a homeless person. A shower and a change of clothes were not just a suggestion on his part, but a necessity. He waited in the car while I made my way back to the room. Maggie hadn't moved since we left, nor had Bitsy. I gathered my change of clothes and went into the bathroom, turned on the shower to just a shade under boiling, and stripped off my clothes. The hot water stung, especially around the tattoo, but the layers of filth that came peeling off my body made the sensation a good one. I used the hotel-provided shampoo and soap and made a mental note to get a razor, provided I wasn't killed before I made it back for my next shower. When I was done, I toweled off, brushed my hair straight back against my scalp, and dressed. The dirty clothes on the floor, which I only just realized smelled of a combination of urine, feces and sweat, I wrapped in a spare can liner from the bathroom trashcan, then I brushed my teeth and left the bathroom. Bitsy blinked at me as I leaned over and kissed Maggie on the cheek and scratched the cat's head. Then I grabbed a spare towel and headed out to meet Taylor.

He was waiting in the parking lot with the windows down in the frigid air in an attempt to let my odor out.

"Sorry 'bout the smell," I said as I draped the towel across the seat.

"I'll get a new air freshener later," he said. Then he put the car in drive and headed toward the university.

Before we crossed the bridge, Taylor took a left and drove down Carson Street.

"While you were playing hide-and-seek last night, we had problems of our own."

Doug's shop still sat empty with yellow tape flapping in the cold air. Maggie's place still looked like an open sore on the street. Beyond I could see the bead shop, its owners looking lost while they swept up glass. A few shops down, I saw flashing lights. Police cars lined the street, each driver taking information from another owner whose business lay in ruins behind them.

"My God..." I whispered.

"Seven shops last night," he said. "With six more people either dead or missing. All the same. They came up through the basement, tore the place apart and left. If someone was there and tried to stop them, they got ripped to pieces."

I could see them. Not just the six, but all the victims. From my apartment. The two cops. More than twenty more, all blinked in and out of time, flashed like dancers under a strobe. All of them stared at me with anguish and pleading in their non-existent eyes. And in front of them stood Shannon, her expression frozen in sorrow. Somewhere deep inside me, I felt something crack and almost break. All those people dead, all those lives destroyed, and there was nothing I could've done to stop it. All I wanted to do was sleep and wake up from the nightmare.

"Just how many of these fucking things are there?" asked Taylor. "And how're we supposed to stop them?"

I wished I had an answer.

We pulled up at Duquesne University. Taylor's badge got him full access to the faculty parking lot, but even that seemed like a hunting expedition for the elusive empty space. We found a space near the far end of the lot and got out. It was cold, even for February, though Taylor didn't seem to notice. Maybe I noticed it more because I was so tired.

We made our way into the massive building and rode the elevator down to Plumb's basement office. On first visits to new places, most folks see the big picture, directions, which door to walk through, that sort of thing. On subsequent visits, a person can pick out more detail. I didn't notice on Maggie's and my first visit that the elevator was located next to the stairs, otherwise we'd have taken it back up instead of climbing two flights. I also didn't notice that the lower level of the building was darker, both in color and in lighting, than the rooms upstairs. The paneling was stained with a deep brown as opposed to the rich cherry of the more prominent hallways, and even the tiles on the floor seemed almost black instead of green. The lights that hung upstairs were fluorescent, bright energy-savers, whereas the ones down here were standard, run-of-the-mill incandescent bulbs. Some burned brighter than others.

As we got to Plumb's door, we heard shouting from inside his office. A woman's voice, angry and threatening, came through the wood, muffled so neither of us could make out what she said. In between bursts, each one rising in pitch a bit, there was silence, which I figured was Plumb's soft-spoken reply. Taylor looked at me, shrugged, and raised his hand to knock. As his fist began its decent toward the door, it flew open and revealed a pretty girl in a skirt with short dark hair and murder in her eyes. She gave us each a withering glance and stormed off down the hall.

I felt something tug at me, like a loose string on a sweater caught on a nail. I turned toward her.

"Andrea?" I called. She froze. The elusive Andi Anthropology. I started down the hall toward her.

"I'm Stan Cooper," I said. "I knew your roommate, Shannon..."

At the mention of the name, Andrea bolted. In a blink she was around the corner.

"Hold it!" called Taylor, but by the time the words escaped his lips, he was talking to an empty hallway.

I took off after her. Tired or not, there was no way I was going to let her go. I needed answers, and Andi Anthropology was, to my mind, my best chance of getting them. I cleared the corner and ran for the stairs, catching just a glimpse of her skirt as it rounded the flight above. Taylor closed the distance between us fast, passed me and gained ground on her. I reached the main level in time to see her throw the outer door of the building open. Taylor was only a few feet behind.

Running has never been my strong suit. I usually only run when chased, and it has to be something pretty damned scary that's bearing down on me. Then, the fear and adrenaline kick in and I can sprint with the best of them. Being the one doing the chasing is another matter.

At the top of the stairs, my heart felt like it was trying to escape my ribs by beating its way out, and my lungs felt like they were on fire. Not to mention that my mangled legs throbbed with every step. I cleared the door and found Taylor on the other side, staring out over a sea of long hair and overcoats, frustration etched on his face.

"Dammit," he spat. "She just ducked into the crowd. I lost sight of her."

"She can't hide from me," I wheezed. I closed my eyes lowered the walls of my perception, and when I opened them again, the campus exploded in a Technicolor wonder. Every hue of the spectrum was there in front of me, blending, ebbing, melding and separating. Every color except for the one I was looking for. There were small traces of red and black, sure, but not the kind I was looking for. She should've put off quite a glow, but it just wasn't there. It was as if she'd vanished.

"I stand corrected," I said. "Where the hell did she go?"

"I don't know," said Taylor. "Maybe she went down the storm drain or something. Who knows. We're not going to find her in all this."

I shifted my perception back to normal and sat down. My head and legs throbbed in time with my heartbeat. I felt like I was going to pass out.

"Now what?" I panted.

"Well, we're here," said Taylor. "May as well go talk to the professor. Maybe he can tell us something about the girl."

I nodded and held up a finger. Just a moment to catch my breath was all I needed. Maybe I needed to get in shape. Because being out of shape really sucked sometimes.

Plumb's door stood open. He stood just inside, writing on a yellow notepad.

"Professor? I dropped by the other day…"

"Yes, Mr. Cooper. I remember you. But where is the lovely Maggie?"

"She's resting," I said. "Not feeling well."

"Oh, well I am sorry for that," he said. "Please give her my warmest regards, won't you?"

"Sure thing. This is Detective Taylor of the Pittsburgh Police Department."

"Charmed," he said. "But despite what you may have heard, I didn't kill anyone with a candlestick or otherwise."

"I used to love that game," Taylor smiled.

Plumb beamed.

"Now, what can I do for you gentlemen? I have a class to teach in a few minutes…"

"We won't take up much of your time, then, Professor," said Taylor.

"That girl," I said. "The one who just left."

"Miss Bedford," he nodded.

"Yes. Wasn't she Shannon's roommate?"

"Haven't the foggiest," said Plumb. "I do know that I saw them together often at the beginning of last semester, but not so much since January."

"Just this semester?"

"Well," he said, squinting his eyes in thought. "It seems to me that they were always together during the first part of the fall, but right around midterm they sort of detached from one another. I didn't think much of it. Why?"

"It's part of an ongoing investigation," cut in Taylor. "We really can't say."

"Are you suggesting that Andrea Bedford might have had something to do with Shannon's death?"

"Not suggesting anything," said Taylor. "But she is a person of interest to us."

"I see," said Plumb. "Well, I don't know if it's worth anything, or if I should even be telling you this... This is for an official investigation, is it?"

Taylor nodded. He had a better poker face than anyone I've ever known.

"Well, it's just that I've not seen her much in class lately. In fact, before you gentlemen came to my door, it was the first time I'd seen her in weeks. She was arguing with me about getting review questions for an exam. I told her that if she'd come to class, the material was presented."

"Do you happen to know if she and Shannon were close?" I figured I already knew the answer, but I'd feel useless if I didn't ask at least a few questions.

"They sat together, whenever Miss Bedford came to class. Though they didn't seem to talk during my lectures so much anymore."

"When Shannon died, did she continue to sit in her regular seat?" Taylor scribbled notes in his notebook..

"She stopped coming to class completely a few days before," he said.

"Thank you, Professor," said Taylor. "This has really been a big help."

"Always glad to help the local magistrate," said Plum, as he shook our hands.

We turned to leave when another question struck me.

"The test she was asking about... What was it over?"

"Our current unit," he said. "Rituals and customs of primitive cultures."

"Was there any information about the rat-plague in South America?"

"Quite a bit, actually," he smiled. "We covered it extensively. Why? You know, you're more than welcome to audit the class. Along with Miss Perry, of course."

"Just a thought." I laughed and waved as I followed Taylor out of the office.

"Andrea Bedford," said Taylor. "I think we have our prime suspect."

"You think?"

"Maybe. It's worth following up on, though. Maybe try to get some evidence that a judge'll buy, get us a warrant to bring her in for questioning."

"If you get her, I want to be there."

What bothered me the most about finally coming face to face with Andrea was that she disappeared in plain sight, and I couldn't puzzle out how she'd done it. Sure dodging into a crowd was a simple trick that every thief knew, but avoiding eyes as trained as Taylor's was no easy task. Even so, she shouldn't have been able to hide from me. It was almost as if she'd stepped out the door and just vanished.

As the elevator doors opened, I took the lead and made my way to the building's exit.

"We're parked over here," said Taylor.

"I just need to check something out."

The crowd outside was thin. It was between class changes, and only a few stragglers remained on the quad. I got to the bottom of the steps, lowered the walls to my perception, and turned to face the building.

"What're you looking for?"

"That," I said, pointing to a pair of storm drains on either side of the building. To Taylor, they looked like snow-covered culverts, but even they should have had some energy left to them, some trace of what washed through. Instead, they were cold and black. In fact, the walls of the building, all around the foundation, was a mass of black stone and brick. She'd infected the building.

"That's how she got away. She ran out, slid into one of these things, and scuttled off."

"It's a good theory," said Taylor. "But where do you think she went?"

"I don't know," I said. "But it's a safe bet she's long gone by now."

"Come on," said Taylor. "Let's get back to the hotel and check on Maggie."

We stopped at a sandwich shop on the way back. If Maggie'd taught me anything, it was that magick was hungry work. The energy expended in any type of spellwork needed to be replaced, and that meant feeding the human machine. If throwing any run-of-the-mill charm could give a person a case of the munchies, the shield-slinging she did last night was bound to make her ravenous. Since it was part of an "ongoing investigation," Taylor was kind enough to put it on the department's bill.

I expected Maggie to still be asleep when we got there.

When I opened the door, however, the bed was empty, the sheets wound and wrinkled on the floor, with Bitsy laying in the middle of one of the pillows. Faint light flickered through the crack under the closed bathroom door.

"Maggie?"

"I hope you brought food," came the reply, followed by the sound of sloshing water. A moment later, steam billowed from the opening bathroom door, and Maggie emerged wrapped in towels. "I'm starving."

To say Taylor blushed would be a gross understatement. On sight of her, his jaw dropped open. Then he became conspicuous in trying to look at anything *but* Maggie's dripping, towel-wrapped body. And if it wouldn't sound ridiculous, I would swear the cat snickered.

"Sorry," she said. "Thought you were alone. Be right out."

She picked up her clothes off the bed and disappeared back into the bathroom.

"Wow," said Taylor.

"Tell me about it."

"I can hear you two, y'know," came Maggie's voice through the door.

A moment later, Maggie came back out, this time wearing sweats and a t-shirt, her hair still in a towel-turban. She unwrapped her hoagie and ate while we told her about our encounter with Andi Anthropology at the college.

"But she got away," she said between bites.

I nodded.

"And now she knows you're looking for her."

"Yeah," I said. I must've yawned while I said it, because Maggie stopped in mid-bite and gave me a hard look.

"Have you slept at all?"

"No time," I said as I sipped my soda. "We've got to get

148

moving before the sun goes down, and we can't track down information at night. Besides, you needed the sleep more than I did."

"You're not going anywhere in your car," Said Taylor. "Remember? It's totaled."

"And gross," I added.

I checked my watch and saw I still had the better part of an hour before my insurance carrier left his office. I dug his card out of my wallet and picked up the telephone to dial.

"Help me..."

Shannon's voice bled through the dial tone. This time there was a chorus behind her, a wailing choir of voices, all of them pleading. My stomach churned. My sandwich threatened an encore.

"I'm trying," I said into the handset. "I swear, I'm trying."

The choir faded. I looked up to see Taylor and Maggie staring at me.

"Was that..?"

"Shannon," I said, pretending to look at the insurance agent's card in my hand. "And the rest. We have to stop this."

Maggie got up and walked to me. I didn't move as she reached up and dragged a finger under my eye. I wasn't even aware I was crying.

"We'll get this sorted," she said, putting her arms around me. "We'll put them to rest."

I nodded as I dialed. When my agent answered the phone, I gave him my information and told him where to get my car. I carried full coverage, so all the damage would be taken care of. It was just a question of how long it would take to get my car back. The agent assured me he would drop a rental off at the hotel before noon tomorrow.

The sun already hid behind a few of the taller buildings, and I knew we had to get moving. They'd be coming, more determined than last night.

"Finish getting ready," said Taylor as he wadded up his sandwich wrapper and tossed it in the trash can. "I'll drive tonight. Just let me get some patrol units over here to watch the place." The door closed behind him as he went to the parking lot and his radio. Maggie turned to me.

"Are you okay?"

"Really tired," I said. "How 'bout you? You spent an awful lot of power last night."

"Some of it was borrowed," she said. "And I used some of yours. I'm surprised you aren't asleep standing up."

"I'll sleep later," I said. I went to the bathroom and splashed some cold water on my face. When I looked into the mirror, I saw someone I wouldn't have bought a used car from. The bags under my eyes were getting darker, and they were rimmed in red. I looked strung out.

When I came out, Maggie went in. It took her a few minutes, but when she came back out she'd replaced her sweatpants with jeans, her long t-shirt with a black one that fit better, and was carrying sneakers. She'd pulled her wet hair up into a ponytail, and a silver chain that peeked from the neck of her shirt let me know that she was wearing her pentacle necklace. A second string around her neck hid another pendant under her shirt.

"New necklace?" I jerked my chin toward the jewelry.

She tugged at the string and pulled the seashell, the only thing left from her shop, from under her shirt.

"It's comforting somehow," she said. "So what's the plan for tonight?" She sat down on the bed and put on her shoes. "We planning for a fight or what?"

"Not if I can help it," I said. "Tonight, we hide while we try to figure out what to do. Maybe they'll lay low."

"They haven't any other night," said Maggie. "What

makes you think they will tonight?"

I didn't have an answer. The truth was, I knew they wouldn't take the night off, and I felt like a coward for trying to run away from them, but I couldn't figure out anything else to do. On the one hand, if we stayed and fought, we'd die, end of story. On the other, if we ran, and more shops got looted, more people would die, and more restless spirits would show up to ask me what the hell I was doing about it. My head swam.

There was a knock at the door.

"We'd better get moving," said Taylor from the hallway. "The sun's going down."

Maggie rode in the front seat while I stretched out in the back. As scared and angry as I was, my own exhaustion won out and, despite Taylor hitting every pothole in the road, I fell asleep. I awoke to the all-too-familiar feeling of falling, only this time the feeling was real. I let out a yelp as my body slammed into the floorboard of Taylor's land-yacht.

"Shit," he spat.

"There's too many of them!" shouted Maggie.

"What the..?"

My body shook and my stomach rolled, the feeling of falling still held firm on my heart. I had to tell myself that I was in a car, that I wasn't plummeting toward concrete, that I wasn't going into that awful blackness again. It was dark, but it was night, not the maddening nothing that came from death. This darkness had voices, textures. I was still alive.

My attention snapped straight as I scrambled out of the bowels of the car to a window. Against the night, I could see dozens of them. Their twisted faces screamed and howled as they ran toward the car on all fours. I looked around at our surroundings and recognized the area as north of Pittsburgh. Why would there be so many of them here, concentrated right on this highway unless…

"It's a trap!"

"Y'think?" growled Taylor. "Little fuckers were waiting for us. Hold on!"

He spun the wheel and hit the emergency brake, twirling the car until it came to rest facing the opposite direction, then he stomped on the gas pedal and paid no mind to the shrieking bodies that bounced off the hood of the car. The engine roared like an angry beast as the car leaped forward.

"Where're you going?" I shouted.

"Anywhere but here," he replied.

In Pittsburgh, there isn't a time when the streets aren't occupied. No matter the time of day, there are always a few cars on the road for one reason or another. I guessed that it was around three in the morning, too late for the drunk crowds, too early for the morning rush-hour traffic. The cars on the road were few, but still in danger. If not from the possessed creatures behind us, then from Taylor's creativity behind the wheel.

"This car might not be as pretty as yours," he grinned. "But it's built like a tank and can outrun just about anything."

In the passing street lamp glare, I could see Maggie, her eyes wide, her expression drawn in fear, either at the monsters or at Taylor's driving. At the time, I'd have been hard-pressed to say which one scared me more.

We cut through the strip district. As Taylor's engine growled, I looked out the window to see all the restaurants, farmer's markets, and butchers with eerie shadowed figures crawling over their facades. They were looting, coming up through the basements, making off with whatever they wanted, and there was nothing we could do to stop them.

"Just a little bit further," said Taylor. Another block or so and he wrenched the wheel hard, sending the car into a skid that turned into a sharp left turn. He pulled a key-card from under his visor and swiped it through the reader by an enormous steel gate.

"C'mon," he hissed as the door in front of us groaned. When it rose barely five feet off the ground, Taylor pulled the car through, then leaped out, ran to a key-pad, and punched in a code. The door lurched and crept closed. In the distance, over the whine of metal gears and cables, there came a chilling shriek as the vermin began to catch up to us. When the door was only a foot from the ground, shadows moved on the concrete beneath the door. At ten inches, the shadows got bigger, closer. At six, one of the shadows congealed and slid under the door, the twisted face letting out a scream that echoed throughout the concrete structure. The door slammed shut on dozens of fingers, leaving us in dim light with one of the monsters hissing and squealing at us.

When the door clicked into place, the creature sprang, both clawed hands pointing straight at me. I threw my left arm up out of instinct, more covering my head than any brave fighting move. The tattoo on my arm burned, and when the creature reached me, it flew backward as if bouncing off a trampoline and sprawled on the floor, shaking its head.

"I'll be damned," I said.

The thing turned its attention to Maggie, who looked less flustered than I thought she would. To be honest, she didn't look scared. She looked angry.

It leaped into the air at her, ready to do her real damage. But Maggie made a grabbing motion in the air and made a sharp pull downward. The creature froze in midair, then slapped onto the concrete. It scrambled to its feet, still hissing, still spitting. It wasn't smart enough to be afraid, nor was it stupid enough to attack either of us again. It went after the only person it hadn't tried. Taylor.

It ran at the detective, raising up and jumping, only to have one of its knees destroyed by a well-placed bullet from Taylor's gun. It landed, but kept coming, the damaged leg still kicking. Four more claps of thunder later, the thing lay twitching less than a foot in front of Taylor. He kept his eyes and pistol on the creature, his finger twitching near the trigger.

"He's down!" cried Maggie.

Taylor shot a glance toward us then back on the fallen man. His eyes were wide, his breaths shallow and fast.

"Taylor?" I took slow careful steps toward him. "It's okay, man. You got him."

His head and gun snapped up toward me. There was no recognition on his face, only fear.

"Whoa!" I said, throwing my hands up. "I'm on your side, remember?"

He looked confused, terrified, as if he expected me to attack him too.

"Matt." Maggie's voice was soft, soothing. She walked past me toward him. "It's okay, Matt. You got him. You saved us both." Her voice was like velvet, sliding over him, easing the terrified creases out of his forehead. She stepped closer to him, her voice never stopping. When she was close enough, she put her hand over the top of the gun and eased it down. He looked lost, unsure of what he'd done or what was going on around him. When his eyes met hers, he let go of the gun and backed away.

On the other side of the door, they were scratching, clawing at the metal, trying to get in. When fingers and claws didn't work, they slammed themselves against the door, cannon-shots of thunder in the structure.

I took Taylor by the arm.

"Matt." He didn't respond. "Matt! Taylor!"

His eyes snapped up.

"Where are we?"

"Safe," he said. "This is the impound lockup. Nothing gets in here."

Hands scraped the steel door, human fingernails torn away from cuticles, fingers worn bloody as they continued their assault.

"Are you sure?" They sounded determined.

He didn't answer, but stared at the door with dread crawling across his face.

"Is there another exit?"

His face twisted as he shot me a horrified look. Without a word, he took off at a dead run toward the other end of the structure, passing impounded cars and steel cages full of contraband. Maggie and I followed. He ducked around the side of one of the lockers and up a concrete flight of stairs where an ordinary-looking door stood.

"It's steel," he said. "The same kind that's at your place. They couldn't get through that one, so this one should be fine."

"Mine was reinforced by magick," I growled. "They'll tear this apart like tissue!"

"Is there a kitchen in here?" Maggie spun as she looked.

"Why? What good is a..?"

"*A kitchen!*" She stared at Taylor. "With salt, maybe?"

Taylor nodded and pointed. Maggie jumped down the stairs and ran for the door across the room. Smart, and something I should've thought of. They couldn't get through my door, sure. The talismans and symbols on the other side kept them from coming through. But more than that, I had the threshold lined with salt. I don't know why it keeps negative creatures out, but I've been damned thankful that it does on many occasions.

The metal of the far door groaned and my stomach fluttered. I've seen some horrifying stuff in my life, but that doesn't mean it doesn't scare me. If anything, because I've seen what the negative entities can do, they scare me more.

"I couldn't find enough for both doors," shouted Maggie over the din. "But this'll hold this one."

She flipped open the spout and poured a line across the threshold of the back door. Then she knelt with her eyes closed. I knew what she was doing, raising power to put into the line. When she touched a finger to the line, even Taylor could see the air above it shimmer for a second.

"Now what?" She rose to her feet.

"I don't know," I said. "Maybe there's something here we can use."

Taylor's blank expression snapped off. His clenched jaw and hard eyes took up their familiar places on his face.

"Of course!" he yelled as he sprinted to one of the cages. "We keep confiscated weapons here! Help me find the right cage!"

We split, each one running to a cage and peering through the bars. One held plastic bricks that I assumed were drugs. The one next to it glittered with stolen jewelry in plastic evidence bags, guitars and even lawn ornaments.

"It's amazing what people will steal," I muttered.

"Over here!" called Maggie a few cages down. "Where's the key?"

In answer, Taylor kicked at the door. When it didn't budge he tried again.

"I don't have one," he grunted.

"Get back!" barked Maggie. "*Aperité!*"

The lock clicked and turned, and the door swung open.

"How..?"

"Later," said Maggie.

The thundering on the door got louder. It sounded like there were hundreds of them out there, all of them throwing each other at the steel door, trying to reach us. It wouldn't be long. I was surprised the door held as long as it had.

I turned to see Taylor methodically searching through boxes, looking past the hand guns and rifles until his face lit up in gleeful smile.

"Hah!" he cried, dragging a box off a shelf like it contained the greatest treasure he'd ever seen. In light of the current situation, I hoped it held some holy relic that could banish demons. Instead, I got the next best thing.

"Grenades?" I yelped.

"I'm going to blow the bastards to kingdom come!" he said with a cruel grin.

Normally, I'm not the type to resort to violence, especially when there's a risk that I might be killed in the process. Standard military-issue pineapples like the ones in the box could create one hell of a boom, but the blasts were comparatively small. The explosion wasn't what caused most of the damage, however. The shrapnel from a fragmentation grenade could make a human body look like linguini, not to mention the damage it could do to the rest of the building. One support gone and we'd all be trapped under a mountain of rubble.

"What about the *guns*?" I shouted.

"No good," said Taylor through clenched teeth. "We keep the guns here, but the ammo gets put back into the department. Cost cutting."

Of course. Everyone wants safer streets, but no one's willing to pay for it. People gripe all day long about losing the battle for crime in the city, but when someone asks for a raise in taxes to pay for things like new computer systems, body armor, or even bullets, there's an uproar. Really, putting it back to good use seems not only cost-effective, but poetic in a way.

"Get to the car," he shouted as he tossed me his keys. "Get it started. We're only going to get one shot at this."

Maggie shot me a worried look before we both ran to the car. She slid into the back seat while I took the front driver's and jammed the key into the ignition. I turned the key and brought the engine to coughing life, slid over to the passenger's seat, then we waited. Seconds ticked by as the sounds of scraping and banging changed to the whine of steel tearing. They were coming, no doubt about it. I looked through the rear window of the car to see Taylor, his jaw set in a hard grimace, a grenade in each hand. As the first hand of one of the possessed poked through the door, he took off at a dead run, pulling the pin as he went. The safety lever dropped away and I felt my breath stop in my chest.

It was amazing to watch, like being in the front row of one of those theme-park action extravaganzas, where the Stallone-like hero defies the odds by doing some crazy stunt. Except Taylor wasn't an actor, and the guys on the other side of the door weren't stunt men. In my mind's eye, I saw Taylor's arm erupting in flame as the grenade went off before he could get rid of it, killing him and dooming us. But it didn't play out that way. He made it to the hole in the door as one of the monsters poked his head through and screeched. Taylor hit him square in the nose with the steel shell of the little bomb and made the monster retreat a half step. The other grenade followed its twin through the hole. Taylor juked right and spun and made a bee-line back for the car.

"Get down!" he screamed as he dove through the open car door and slammed it. Maggie ducked into the floorboards. I covered my ears and turtled down into my seat. Taylor grabbed the gear-shift and stared out the window.

And then God spoke.

Flames belched through the hole on the door, accompanied by the loudest *boom* I'd ever heard. Bits of metal sailed through the air, clanking off the hood of Taylor's car. He pushed the gas pedal to the floor and aimed squarely for the hole, much larger than it had been a moment ago, and crashed through it onto the street. I barely got a glimpse of what lay on the other side before we were around a corner and gone in the darkening night. What I saw made me sick to my stomach.

There weren't nearly as many of them as I thought there were, maybe only twenty or so. The grenade had landed right in front of them, and the impact killed at least five outright. Several others lay on the ground clutching their arms or bellies. The sidewalk was awash in crimson-burned-black.

"They're people," said Maggie through tear-filled eyes. "You killed them."

"They were already dead," I said. "They were just shells for the demons." I said it, but it didn't make their agonized faces fade from my memory. It didn't soak up the blood on their mangled bodies. It couldn't stop their squeals of pain.

The sun peeked over the horizon and between the buildings. I've always thought sunrises were beautiful, but this one was more so than most. This one meant that, against all odds, we got to live for another day.

Taylor got us back to the hotel and walked us to the door. He and Maggie spoke briefly, but I didn't hear their terse conversation. From the way they parted, I guessed he'd be back. She tried to get him to stay, but he said he had business to attend or something like that. I slumped into the bed without so much as taking off my shoes. I'd swear I was asleep before I hit the pillow.

When I woke up, it took me a few seconds to realize

what felt different. Not wrong, exactly, but something was out of the ordinary. Sure, I wasn't in my apartment, in my bed, but that wasn't it. Maggie's arms around me felt good and warm, and not what I was used to, but that wasn't it either. I sat up and swung my legs over the side of the bed, annoying Bitsy. She humphed then pushed her head under my hand until I scratched her ears. But I still couldn't figure out what was out of the ordinary. I didn't feel sick. In fact, I felt great, the best night of sleep I'd had in years. Five years. Then it hit me. I hadn't had the dream. I didn't wake up to the nauseating sensation of falling, wasn't bathed in sweat, wasn't reliving the final three seconds of my life again. I felt myself smile as Maggie stretched beside me.

"How'd you sleep?" she said.

"Well," I said. "Better than I have in years."

"Good. I figured you deserved it."

"You?"

She nodded.

"Just a little spell. It only worked because we were in physical contact. I can't stop them completely or anything, but like I said. I figured you deserved a real rest."

"Thank you," I said. It was the nicest thing a person had done for me in years, and it was something so simple, so easy. By lying next to me, by touching me, she made it stop, made the nightmare go away. The way a mother makes the darkness seem not so bad by stroking a child's hair.

"So," she said as she sat up. "Have you figured out what we're going to do?"

"Yeah," I said. "I'm tired of running from them."

"What do you suggest we do?"

"We start hunting them. I need to call Taylor. We've got some planning to do."

13

My plan, if it could be called that, sounded a lot better in my head than it did in practice. Sometime during my non-nightmare-enhanced sleep, I decided that I was tired of being hunted. The more we tried to run, the more they blocked us in. Last night, every road out of town that we tried was crawling with them, and I'd just bet the roads we didn't try were blocked as well. They were smart, or at least whoever was controlling them was.

All signs pointed toward one person: Andi Anthropology. She had direct contact with Shannon, her other roommates showed the same signs of infection, and she had access to the kind of arcane knowledge she needed through Doctor Plumb's class. If I was right, and she was the person pulling the strings, she was in for a rude shock. Instead of waiting for her to send the rats after us, we'd hunt her. There were only two small problems with my plan. First, we didn't know how to find her. I doubted she'd go back to her house, and she'd already proven she could disappear in a crowd, which I still hadn't figured out. Second, I knew nothing about hunting. While most other red-blooded men my age in Pennsylvania had been hunting since they were kids, I couldn't bring myself to hurt so much as a frog. Hunting wasn't something that interested me at all. I even hated camping. At best, I'd shot a bow-and-arrow in Boy Scouts when I was a kid at summer camp, and I was terrible at it. That was where Taylor came in.

I explained the plan to him over the phone, and he told me he'd been hunting since he was little. His father was a gun nut, and made sure Taylor'd been on the right side of a rifle since he was around six. The thought of Taylor as a six-year-old with a rifle sent shivers down my spine, but at the time, I was glad that one of us had some kind of hunting know-how.

When Taylor arrived, I had no question that he knew what he was doing, and that he meant business. He was dressed like some sort of commando from one of my beloved video games, in grey, urban-camo pants and a black vest covered with pockets. He carried a large black duffel. Inside it were several rolls of duct tape, two electric stun-guns, ropes, and a couple of bottles of something he called "Deer-Stink."

"Rats track by smell," he explained. "If they're following us, they've got our scent, and we won't be able to get anywhere near them. This'll make us smell like some other animal, and they'll leave us alone."

Sure, I thought. Just as long as they think that there are three rogue deer walking through downtown Pittsburgh, we'd be perfectly safe.

Maggie and I didn't look particularly stealthy, but if luck was on our side, for once, we might be able to catch the rat queen, and we might be able to put a stop to all this insanity.

We climbed into Taylor's car and drove to Carson Street, past rows of taped and closed storefronts until we came to a few shops that were still in business. Even though the sun was still up, the shops were closing early.

Taylor parked several blocks away and we hoofed it to an alley near the closest untouched shop. The looks we got from passers by as we walked down the sidewalk in the dimming day-light were priceless. We looked like we were ready for war. Well, Taylor did at least. Maggie and I looked like we were out to pick a fight. And we were.

We also stank to high heaven. "Deer-Stink," as it turned out, was a bottle of concentrated pheromones and deer piss. I wish I'd known that before I splashed it all over my clothes and my only winter jacket. As it stood, unless there was some miracle soap that could get it out, I'd have to burn my clothes when all this was said and done.

"Did you catch much flack for the impound?" I asked Taylor as we walked.

"Yeah," he said, his eyes never shifting. "The security cameras were damaged in the blast, but the ones inside showed all three of us. They know I was the one that threw the grenade."

I let the phrase hang in the air for a moment before I asked the next inevitable question.

"What..?"

"Suspension pending a full investigation," he said. "They're talking jail time."

"I'm sorry."

He shrugged as he walked.

"I'd do it again," he said. "It'll work out."

Tracking Andi Anthropology wasn't an easy thing. For starters, we had no idea where she was. The only address listed for her by the school was the house she shared with her zombified roommates, and it was pretty clear that she hadn't gone there in a while. We figured she was still in town, having just seen her at the university, but other than hanging out on the campus all day and praying we could make her face out from a sea of identical students was hopeless. I asked Maggie about a tracking spell, but she snorted and told me I'd been watching too many B-movies.

Besides, she'd need something personal of hers to do such a thing, and as I wasn't going anywhere near that house again, there wasn't much chance, which left our only other thought. Carson Street.

Rats are creatures of habit. They're not random in their hunting or attacks.

If they started at one end of the street, we figured, they'd continue up the street until they were done. Then they'd move on. It seemed that the best idea was to sit and wait in the cold February night and hope that she showed up to one of the raids.

I know. Fat chance, but it was all we had.

And it was starting to snow.

The weather in Pittsburgh is predictable only in that people are certain they have no idea what it's going to do. Winter lasts far longer than most people like, and snow storms are random at best. It's normal for us to have no snowfall whatsoever from November to New Year's, only to have eight inches or more every day in January. In February, all bets are off. It could be nice and pleasantly cool one day, freeze your butt off the next, and balmy hot the day after.

As fat white flakes began to fall from the sky, I could only think of one word.

"Perfect."

"Here," smirked Taylor. He tossed a silver packet to me and one to Maggie. "Bend it and put it in your pocket. It'll keep you warm." Hunter's wisdom.

We took our positions, Maggie and I in separate alleys a few blocks from each other, Taylor across the street and between us. We could see each other if we looked hard, but I still felt very alone, and that little voice in my head kept telling me that I was going to die a painful death. I told the voice to piss off as I sat down next to a dumpster and waited.

And waited. And waited some more. I didn't have a

watch on, but as the darkness deepened and the cold started slicing through the layers of my disgusting jacket, I began to question my own sanity. Here I was, ostensibly alone, covered in deer piss, in an alley, waiting for what? A demon-possessed monster who could tear through steel doors like tissue paper, with the delusion that if we somehow managed to catch the queen, the power source behind all of them, that we might be able to subdue her and break the spell. With duct tape. It sounded really stupid to me too. I don't fight, I've never fired a gun (which didn't keep me from keeping my hands tight on the Beretta 9mm Taylor'd loaned me), and wasn't sure what we'd do with her *if* we even managed to catch her. Taylor was armed to the teeth, sure, and Maggie had her magick, which she'd already proved to be formidable, but what the hell did I have? I could see them coming, maybe, if they were above ground and in the open, but other than that, I was pretty much useless.

You're not useless.

I froze, and not because of the falling snow. I knew the voice. It haunted me with its plaintive moan. I might not have sat around weeping, but Shannon's voice was never far from the front of my mind.

Help me, she said. *Help us. We're slipping away.*

My eyes stung with angry tears and a lump wedged tight in my throat, but I didn't turn around. I knew what I'd see if I did, and I'd seen too many dead people walking around to want to subject myself to it voluntarily.

"I'm trying," I whispered. "We're all trying."

She didn't answer. I sat there, not breathing for a few seconds before I chanced turning my head. The alley was dark and empty. No phantoms or wraiths there to wag their spectral fingers at me, but it didn't change their message. Time was running out for them.

The human soul is an interesting thing. When a person dies, the energy that most folks think of as a soul leaves the body. Where it goes from there is a matter of opinion. Some say Heaven, others say it reincarnates. I have no clue. My own experience didn't shed any light on the subject. But I do know that when the soul doesn't go where it's supposed to, when it hangs around here for whatever reason, people call it a ghost. Most ghosts go where they're supposed to after taking a little time to figure things out, but there are some that don't get that chance. When something like our rodent-friends invade a body, they keep a link to that life force and feed off of it. They literally kill the ghost. If there's even a chance that there's a Heaven, an afterlife, or even a chance to be reborn, I couldn't just walk away.

They were dying. All of them. Draining down like the final wisps of electricity in an aging battery.

I was cold and wet. The snow seeped through my urine-soaked jacket, wetting my shirt beneath, and my shoes weren't made for skulking around in snow-filled alleys. The hand-warmer in my pocket had lost its heat a while ago, and I was beginning to think we should just pack it in when a little luck shone down on us.

I looked up the street and caught a glimpse of Taylor pointing toward Maggie's position. He crept forward and knelt, leveling his rifle as he did. I moved as quietly as I could and leaned around the corner until I spotted her. Andi Anthropology, skulking around in the shadows. She was moving toward the shop next to Maggie. It looked like she had a bag in her hand, no doubt a way of marking the shop for the next hit. The muscles in my body tensed in anticipation of the report from Taylor's rifle as he took her down. Then I felt the bottom drop out of my stomach when Maggie stepped out from around the corner and faced her.

"What sort of bullshit movie heroics..?" I spat under my

breath. Andi Anthropology did what a normal person would've done. She turned and ran. I thought she'd have torn Maggie to pieces, but I decided to figure out why she didn't later. Now she was running top speed right toward my position.

Taylor followed her with his rifle and fired a sharp bark in the darkness, which missed her. She yelped, ducked her head and kept running. When she was only a few feet from me, I swallowed hard and hoped I wasn't making a colossal mistake. I stepped out of the alley and jumped, putting my shoulder right at her waist, and took her down to the ground. She went down a lot easier than I thought a demon-possessed rat queen would've. But she didn't go without a fight. I took a hard punch to the jaw and a solid knee to the coconuts before Maggie and Taylor got there to pull her off of me. I lay in the snow wheezing and gasping for breath while they worked to subdue her. For a little wiry thing, she sure could pack a punch.

"Let me go!" she screamed. "Somebody help me!"

She didn't squeal or let out some unearthly howl. I lowered the walls to my perception. There wasn't a single trace of black on her. In fact, her aura was shades of blue and green with areas highlighted in white. Of course there were little tendrils of red here and there, but I figured being pissed about being ambushed was normal. And very human.

"She's not one of them," I coughed. "She's clean."

"What?" snapped Taylor. "It's gotta be her!"

"Get your fucking hands off me!" she spat as she struggled against the duct tape that Taylor was still applying to her hands.

"If she's not the one," said Maggie, "then…"

A howl split the snow-filled air like a bone-chilling knife, and I felt my stomach roll again.

"We've got to get out of here," said Taylor. His eyes darted up and down the street. "Now."

"Let me go!" screamed the struggling girl.

Taylor slapped a piece of duct tape over her mouth, hoisted her kicking form over his shoulder, and took off at a sprint in the direction of his car. Maggie and I traded bewildered looks before another shriek motivated us to follow him.

14

"Have you lost your fucking mind?" I screamed as the car skidded around an icy corner. "She's clean! She's not one of them!"

"What'd you want me to do," Taylor growled. "Stand there in the middle of the street and have a chat? Those things were coming and it didn't seem like a good idea."

"You duct-taped her mouth shut!" shouted Maggie. "Then you threw her in the trunk!"

Not that I'm some kind of misogynistic pig or anything, but the image of Taylor running down the street with Andi Anthropology over his shoulder like some kind of cave-man-era prize made me sick. The thought of taking her down when I thought she was the queen rat was one thing, but now that I knew she was clean, I felt guilty about tackling her. Even if my aching groin did seem to ease the guilt a bit. But she was a full foot shorter than Taylor, and couldn't have weighed more than a buck and change, and the whole thing just seemed even more wrong that it was.

"Couldn't you have, y'know, zapped her or something?" he demanded.

Maggie's eyes burned into narrow slits. I'd seen her angry, but never like this. The old saying "if looks could kill" holds an entirely more important meaning when applied to a witch, and for a moment I was afraid a corpse would be driving the car.

"Could," she said, her voice an intense rumble. "But would never, you son of a bitch!"

"I panicked!" he shouted. "I'm sorry, okay? I figured getting her out of there was better than letting her be torn apart!"

"You didn't have to put her in the trunk!"

"Guys!" I shouted. "We have more important problems right now! Like where are we going, and what're we going to do about her?"

"I don't know!" Taylor pounded the wheel with every syllable. "All I could think of was to get away! I need to think! We need a safe place!"

"Where?" I screamed. "It's not like we can go waltzing into some convenience store with a hogtied girl over our shoulders, now can we?"

Without a word, Taylor wrenched the wheel and headed south down 21st Street. When we sped through the entrance of Southside Park, I figured he'd lost what little part of his mind was left. When he slammed the car into park, I knew he was nuts. Out in the open? Just waiting for those things to find us?

"What the hell are you thinking?" I said. "We need to be inside somewhere safe!"

"We did that last night," said Taylor as he got out of the car. "Damned near got us killed for being trapped. I'm not doing that again. This way, we at least have a chance of getting away from them. Now help me with the girl."

I couldn't argue. Maggie was still fuming, but she got out and made her way to the trunk. When Taylor opened it, I expected her to fight, to scream, to attack us like some feral beast. Instead, what I saw was a small, frightened girl, sobbing in the dark. Taylor reached down and pulled the tape off her mouth. He ripped it fast, which brought a gasp of pain from her, but pulling it slow would've hurt worse.

"Please," she sobbed. "D… don't hurt m… me."

Taylor's hard expression faltered into something that re-sembled regret. He reached into the trunk to help her out, but she shrank away from his hand as if she thought it would bite her.

"Get away from her." Maggie pushed him aside.

"I'm sorry," he said. "I was trying to…"

"Like she's going to trust you, after the way you manhan-dled her."

Taylor looked stunned, then he turned and walked a few yards into the darkness. Maggie didn't turn to watch him go, but turned her gentle voice and eyes toward the cowering girl.

"No one's going to hurt you," she said.

"Don't touch me!" screamed the girl. She swung at Mag-gie with her taped hands. Maggie backed up a few steps.

"I'm sorry," she stammered. "Let me…"

"You let them!" she cried. "You let them!"

Maggie expression sank. For a person whose central be-lief system could be summed up in the phrase "Do no harm," it was a crushing blow. Bad enough that we'd gone after the wrong person, but for the wrong person to be around nineteen years old, and to have scared the hell out of her, was probably more that Maggie could bear.

"Let me," I said, then took Maggie gently by the shoul-ders and guided her around to the front of the car.

"It was a mistake," she said, like she needed to explain to me. I knew it was a mistake, and a horrible one at that. Now all that was left was damage control.

"I know," I said. "Just give me a minute."

I walked back to the trunk of the car, unsure of just how

to get the girl out without doing any more damage to her. I sat down on the bumper with my back to her. It wasn't disrespect or anything like that. I just couldn't face her. I couldn't stand to see her like that.

"Andrea," I said. "My name's Stan. Stan Cooper. I knew your roommate, Shannon."

"You killed her, didn't you."

It wasn't a question. In her mind, I was the one who dragged her into that alley and took her life. To her, it was probably the three of us together.

"No," I said. "I didn't. I was trying to help her. I promise you, we're not going to hurt you. We made a mistake, and if you'll let me, I'd like to try to explain. We'd just like to talk."

"You called the house," she said.

"I did," I nodded. "I was trying to warn her. I guess I was too late."

"Why should I believe you? How do I know that you won't kill me?"

"You don't," I said. "But please believe me, I'd rather die myself than hurt you anymore. I promise you, I won't let anyone hurt you."

"Let me out," she said.

It was a risk, one that I couldn't take. As much as it pained me to see her locked in the trunk of that car, I knew if I let her out without saying my piece, she'd run. She'd never know what we were trying to do, and would probably run to the police, which, given our current popularity, would make our lives much more difficult.

"I will," I said. "But first, please listen."

Deep breath. How could I even begin to tell her about demons and ghosts without coming off as a lunatic? The answer was I couldn't. If I started the conversation telling her about all the people possessed by some South American rat demon, chances were I'd just scare her more. Not only would she be trapped, but in her mind she'd be trapped by crazy people. Better to fudge a bit on the facts.

"When Shannon contacted me, she told me that there was something wrong with the people in your house. They were... getting sick. I'm betting you noticed it too. There've been a lot of people who are sick the same way your roommates are, and they're doing terrible things. Robbing stores, killing people. We were trying to stop them. We were trying to find the person directing them. We thought it was you, and I'm so, so very sorry that we thought it was you. People's lives are being changed, people are being killed, and we would do anything to stop it. We've spent the last few nights running from the infected people, and tonight we went looking for them. You showed up, and we thought it was you."

I turned to face her, but I still couldn't look at her. I just wanted her to see my face, to see that I was sincere.

"I am so sorry. We're in the middle of a crisis, and I guess none of us are thinking too clearly."

I left out the bits about magick and the creatures tearing through steel doors, but I thought that summed up the situation. Bad guys on the loose, we fucked up, we're sorry. End of story.

"I don't expect you to forgive us," I said. "But I hope maybe you'll understand, or at least see what we're trying to do."

"What do you want?" Her voice was still raw, but she was no longer crying.

"We just want to ask you some questions," I said. "We just want to talk, and we'll leave you alone.

"You'll keep those other two away from me?" She sounded plenty scared, and I couldn't blame her.

"I will," I said. I stood up and turned to face her. Her face was still wet with tears, eyeliner running down in huge smudges. She was shivering in the cold. Heartless bastards that we were, we didn't even think of putting a blanket with her. We sat warm in the car while she froze in the trunk.

I took her trembling hand and helped her out. She came out slowly, like a frightened animal emerging from a cage. Sure, the outside promised freedom, but the cage was more secure. She might not able to get out, but at least in the cage she knew where she stood.

I took off my piss-stained coat and draped it over her shoulders.

"Sorry about the smell," I said as I tried to tear the duct tape. It took me a few minutes, and I know it hurt like hell pulling it off her bare skin, but I did my best. When I was done she didn't smile, and looked at me like I might still attack her at any minute, but at least she didn't run from me.

Maggie and Taylor came closer. I made sure to keep myself in between her and them.

"This is Detective Matt Taylor," I said.

"You're a cop?" she half-shouted. "What the fuck?"

"I'm sorry," he stammered. "I thought you were…"

"What?" she screamed. "What'd you think I was? One of those monsters?"

"He did," said Maggie. "We all did."

She turned on Maggie, eyes blazing.

"Don't talk to me," she snarled, then turned back to Taylor. "You just pull random people off the street? Aren't you supposed to be protecting people?"

"I thought I was," he said.

"What about me?" she screamed. "Who's going to protect me from those things? Who's going to protect me from you?"

He didn't say anything, to his credit. He just stood there

and took the punishment. He could've done anything, yelled back, knocked her to the ground. A lesser human being would've, but he didn't. He was in the wrong and he knew it.

"What were you doing out there?" I tried to distract her from her anger.

"What does it matter?" she said, still shaking with rage.

"Did you know what was going on?"

"I knew shops were being vandalized. I knew people were getting killed and hurt."

"So why were you there?" Taylor kept his voice soft. "Didn't you think it could happen to you too?"

"I was trying to protect the shop," she said, looking down at her shoes. "I know the old couple that own it. I didn't want anything to happen to them."

"Protect it how?" Maggie took a step forward. I could tell by the tone of her voice that something struck a chord with her.

"It doesn't matter anyway," said Andrea, her voice cold. "It probably wouldn't have worked. Like you care."

Maggie glanced into the trunk of the car where Andrea's satchel still lay. She made to reach for it before I could stop her. She was met with a straight right punch to the chin from Andrea.

"Don't you *dare*," she spat.

Maggie scrambled to her feet, anger and shock arcing between the two. I did my best to get between them, but I'm not stupid. One thing my father always told me was to never get between two fighting cats, dogs, or women. In all three cases, a body stood a better chance of getting hurt and looking damned silly than he did of stopping the fight. Taylor, on the other hand, was a little braver and a lot less smart than me, it seemed. While Andrea was distracted by Maggie, he darted in and grabbed the bag.

"No!" she shouted as he flipped open the top. "Don't!"

Taylor's expression went from hard to confused to incredulous. He reached into the bag and pulled out several Ziplock baggies. One was full to bursting with salt. Another with rose petals. A third held another powder I couldn't identify, save that it looked like it was made from kitchen herbs.

"Give that back!" she shouted as she snatched the baggies away. "Those are mine, asshole!"

"Oh, my gods," said Maggie. She'd forgotten about her swelling chin, which hung loose in surprise. "You're a witch."

"What about it?" snarled Andrea. "You got a problem with my religion?"

Another witch? What, was there a convention in town I didn't know about?

Maggie reached into the neck of her t-shirt and pulled her pentacle out.

"Not at all," she said.

"You don't deserve to wear that," said Andrea. "'*An it harm none*,' right?"

That stung her. The first, and only law of the Wicca was pretty much the only thing that all pagans believed. It wasn't even directed at me, and I winced with sympathy pain. Taylor must've realized he was out of his element because he took a couple of steps back before becoming very interested in the park's trees. Coward. Or genius, I couldn't decide which. Given the situation, I'd have rather been in his place.

"I said I was sorry," snapped Maggie. There was no more trace of wonder or sympathy or even tenderness. Now her voice was sharp like ice. "What would you have done?"

"Well I wouldn't go beating the shit out of random people on the street, that's for damned sure!"

A howl cut through the air and brought the conversation to an abrupt end. The sky grew lighter with the sunrise.

"Guys," said Taylor as he hurried to the front of the car.

"They're coming this way."

"How many?" I said, like it mattered. If there were more than one of them, I wasn't interested in sticking around. One was bad enough, but it took all three of us to put just one down before. Two, I'm not sure we'd be so lucky. More than that, we'd die for sure.

"All of them, I think," he said as he slid behind the steering wheel. "You coming, or do you want to be here when they catch up?"

The three of us looked at each other, blinked, then ran for the car. Maggie and I climbed into the back leaving the front seat for Andrea. I figured it was the least we could do. After all, she rode in the trunk, so now she could at least get the full benefit of the heater. Even though the snow had stopped falling, it was still bitter cold outside.

Taylor started the car and threw it into gear, spitting up snow behind us as it pulled out. As we followed the winding road out of the park, I could feel them coming, hundreds of them bearing down on us. I lowered the walls of my perception and looked behind us, into the woods. The trees were awash in black fire.

15

We drove into the sunrise, the sky tinted vivid shades of pink and yellow, the light dancing off the freshly fallen snow. The morning commute was already well underway, making the highway look like an artery carrying life back into the city. When we crossed the 10th Street Bridge, I tapped Taylor.

"The hotel's that way," I said.

"Not going to the hotel," he said. "Unless you want to walk in smelling like that."

He had a point. We all smelled horrible from his "Deer-Stink." The cold outside made the stench tolerable, but with the heater going full blast, the car reeked to high heaven. The smell made my stomach roll more than once, and I wondered what kind of impression I would make if I just gave up the pretense of civility and threw up in the back seat of Taylor's car. I could only imagine what the hotel staff would think. Not that I cared much. If they knew that we were out all night fighting monsters, they'd probably not even bat an eyelash. But then, they didn't, couldn't know that. And bringing Andrea to a hotel room looking like she'd been abducted probably wasn't the best of ideas either.

"So where are we going?" asked Maggie.

"My place," he said. "I figure you two can clean up there,

then go back to the hotel for some rest."

It was a good plan, flawed by the fact that I didn't have a change of clothes. Of course, I didn't have anything clean at the hotel either, so it didn't really matter.

"They're demons," blurted Andrea. "Aren't they? I mean, I know what you said, but you were just... They are, aren't they?"

Maggie and I glanced at each other, and I caught Taylor's eyes in the rear-view mirror. Moment of truth time. Did I trust her with the awful truth, and possibly gain her trust or solidify her thought that we were all crazy, or lie to her?

"Yeah," I said. "They are."

She nodded.

"Tell me where you're staying," said Taylor. "I'll drop you wherever you want to go."

She didn't say anything for a moment.

"I think I'd rather stick with you guys," she said. "You seem to know more about what's going on than I do."

I caught Taylor's eyes in the rear-view mirror again. He was leaving it up to me.

"I don't think that's such a good…"

"Please," she said without looking up. "I want to help."

That other part of my brain, the one that usually uses silly things like logic and rational thought, told me to send her home and tell her to lock the doors and let the grown-ups handle the big nasty monsters, but the truth was I didn't know what I was doing any more than she did. Maggie knew a little bit more about what we were dealing with, and Taylor had his police sensibilities, but me? I was lost as a goose. We all were.

"Are you sure?"

She nodded.

"Alright, then," I said.

Taylor drove us into the Oakland suburb to a stretch of

row houses usually reserved for University of Pittsburgh students. It was an area I knew from a few years ago when a guy dug a hole through the wall he shared with his neighbor, climbed through and murdered her. I was called by the woman's family to see if she was haunting the place, and if she'd left a will. Nothing like a family tragedy to bring out the vultures. She wasn't, and didn't, but the killer, or rather his madness, was. The guy committed suicide in the house when he realized what he'd done, and never left. I let out a breath when we passed by the street. Funny that I hadn't even realized I was holding my breath.

We pulled up in front of one of the row houses and Taylor shut off the engine.

"Don't expect a whole lot," he said as he got out. "Remember, I'm just a cop."

The first thing that struck me about the inside of Taylor's home wasn't how clean or dirty it was, but that there was so much about the man I didn't know. But it was all here, in every detail of the place, his whole personality made into furniture. Through the front door was a dining room that he used as an office. The big table was covered in file folders and photographs stacked in disheveled piles around an old computer. Tacked to the walls were newspaper clippings, most of them about the rash of robberies and murders, and photos. A giant map of Pittsburgh was thumbtacked to one wall with big red circles around certain areas. I didn't even need to look to know they were the sites of robberies.

Further in, the kitchen was more or less clean, with only a stray dish or two in the sink. A coffee pot sat on the counter, thick cold sludge in the bottom of the carafe. Taylor went straight to it and began to make coffee. Outside the kitchen was where I guessed Taylor did his relaxing, if he ever relaxed. There was an easy chair, a sofa, and a television. On either side were two wooden racks full to the top with DVDs. I smiled. It was almost like looking at my own entertainment system.

"I've got some clothes you two can borrow," he said as he handed me a trash bag. "Shower's at the top of the stairs. Towels are in the cupboard beside it."

I turned in time to see Maggie disappearing up the stairs and cursed myself for not being just a bit faster.

"Make yourself comfortable," he said.

Andrea sat down at one end of the couch, her bag clutched tight against her hip.

"Relax," said Taylor from the kitchen. "You're safe here."

She didn't move, and didn't say anything. It was easy to see she was still scared, but I didn't know what to do about it. I've never been very good with saying just the right thing, and I was afraid I'd just scare her more. Maggie was better at talking to people. What would she do? What would Jake Steele do?

I sat on the floor across from Andrea.

"Why'd you really want to come with us?" She kept her head down. "It's dangerous. I know you want to help, but there's more to it, isn't there?"

She nodded.

"Shannon was my best friend," she said. "We moved into that house, and when everyone started acting weird, I just left. I started staying with my boyfriend."

"Does he go to the college?"

"He's a musician," she laughed. "I met him at a bar."

Her smile faded as she looked down.

"I didn't *love* him. He just... y'know... was there when I needed someone," she said. "Then one night he went out for a gig and when he came back he was acting strange."

"Strange how?" Taylor stood in the kitchen doorway.

"I thought he was high," she said. "But that wasn't it. He started acting like my roommates. He left a couple of nights ago and didn't come back."

"Any idea where he went?"

"Wish I knew," she said. "It's weird. I don't love him, but I'm worried about him. I miss him."

There was nothing I could've said that wouldn't have sounded like a cheap, after-school movie, so I said nothing. Taylor must've felt the same way because he fidgeted in the doorway before turning back to his kitchen.

"Anyone hungry?" He opened the pantry door and gestured inside. "I don't have much, but you're welcome to whatever's in here."

In my mind I laid odds that he'd regret the invitation, but I didn't question it. My growling stomach made a pretty convincing argument to raid the man's refrigerator.

The icebox was full of frozen Hungry-Guy dinners, the kind that taste so good that they can't be even a little bit healthy. I once heard that if a person ate enough of them he'd have so many preservatives in his body that he wouldn't have to be embalmed when he died. The pantry told a similar story. Pop-Tarts, popcorn and a bag of rice were pretty much the entire contents. It was guy-living, something I was comfortable with. I'd bet the man hadn't had a date in at least as long as me.

I rummaged until I found a frozen Salisbury steak dinner with mashed potatoes, and tossed it into the microwave. Three minutes to nuclear food nirvana. I glanced through the doorway and watched Taylor give Andrea a cup of coffee. She flinched when he held it out, but took it anyway and held the cup in both hands while she sipped.

I pulled a cold soda from the refrigerator when my meal was done and tried drawers until I found one with a fork, then I carried my hot plate back to the living room and sat on the floor while I ate.

Taylor disappeared at some point between bites, ducking away into his "war room," which left Andrea and me alone together.

"Mr. Cooper," she said.

"Stan."

"Why did she call you?"

I stopped chewing and swallowed a big chunk of beef.

"She was worried about what was going on in the house," I said.

"Yeah," she nodded. "But why you? Why didn't she call the police or something?"

I wished I knew the answer. The police would've claimed drugs to be the cause, but they would've gotten everyone out. Or they would've died in the process. Why did anyone ever call me? Sure, telling people that they thought their house was haunted or their kid was possessed might be a one-way ticket to goofy-land with rubber walls, but why come to me? There were hundreds of people who claimed to be clairvoyant, hundreds more who had greater abilities than me. But somehow, I got a reputation of being the real thing, unlike most of the so-called psychics. That was how I wound up on most cases.

"I help people," I said. "At least I try to. When she called me, she mentioned a family that I helped a couple of years ago. Maybe she knew them, or read about them, or something."

"What makes you so special?"

Oh boy. Here it was, the conversation that I knew I had to have if I was going to keep her trust, but the one I was really afraid to have.

"A few years ago, I died."

I said it as plainly as I could. I said it just like I would say, "I wore a jacket." Either she'd believe it or she wouldn't. I couldn't afford to skirt the issue with her, not since she'd asked me directly.

"I didn't stay that way, obviously. When I came back from... wherever I was, I could see dead people, energy patterns, that kind of thing. I kind of just fell into this 'psychic investigator' crap."

"What was it like?" She stared at me, wide-eyed. "Dying, I mean."

"It sucked," I said, no longer hungry. I got up and put my half-eaten meal in the kitchen. Maggie padded down the stairs in bare feet and sweatpants and an oversized t-shirt, her hair bunched into a wet bun on top of her head. I took the opportunity and made a beeline for the stairs.

I didn't notice when he did it, but Taylor had left some clothes for me on a small table outside the bathroom door. I took up the pile, grabbed a clean towel from the cupboard, and locked the door behind me. The mirror was still steamed from Maggie's shower, but I didn't care. I wasn't planning on admiring myself in a mirror. I just wanted to get the smell of deer piss off me.

I emptied my pockets and stripped, then stuffed my clothes into the trash bag Taylor gave me. It was a shame, too, because I really liked the shirt I was wearing, and my poor jacket was less than a year old. Then I turned the shower on and climbed in. The warm water made my muscles melt as I imagined it pulling every scrap of grime and fear and negativity off my skin. As I stood there, warm bliss pounding down on my scalp, I started thinking about rat-people.

They only came out at night, but it was almost daylight when they came after us in the park. I couldn't figure out how they'd tracked us, and why they were coming for us at sunrise. Then, somewhere between lather and rinse, my tired brain clicked into gear.

Unless they weren't coming for us. They came up the hill, but none of them chased us as we drove away. I knew they liked chasing. Hell, my car was a testament to what they could do if they caught up to someone. So why didn't they chase us? Unless they didn't even notice us. They weren't coming to kill us. They were going *home*. They'd finished their raid and were returning to their nest. That had to be it. First rays of light, they scampered back into their holes, just like real rats.

I finished rinsing and shut the water off. When I pulled the curtain aside, Shannon, what was left of her, was standing in the bathroom, her eyeless sockets staring at me.

I'd like to say that spirits in my bathroom have happened to me so many times that I hardly even blink anymore, but it would be a lie. I warded my apartment years ago, after one too many such encounters, and hoped never to get another. Of course, Taylor's house wasn't warded, but I hadn't thought of that when we came. Just like a scene from a horror movie, I let out a startled yelp and almost fell backward into the tub.

Her form shimmered and twitched, like she was trying to find the right frequency to broadcast herself. She was getting weaker. The image of her was fainter than the last time I saw her, smeared like charcoal on paper.

Hurry, Mister Cooper, I heard, more in my head than in my ears. *Hurry.*

"I'm trying," I said.

I can't hold on, said the voice.

"I said I'm trying, dammit!"

Her form shimmered and disappeared.

I stood there, dripping and naked and shaking for a moment, and tried to make myself feel brave or determined, anything but useless.

I toweled off, brushed my hair back, and dressed in whatever Taylor left for me. Sweatpants and a t-shirt, almost identical to what Maggie now wore. Great. We could be twinkies.

I left the door open to let the steam dissipate and made my way back downstairs. I was surprised to see Maggie sitting on the couch next to Andrea, the two of them actually talking instead of being at each other's throats. Taylor was conspicuous in his absence. Smart man. More than likely he was busying himself in his office. Hell, I'd almost have rather been outside in the snow and cold. I could understand Andrea's point of view, especially since Maggie helped us throw her in the trunk, but I've also seen Maggie when her temper's up. Hell hath no fury, and all of that. I didn't want to interrupt, but I had to.

"We can't stay here," I announced as I came down the stairs. "We have to get back to the hotel."

Andrea looked uneasy. "Why?"

"Because the house isn't warded," said Maggie, her eyes reading my expression. "You saw one, didn't you?"

"Her," I replied. "In the bathroom."

"'Her' who?" Andrea looked from Maggie to me. "You mean Shannon?"

I didn't say anything. I didn't have to. I'm pretty sure the expression on my face answered for me, and I didn't feel like discussing it further.

"I think I may have figured something out," I said. "Where's Taylor?"

"Here," he said as he entered from the front room.

"Those things only come out at night, right?"

"So far," he said.

"But they came after us when the sun was coming up, and they didn't exactly chase us down like they usually do."

"Which means," said Taylor, "they weren't after us. They were on their way back home. Or to their nest, or whatever. Come in here."

Damn. He stole my thunder. Just once, I'd like to be the

guy that figures everything out and explains it to everyone else. I bet this kind of thing would never happen to Jake Steele.

Maggie and I followed him with Andrea trailing behind. On the wall of his office, the huge Pittsburgh map had some new color, a giant green circle that encompassed Southside Park, as well as the suburbs of Arlington, Mt. Oliver, and Allentown.

"I figured, with the light coming up, they had to have some place close by to hole up in," he said as he pointed at the map. "I don't think they're actually living in the park. Someone would've seen them. So that means they've got to be hiding somewhere where they can get underground."

"Basements," said Maggie.

"Right. I'm figuring they're in one of these places that butts up to the park."

"That's a lot of ground," said Andrea from behind us. "How're you going to find them?"

"That's where I come in," I said with a shudder. "They leave a kind of... trail. I think I can track them."

"Then we should go now," said Andrea. "While they're still sleeping."

"What do you think we're after here, vampires?" I turned to face her. "We don't know if they sleep during the day, or even how many of them there are. We could walk right into a room with a couple of hundred of them inside. And the way their numbers are growing, who knows how many there are!"

"And just what do you propose we do with them once we've found them?" Maggie crossed her arms and fixed her with an icy glare.

"I hadn't thought of that," said Andrea, shaking her head.

"Plumb said the tribe in South America performed some kind of exorcism on the king rat, didn't he?" Taylor was looking from Maggie to me. "You guys know about this stuff. Don't you have some sort of exorcism... thing you could perform?"

Sure, I knew several, but I didn't look forward to performing any of them.

People think exorcisms are like they are in the movies, with one person tied to a bed and a young priest and an old priest reciting biblical lines at them until the demon voluntarily leaves or is forced to release his hold. But the truth of the matter is that it's much more serious than that. It's a fight between the will of the demon and the exorcist. Their energies entwine, ripping and tearing at each other, vying for dominance over both physical forms. I've watched it, seen it for myself. I've done it a few times, and watched as my aura was torn to shreds, ripped like tissue from around me. In some cases, the exorcist is able to pull the other energy out of the victim. Of course, the Vatican never really advertises the cases where things don't go quite so well. For priests, their faith gives them an edge, an extra boost of energy to fight with. But even so, there are too many that end up on the losing end of the stick, or that never recover. The losers wind up infected with the demon, locked inside their own bodies and able to see everything, hear everything, and unable to stop themselves from committing all kinds of atrocities. For others it's even worse. They wind up locked away in monasteries, drooling and catatonic, with friars to feed them and bathe them and clean up after them when they shit themselves. I've never seen one, but it wouldn't surprise me to find out their energies are just as empty as that kid in Shannon's house. They're just empty shells. Like I said, I don't have that kind of fire-power. I have my own energies, my own beliefs, but no real faith. The last time I performed an exorcism, it took me more than a month to recover. I had a feeling this rat demon was stronger and meaner than the last one I faced.

"I know a few," said Maggie. "But it might help to know more about the ritual they used in South America."

"I tried to find out," said Andrea. "That day you saw me at Plumb's office? That's what I was asking about. He wouldn't tell me, though. Just kept going on and on about skipping his class and was I on drugs and how the material was provided if I had gone to class. That guy's a total prick."

"I might have more luck," said Maggie. "He likes me."

"Of course he does," snorted Andrea. "You have tits. He hits on every girl in class. He takes grad students to digs in Paraguay every summer and half of the girls come back with herpes or something. From him."

The thought of the old man chasing co-eds made me equal parts nauseated and giddy. Even more so was the thought that he'd been doing it for years, gotten a reputation for doing it, and *still* managed to find students willing to bed him. He was probably a legend among frat boys, but did no favors for the reputations of good men anywhere.

"He's even gotten to the point that he tries to recruit in the middle of the school year. No one seems to care that he's banging half his class."

I thought about it for a moment, and things seemed to click into place.

"What was the age of the infected guy you pulled into lockup?"

"I don't know," said Taylor. "Looked like early twenties to me. Why?"

"Anyone identify him yet?"

"Don't know. Why?"

"Can you find out?"

"I'm on suspension, remember? I can't just waltz in and ask for information on a case. Why do you want to know?"

"Because this is starting to make sense to me."

Finally, I got to be that guy.

16

We dropped Maggie and Andrea back at the hotel, ostensibly so Maggie could check on her cat. It was a lie, of course. That cat was more self-reliant than any four-legged animal I'd ever seen. It wouldn't have surprised me to walk in and find she'd grown opposable thumbs and was using the can opener on her own. The truth was I didn't want either of them coming with Taylor and me. Pig I may be, but if what I suspected was true, the safest place for them to be during the day was where they could sleep and recharge. Besides, I needed Maggie at her strongest, and I didn't need the chip on Andrea's shoulder making decisions for her.

As we crossed the 10th Street Bridge, I rubbed my eyes and yawned. Nothing quite like a little terror and mortal peril for a week to just drain all the energy a person has right out of them. When this was over, assuming I lived through it, I was going to need some serious rest. I shuddered. It was the first time I'd really considered that I might be walking into that cold blackness again.

"You okay?" asked Taylor. "Maybe you should've gotten some sleep too."

"No time," I said. "They're going to come again tonight, and I'm tired of running."

"If you're wrong..."

"Then we spend tonight running again, and more people get hurt or killed," I said. "But if I'm right, we might be able to stop this."

"Or we might get killed. Ever consider that?"

I didn't answer him. I was trying not to think about it.

We pulled into a space in front Duquesne University and got out. The frigid air smelled clean for once, or at least cleaner than the inside of Taylor's car, which still smelled like deer piss. I couldn't imagine how he was going to get that smell out of his upholstery. We tromped up the salted sidewalk and through the doors. When a couple of students stopped and stared at us, I realized how I must've looked. "Homeless" was a word that came to mind. So was "ridiculous." I probably smelled bad too, thanks to the ride in Taylor's car. Fabulous.

We opted for the stairs and made our way down to the bottom floor, to Plumb's office. The door was closed and locked, but the schedule on the door told us that he was in one of the large teaching theaters in the building.

It took us a few minutes to find the right room in the labyrinthine building, but our search eventually led us to a set of double doors, through which I could hear Plumb's booming bombastic voice.

"The Yanomamo tribe of South America holds fascinating funeral rituals," he said. "Not for the faint of heart at all. Before we view this film, I must ask that anyone with a weak stomach please do yourselves the courtesy of exiting the room."

I pulled the door open a bit so I could see inside. The huge room seated more than four hundred students at a time. The stage area was backed by a large screen, in front of which stood a lectern with a microphone. Plumb stood with the patient look of a saint while his students shifted and adjusted. A few got up and exited, brushing past me as they did, but the majority of the packed house stayed. I closed my eyes and lowered the walls in my perception, held my breath and took a good look.

The room was awash in every color imaginable, all clumped together. There were patches of blues and pinks surrounded by a field of green and gold, testaments to the personalities of the students. Many of them were idealistic, from what I could see. Amid the colors were horrifying patches of black. They were like tears in the multicolor fabric of the room, their black energies stretching and growing, tearing a little of the color away at a time. There were less than ten in the room, but they were infecting all of those around them.

On the stage, Plumb radiated darkness as if he were made of it. In the students, I could still see that thin corona of blue or green where the darkness kept them down, but Plumb had no such aura. The energy that radiated from him was darkness, pure and simple, a cancerous evil that was using his position to infect young minds.

"It's him," I whispered. "I was right."

My stomach rolled as he raised his head, as if he'd heard me, and stared right at us. He fixed us with a pleasant smile and waved, motioning for us to wait for a moment. He clicked a button on the lectern, dimming the lights, and the screen leaped to life with an old documentary. Plumb hurried down the aisle toward us. I shut my eyes and threw my walls back up. If I continued to see him for what he really was, I might not be able to fake not knowing, and then we'd really be screwed.

"Mister Cooper," he said, shaking my hand. My flesh crawled where he touched it, but I tried not to let on. "Detective Taylor. How pleasant it is to see you both again. How's the case going? From the looks and smell of you, not well at all."

"Rough," I said. "But nothing we can't handle. We think

we may have tracked down Shannon's roommate. We're pretty sure she's the cause of all of this."

"Really," he said. "That angry young girl? She hardly seems the type."

"We were hoping we could ask you a few more questions," said Taylor, poker-face firmly affixed.

"Certainly," said Plumb, his eyes fixing on mine. "Is there some problem?"

"No," I said, probably a little too quickly. "Just a few details we wanted to verify."

Taylor nudged me as he took a small notebook from his pocket and a pen. I took it for what it was, a non-verbal command to shut the hell up.

"The student that we saw at your office during our last visit," he said. "Shannon's roommate. What was her name again?"

"Andrea Bedford," said Plumb. "She'd be, I believe, a sophomore or a junior, though I don't really recall which."

"And I assume the school will have records of her local and permanent address."

"Yes," nodded Plumb. "Though I don't know what good that will do you. Most of these students move around like nomads and never remember to update their local addresses in the directory."

"But the permanent address stays the same," said Taylor. He shook his head. "All these students must really choke off the area. Doesn't it make it hard for you to get to work? I mean, especially in all this snow."

"Oh my, no," smiled Plumb. "Many of my colleagues prefer to live out of the city, but I live just across the river."

"Oh?"

"In Arlington Heights," he said.

Right across the river, and butting up to South Side Park.

Scott A. Johnson

It made perfect sense, and was exactly what I suspected.

I must not have been as good with a poker face as Taylor, because Plumb's eyes fixed on mine, and the corners of his mouth twitched the tiniest bit.

"In fact," he said, his voice frosting. "I'd love to show you the place some time. It's quite roomy. Enough room for plenty of friends. Now, if you two gentlemen will excuse me, I've got a class to teach."

Taylor didn't say a word on our way back to the car. I could tell he was angry by the way the muscles in his jaw throbbed. My father used to do the same thing when he ground his teeth to keep from saying something he might regret, or when he didn't want to make a public scene. I guessed Taylor was following the latter.

When we got to his car, he knocked snow out from in front of the headlamps with a stiff backhand swipe, then unlocked my door. I got in, making as little noise as possible. I screwed up and I knew it. Something about my nature makes me a chatter-box when I'm nervous, and knowing what Plumb was gave me all kinds of heebie-jeebies. I also knew I couldn't keep a straight face if my life depended on it. I may as well have held a neon sign over my head.

Taylor slammed the door, sending tiny avalanches of snow down the windshield.

"That could've gone better," he said between clenched teeth.

"Sorry," I replied. "I'm rotten at this, I know."

"You suck," he said as he turned the engine on. "Now he knows we suspect him, and he probably knows we're coming after him."

"Do you think he knows we know he knows?"

Taylor turned furious, buggy eyes on me.

"How could he *not* know?" he spat. "You practically pissed yourself when he looked at you!"

"At least no one will notice the smell," I deadpanned.

Taylor blinked, then snorted in laughter.

For once, my instincts proved right. One of Taylor's associates gave him intel on the incarcerated man. His name was Sean Prather, he was college-aged, and was a student at Duquesne. A bit of digging revealed that, not only was he one of Plumb's students, he was also with him on his last trip to Paraguay. I figured that last trip was when he found the demon, and spread his infection to his students. Everything made sense except for why. A tenured professor at a college like Duquesne pulled down a lot of money, and most of them were content to rule their petty little kingdoms. I thought about it again until something else clicked in my brain.

"My god," I said. "He's dead."

"Who?" asked Taylor.

"Plumb!"

"What're you talking about? We just saw him alive, plain as day."

"We saw his body," I said. "But what was in there wasn't Jason Plumb."

The black that oozed from his body dripped with negative energy, but it was more than that. In every other case I'd seen, a thin corona of the person's energy remained, sometimes buried beneath the power that pushed them down. But in his case, there was nothing left, no thin blue line, no hint of the human that once lived in that sack of flesh. There was just the negative energy of the entity inside. Of course, it was just a theory, but at the time I didn't have anything else to go on. Besides, it made me feel almost better in a way, that what we were going up against was a monster in human skin. If there were any trace of Plumb in there, I doubt I could do what I suspected had to be done. If I could even do it at all. The only way I could break his hold on the others was to catch him. Maybe even kill him. I didn't know if I even could do such a thing, but time was running short, and I had a feeling that now, since he knew that we knew, it was going to be either him or us.

The snow stopped falling as we pulled back into the hotel parking lot, but the heavy grey clouds threatened to dump another load of white on the city. Plow trucks did their best to clear and salt the roads as they careened around corners before it all started again. Someone on the radio said that by five o'clock in the evening, Pittsburgh was going to be hit with a major snow storm. Somehow, it seemed fitting. No sense making anything easier for either side. They didn't seem to be bothered by the cold, but maybe even they would have trouble getting through the icy streets. It was something to hope for, anyway.

The schedule on Plumb's door said he taught classes until two o'clock. It was just after ten, which gave us precious little time to plan our own deaths. My mother would've called it pessimism, my father realism. I just called it fate. I was tired of running, tired of seeing tortured phantom faces wherever I went, and just plain tired. Seeing Shannon in the shower gave me enough of a what-the-hell attitude to think I might be able to do some good. By the time we got back to the hotel, that tiny voice in my head was screaming and banging pots and pans, telling me to get out of town while I could, and never look back.

We walked through the door of the hotel room to find

Maggie sitting in one of the room chairs with a white candle burning next to her and Andrea curled on the bed in a deep sleep.

"She has nightmares," said Maggie as I closed the door. "Not like yours, but bad enough. Keeps whimpering in her sleep."

"After what she's been through? Go figure. Is that the same spell you used on me?"

She nodded. "A little different. I didn't feel comfortable touching her, but the lower power seems to work. I figured everyone needs a moment or two of peace."

"Wake her up," I said. "We don't have much time."

"Why?"

"Because dipshit here," said Taylor, jerking a thumb at me, "tipped him off that we know about him."

"Oh, merciful Mother," gasped Maggie.

"He'll be coming for us," I said. "Wake her up."

Maggie said a few words under her breath and pinched out the candle. Then she went to Andrea and put a gentle hand on her shoulder. The girl awoke with a start.

"You have to get out of here," said Taylor. "They're coming for us, and I don't want you hurt."

"I can help," she said.

"No," I said. "I've already got too many deaths on my hands. We can give you cab fare to get out of town. Where are your parents?"

"Europe," she said. "They shipped me off to college and took an extended vacation."

"I'm sorry," I said. "Is there anyone else you can go to?"

"I don't have anyone else," she said, shaking her head. "I can't go back to the apartment, and I'm not going anywhere near that house."

"Then you'll stay here," said Taylor. "Where it's safe."

"The hell I will." She stood and fixed Taylor with a vicious glare. "They've taken my best friend, my roommates, and my boyfriend. By now they're looking for me too, so unless you want them to shred this hotel, you have to take me with you."

She had a point. Images of my apartment building sprang to mind, echoes of the screams flooded my memory. If we left her, no one in the hotel would be safe. They'd tear the building and everyone in it apart to get to her.

"Look," snapped Taylor. "I carry a gun, she's got magick, and he's a fucking psychic who can see 'em coming. No offense, but we're outnumbered, and we can't be worried about what happens to you if you fall behind."

"You think I'm worthless," she seethed. "You don't think I can't help?"

I didn't see her energy rise, but I felt it. Hell, anyone could've felt the swell of heat that came out of her. Her rage built inside her until it burst forward in a palpable wave. The picture frame behind the bed shifted, the chair behind me scooted and bumped the wall, and Taylor had to take a few steps back. There was a crash as the mirror in the bathroom shattered.

"We're going to have to pay for that," I said.

"I'm not some helpless little waif," she said, her voice a low growl. "And I'm not going to let you treat me like a child! You either take me with you, or so help me, I'll follow you anyway!"

Maggie raised her eyebrows and shrugged. Taylor's hands shook as he fought to wipe the surprise off his face.

"What the hell was that?" I said.

She dropped back down to the bed.

"I don't know," she said. "I started doing that before... before I started college."

"Why didn't you do that last night?" blurted Taylor.

"It doesn't always work," she said. "I was too scared. Fear doesn't always do anything. Anger... now that works."

"Welcome aboard," said Maggie.

My father always said, "never bring a knife to a gun fight." The fact of the matter is that if a person goes into something outnumbered, and with not enough firepower, he's going to lose. He'll also wind up looking very silly in the process.

As it stood, even if there'd only been four of those demon-possessed things crawling the streets, we'd still be outnumbered. At last count, there were more than a hundred of them, and our chances of beating them hand-to-hand was about the same as Maggie joining a convent. Possible, but highly unlikely. It just wouldn't work. But, my father also used to say, "Lack of manpower can be made up for with more firepower." To be honest, I think he got that last one from a movie, but it was still a valid point. We waited for Maggie and Andrea to put their shoes back on, and for Maggie to feed Bitsy, and went back to Taylor's rolling porta-potty.

"Where are we going?" Andrea slid into the back seat, entirely too eager for the coming fight. "Unless you've got an arsenal at your place..."

"I do," grinned Taylor. "But it's not nearly enough for what we have to do. But I know a guy."

We drove until we came to more boarded up shops and graffiti. Angry eyes lined the streets and watched as Taylor's car rumbled past. We were in the poorest section of Pittsburgh, a suburb called Wilkinsburg.

The place was strange to me, in the sense that once, it had been *the* place to be, with fine restaurants and automobile boutiques, locally owned shops and real pride. Then something happened, about twenty years ago, and no one could really place what. The businesses all moved a dozen or so blocks down, and the town just started to die. Drugs began to appear on the streets, and it seemed as if everyone just gave up. Then, a few years ago, a group got tired of all the gangs and the violence, and got tired of being thought of as second-class. They started cleaning up the town, one block at a time. Far from gentrification, the group was made up of locals. They kept the rents low and pushed local pride as a way to make the little suburb shine. They just hadn't made it to the block we were on yet.

Taylor pulled his car up to the curb and killed the engine. The storefront beside us was painted in camouflage with stickers with names like "Winchester" and "Beretta" and "Remington" on the windows. My guess was that this shop was one of the only safe havens in this part of town. Who would be dumb enough to try to rob a gun shop?

"Come on," he said.

"Maybe we should wait here," said Andrea, looking nervously around.

"In this neighborhood? Be my guest," said Taylor with a grin.

Maggie and Andrea traded looks before scrambling out of the back seat to catch up to Taylor, who was already pulling the shop door open.

"Hello, Walt," said Taylor with a stony face.

The shopkeeper looked up from his chore of cleaning the rifles, and all the color drained from his face.

"Officer Taylor," he stammered. "Good to see you again. What brings you out here?"

"I have a problem," said Taylor. "And you've got a whole shop of solutions."

"Sure thing," said Walt. "Anything I can do to help."

It was fascinating to watch Taylor when I wasn't on the

other side of that cutting stare. Taylor's eyes never shifted, he never blinked. The guy behind the counter broke out into a cold sweat before Taylor'd even said a word. That took talent, the kind I wished I had sometimes. It would make negotiating for a new car easier.

"I need guns, Walt. You know what kind I mean."

"Sh… sure," he said. "I got handguns, rifles… You going hunting or something? I just got in the new Henry rifles…"

"Cut the shit," said Taylor without moving. He didn't have to. He had Walter pinned to his spot with his eyes. "I need something a little special."

Walt forced a smile, but his eyes told me everything. Taylor had him by the short and curlies.

"I only got what's in the cases," he pleaded. "I run a clean shop here!"

Taylor shook his head and straightened. I'd seen this act before. Not from Taylor, but from late-night cop movies. He was playing the heavy, and laying it on thick. From the looks of Walt, he didn't watch those same kinds of movies.

"You know how many guns we pull off the street every day? And how many of them I can trace back to you?"

Walt's face went from pale to chalk-white.

"Every time some gang-banger with an Uzi gets popped, he sings to keep his tender ass from spending too long in the feeding line. They like tough guys in prison. Like breaking them. It doesn't take much to make them roll over. You get me?"

"You got nothing on me," stuttered Walt. Geez, it really was like watching an old movie. All that was missing was Walt on top of the building screaming "Top of the world, Ma!"

"Wanna bet?" said Taylor with a sly grin. "You show us your private stock or I make a phone call and you'll have so many cops here that your clients'll think you've turned rat on them. I wonder how well that would sit."

"Fine!" shouted Walt. "Fine! Of course I'll help! Hey, because it's *you*, right?"

Walt shoved his way to the front of the shop and flipped the sign over, then turned the deadbolt, all the while muttering curses to himself. When he turned around he wore a fake smile and had hatred in his eyes.

"Right this way, folks," he called as he passed behind the counter and through a beaded curtain in the back.

Maggie and I followed Taylor with Andrea coming up close behind. Behind the curtain was a door that looked like it belonged on the front of a walk-in freezer. Walter fumbled with the padlock on the handle, snapped it open, and threw the door wide. My jaw dropped and I half-expected to hear military music full of drums and trumpets come blaring out of the room.

If Taylor appreciated the sight, I couldn't tell. His jaw stayed set and his eyes stayed stony. Maggie goggled at all the matte and shiny black barrels. The room was lined on every wall with racks containing assault weapons, some of which I'd never even heard of.

To be honest, I wouldn't know the difference between an automatic and a semi-automatic if a Marine showed me. All I know is which end of a gun I don't like to be on.

A wooden crate at the far corner sat open revealing familiar shapes.

"Grenades?" I stared at Walt. "What is it with you guys and grenades? Where the hell do you even get these things?"

"I know a guy," said Walt.

"You'll have to acquaint me with him," sneered Taylor. "There's what I'm looking for."

The thing he pointed at didn't look like any gun I'd ever seen. It had four barrels on it, all of which were covered by egg-shaped bulbs. The barrels didn't aim straight, but went away from the center.

"It's a net gun," he said, reading my expression. "Riot cops use 'em all the time. The mesh is a metal weave, and there's a draw cable attached. Good for catching big rats."

"Even ones who can chew through steel?" I asked.

"Maybe for a minute," shrugged Taylor. "Might give us time we need."

Andrea stared around, wide-eyed, her hands clasped in front of her. She looked so young, so much like a child instead of the young woman she was. She slowly raised her hand and felt the metal of one of the barrels, then pulled it back away.

"I don't think I can do this," she said.

"Then go back to the hotel," said Taylor. "Makes me no nevermind. You go with us, you have to be sure."

Defiance burned in her eyes as she glared at him for a moment, then she took one of the guns from the wall, one I recognized from a Pacino movie, and held it out to Taylor.

"Show me," she said.

17

In the great, long list of things I've done that later turned out to be bad ideas, there are some real doozies. Bragging to some girl in the seventh grade that I was a championship diver when I knew damned well I couldn't even swim is on that list. So is trying to bathe my mom's twenty-two pound cat.

As I headed back toward Carson Street and the park, I had a sneaking suspicion that this plan of mine would knock all others down a peg on the list. The trunk of Taylor's car was so full of weapons and other evil-looking things that I winced every time we hit a bump in the road. Maggie hadn't spoken in almost an hour, and neither had Andrea. Taylor seemed happy as a clam, humming along with the radio as we went to meet our deaths.

It was snowing again. Not just fluffy puffs of delicate flakes, but angry buckets of white powder that blanketed the city in ice and death. I wasn't sure if Taylor could even see to drive. If he'd been nervous or overly cautious, I might have felt better, like maybe he was aware of the reality of the situation. But the more he hummed, the more he sat with that eerie smile on his face, the more tense I got. Maggie and Andrea weren't helping matters with the silent treatment. The snow made it feel like we were trapped in Taylor's boat-sized coffin, with the three of us already dead and Taylor some demented mortician.

"Lots of snow," I said. Maybe some small talk would break the tension.

"Uh-huh," grunted Maggie. Andrea said nothing.

"Yep," said Taylor.

The sun already hung low, dipped below the tops of the buildings. Night was coming fast, and I wished I could be anywhere but here.

"It's weird," said Andrea. "Plumb is so well-respected at the college. He's... everyone likes him. But he's a demon."

"How long has he worked at the college?" I was thankful for the conversation.

"Years. He built that department from nothing."

"How do you know that?"

"He told us. First day of class. That and his yearly trip to South America were his pride. He almost didn't make it back from the last one."

That got my attention.

"Why not?"

"He got lost during the last one. Went missing for like five days. He said he was in the rainforest when he found a temple that looked like the jungle had reclaimed it. Covered in vines, crumbling walls. He said he was so fascinated that he started exploring it and lost track of time. He didn't even realize how long he'd been gone until a search party found him. He said he spent the rest of the trip with his students going through the ruin. It was a great find for the university."

The tiny engine in my brain turned over and revved.

"Did he mention what kind of temple it was?"

"He couldn't shut up about it," she said. "It belonged to an old civilization that was into animism. They worshipped..." Her face turned ashen.

"Rats?" I ventured.

"Yeah," she said.

"So," said Taylor. "This guy goes to South America, finds some moldy temple, and what? He brings back a really unique kind of souvenir?"

"No," I said. "More like an illegal alien."

"Who wants to bet me that Plumb died out there somewhere, and what came back isn't him?" said Maggie.

"Sounds plausible."

"Plausible?" laughed Taylor. "Are you even listening to yourselves? What, like some monster just put on this old fart's skin like a suit? Are you kidding me?"

"It makes sense," I said.

"On what planet does that make sense?" he yelled.

"Do you have a better explanation?" shot Maggie. "For anything we've seen?"

Taylor didn't answer, but the weird little smile on his face faded, and he stopped humming along with the radio.

The snow fell harder, wiped away the landscape canvas with a wash of white as we passed through Oakland. Aside from the occasional plow-trucks, there weren't many people on the road. Drifts buried the parked cars up to their frames and doors. Whoever owned them weren't going anywhere anytime soon. Taylor's car skidded along the salted streets, which only served to point out just how crazy we were to be out in weather like this. By all rights, I should've been holed up in my apartment, with a mug of hot chocolate in my hand and watching the snow fall in between levels on a video game. But we were about to walk straight into one of those games, and somehow it didn't seem fun anymore.

We passed by Duquesne University, rounded a corner, and came to the tunnel that led to the 10th Street Bridge. The snow built up around the opening made the thing look like a gaping hole in a blank canvas. Or like a hungry mouth. The sun was just a trace of orange on the horizon by the time we got there, and that nagging voice screamed at me to run and hide. But I couldn't. We'd come too far, and, like it or not, we had to see it through. I hate being noble.

We turned into the tunnel and I was struck by how dark it was inside. Most of the tunnels in Pittsburgh were well lit. It cut down on muggings, and it helped prevent wrecks. The 10th Street tunnel was usually lit too, but because of a strange bend in the construction, it was easily the creepiest tunnel in the city. And the lights were out. The only thing that illuminated the sides and street were Taylor's snow-encrusted headlamps.

In the back seat, Andrea stiffened and gasped. Taylor slowed the car to a crawl and rolled his window down to listen. In the icy blast that came through, there came a low murmur, not words but a hundred voices chattering. Then came an ear-splitting squeal that made the muscles in my back clench. I shifted my perception to see what was coming.

I really wished I hadn't.

The walls and the floor of the tunnel were black. Not just dark, but flat black, as if they just weren't there. Whatever energy the tunnel had from millions of cars passing through, there was none left. Just like the house, just like the alley, just like every other place those bastards went, this tunnel was dead.

"What's that glow?" Andrea pointed up ahead, her whisper trembling.

We rounded the corner. More than a dozen of them clogged the end of the tunnel, all with hungry eyes and snapping teeth. It was hard for me to remember that these things were once human, once had souls of their own. But that was before Plumb, or whoever he was, sucked the life out of all of them. In my shifted perception, darkness poured off of them, blended the creatures with the tunnel walls. Their auras were black with spikes of red, with just the thinnest blue ring closest to the bodies the monsters inhabited. They were as good as dead already. Even if we could save them, somehow pull the invading darkness out, they'd still spend the rest of their lives like what's-his-name back at the house, mindless vegetables that could do nothing but stare out at the world with unseeing eyes until their bodies shut down and crumbled like empty corn husks. Between them sat the source of the glow.

"Fire barrels," said Taylor. "They're blocking us off."

"In," said Maggie. She faced the back window. "There are more coming up behind us."

I spun in my seat to see behind. Sure enough, there was another group, larger than the one in front of us, between us and our only exit. If we'd been playing a video game, I'd have called it the "Impassable Level," the one where, unless the player knew some trick or a cheat code or two, there was no hope of getting out. Andrea summed it up in two words.

"We're fucked," she said.

My heart pounded in my chest while my stomach did backflips. I could see the panic etched on Andrea's face, and I was sure I didn't look much better. Maggie whipped her head around, stared out the front and back windows, her hands clenching into fists. Taylor threw the car into neutral and revved the engine.

"What're you doing?" I screamed.

"Demons or not," he growled, "They're still flesh and bone, right?"

"You can't be..." gasped Maggie.

"You want to get out and talk to them? Go right ahead and be my guest," he said.

They stood, a giant throbbing mass in front of the fire

barrels, defiant. The group behind us skittered forward, though not as fast as I'd seen them move. It was almost like they were waiting for us do to something. Then one of them let out an ear-splitting shriek, echoed by the others, and the whole world was lost in the chaotic din. Andrea screamed. Maggie screamed. Hell, I screamed right along with them. The only one who didn't was Taylor, who wore a huge grin as he stomped on the gas and threw the car into drive.

The vermin sprang forward as the car's tires spun on the salted wet pavement, then lurched forward. Whatever their plan had been, they didn't on a ton of rolling steel being driven by a lunatic. As the first few bounced off the hood in a display of broken bones and gore, I couldn't think, couldn't focus. All I saw was face after twisted face as they smashed into the windshield and streaked it with blood as broken bodies fell by the wayside.

The car slowed as we moved into the thick of them. They banged on the back and climbed up on top as they tore into the roof with clawed fingers. They banged against the side with their fists. Around us, the air vibrated with their howls and the harmony of squealing twisted metal. They were coming in. They were going to peel the car apart like a banana and eat the soft fruit inside. Us.

"Why're we slowing?" screamed Andrea.

"There's too many of them!" cried Taylor. "Almost there!"

"We're not going to make it!" I screamed.

"We'll make it!" he said.

We were within a few yards of the fire barrels. The top of the car was peeling away in layers as the vermin fought to get through to us. The back glass shattered as one filthy paw reached through and swiped at Maggie and Andrea. I know I screamed again. I couldn't hear it for everything else going on, but I could feel my throat go raw and tasted blood in the back of my mouth.

"Hang on!" screamed Taylor as he jerked the wheel. The great barge that was his car spun sideways, throwing a few of the monsters off. When it was completely backwards, he shifted it to reverse and floored it again. The back bumper struck the fire barrels and spilled the flaming contents all over the road.

"Maggie!" he shouted.

She thrust her hand through the broken side window and screamed.

"Flambé!"

Her will leaped from her fingertips and streaked like lightning toward the overturned barrels. The spilled fires belched up high into an angry wall of heat. It raged like she'd doused the ground and walls with gasoline. From inside, howls of rage and pain echoed as the vermin tried to leap through the flames. One or two of them made it through only to squeal and twitch on the ground until their bodies were nothing but smoking meat. Taylor let the car idle for a moment as he watched the hellish inferno melt the snow around the tunnel and scorch the brick. Then he put the car in drive, stomped on the gas, and turned the car around toward the bridge.

"That won't keep 'em long," he said.

"How did you know she could do that?" I demanded. Hell, *I* didn't know she could do that. Maybe it was just stupid pride, but I felt a little jealous that he knew something about Maggie that I didn't.

"I didn't," he said. "But I figured that if anyone could do something, it was her."

"What if it hadn't worked?" yelled Maggie, punching the back of the chair.

"Same plan," he said. "They'd just be behind us now. This way, we've got a head start."

"Flambè?" said Andrea. "That's your magick word? A

cooking term?"

"The words you use aren't so important," said Maggie. "It's the intent behind them."

"Besides, they're cooked, aren't they?" snickered Taylor.

I didn't want to laugh. I was too scared and angry, but I just couldn't help myself. Maggie fixed Taylor with a steely glare before the corners of her mouth twitched and she snorted too. Andrea sat looking dumbfounded in the back seat.

"So now what," she said. "That fire wall can't burn forever. They'll come after us."

"I know," I said. "We have to find the source before they find us."

"And how do you propose we do that?" asked Taylor. "Do you have Plumb's address? Or are we just going to go door to door? 'Hello! We're looking for people infested with rat demons. Seen any around?'"

"I don't know," I said. "Maybe if we can get to the park, I can track them from there."

"Then what?" said Andrea. "Assuming you can find him, then what're we going to do?"

I was still working on that part of the plan.

18

When dogs chase cars, I always wonder what is going through their minds. They run down the street, barking like lunatics, like they just *have* to catch that big hunk of metal that invaded their territory. The thing I could never figure out is what the dog was going to do with the car if he ever caught it. They can't drive, they're not going to wrestle the thing to the ground and tear its throat out, so just what the hell *do* they think they are going to do once they catch the car?

Kind of like us. We left a wall of smoke and fire behind us as we crossed the 10th Street Bridge, with more than a hundred possessed things ready to follow, and we were on our way to find the head rat. And for the life of me, I couldn't figure out what we thought we were going to do once we caught him. Sure, Taylor could shoot him, but that wouldn't really solve the problem. If Plumb was really dead and this thing set up shop in his body, we had bigger problems.

"Say you do shoot it," I said as Taylor drove. "I'm pretty sure that won't kill it."

"What makes you think that?" He glanced at me in the rearview mirror.

"Because it's been around for more than a century," I

said, "and if it could jump into Plumb's body, what makes you think it can't jump into yours?"

Taylor's smile flickered for a moment.

"So what're we supposed to do?" He turned his eyes back toward the road. "Knock on the door and ask him to quit?"

"I think we can force him out," said Maggie. "Perform an exorcism."

My stomach wriggled and tried to climb out of my body through my butt.

Exorcisms are risky affairs, and not just for the exorcists. For everyone concerned. For the demon, if the host is killed, the demon has nowhere else to go. For the exorcist, that "nowhere" could easily become his body. And for anyone left observing, there's always the chance of becoming collateral damage. I've been in on a few exorcisms, and not only was I left sore and broken, but they also scared the hell out of me. And none of them had the kind of power this thing had. Most of them squatted like toads in their victims. This one spread like an intelligent plague, contaminating everything in its path. I had a feeling that, if we got into a pissing contest with this thing, we would come up on the losing side.

"I'm not so sure that would work," I said.

"Then what're we doing?" barked Taylor. "Why'd I lose my job? Why'd those people die? Why are we going after this thing if nothing's going to work? What is this, a suicide run?"

"We have to try to do something," said Maggie, her voice low. "No one else will. The other cops wouldn't believe this, would they? And even if they did, they'll die if they try to go after him. Or worse."

"So what do we do?" Andrea looked from me to Maggie, then back again. Fear lined her face like age.

I thought about the net guns in the trunk. When I was

a kid, one of my favorite games was based on the Rube Goldberg machines of the 1930's called "Mousetrap." I spent hours playing that game with my friends, building the most intricate and convoluted gizmos our minds could produce, all for the sake of ensnaring a mouse in a net. The direct approach would never work because the mouse would simply move. The more intricate the trap, the bigger the chance of catching the mouse because he wasn't aware of what was going on.

"We set a trap," I said.

We didn't dare risk a stop at the hotel. We had no idea how long the fire spell would last, and if our luck until now was any indicator, they were only a few minutes behind us. We passed by the hotel and Maggie pressed her hand to the window.

"Be safe," she whispered to her cat. I wasn't sure why she was so concerned with Bitsy. The room was warded, and I'd be willing to bet when we came back the cat would be sitting on the middle of the bed, waiting for us and demanding to know just where the hell we were.

If we got back.

The thought made my spine jump, and I understood. "Be safe," she said, just in case none of us got back and she wound up the pet of some chambermaid.

We pulled into the mostly empty parking lot of the wholesale club where I used to work, got out and made a mad dash for the door, more out of fear than the snowstorm. At the door, the greeter asked to see our memberships before she recognized me, then stuttered. Taylor flashed his badge and pushed his way past. We followed as the greeter spoke into her walkie-talkie. A few minutes later, the walrus-shaped bulk of Mike Millman blocked our path.

"I told you not to come back here," he sneered.

Before I could answer, Taylor stepped up between us and flashed his badge.

"He's here on official business," barked Taylor. "And if I were you, I'd start looking for another job because he's got one hell of an unlawful termination suit coming against you. And unless you want me to haul your giant ass in for obstruction, I'd suggest you point me to the road salt, pronto."

The walrus shrank under Taylor's glare.

"And get some of your boys to help us carry this shit!" he growled over his shoulder as he made his way down the aisle.

"Laying it on a little thick, aren't you?" I couldn't help but smile at the notion of Millman cowed by Taylor.

"The guy's a prick," he said. "Thinks he's a big man. I just showed him that I can be a bigger bully."

There was something in his voice, something about the way he kept that damned smile plastered to his face that had me worried. Being chased down by the Rudy Rat club in the impound did a number on him, I was sure, but I thought he was over it. Now I wasn't so sure. I asked Maggie and Andrea to grab a first aid kit from near the front of the store. When they left, I took Taylor by the arm.

"Matt," I said. "Are you okay?"

Taylor turned to me and I shuddered. What I took for a smile flickered at the edges and was more of a grimace. His eyes were a little too wide to be normal. He was cracking, and all I could do was stand there and watch.

"No," he laughed. "No, I'm not. This isn't my world. I mean, I thought it was. I believe in you and everything you said you could do, but this? I live in a world where there're things like rules and logic and evidence. And I'm about to go face down what? The king of the rat demons? I mean, after everything I've seen, yeah, I believe it, but part of me just can't. Part of me keeps hoping to God that I'll wake up. Part of me just wants to tell you guys to go fuck yourselves and go drink a beer in happy ignorance. But I can't, can I?"

I shook my head.

"And now look at me. I lost my job because of those damned things, and even if we do stop them, how're we going to not wind up in jail?"

I didn't have an answer. I knew why I was chasing after them, but I couldn't decide for anyone else. When the movie's over, people like to think the surviving characters go back to their lives, but it never works out that way. The things that happen to people change them forever, and Taylor would never be able to un-see what he'd seen.

"Truth be told," a sob caught in his throat. "I could really use a drink. I've been sober now for three years, but I gotta tell you, a good old fashioned belt of Jack Daniels would really do me good right now."

A couple of teenagers in blue smocks showed up to help us load four of the fifty-pound bags onto a flatbed, then we hurried to the other side of the warehouse to get a case of chemical light sticks and a spool of nylon rope. Taylor also grabbed a four-pack of duct tape rolls. On the way to the checkout station, he grabbed a large box of Pop-Tarts and tossed it onto the pile.

Maggie and Andrea met us halfway up the aisle at a sprint.

"They're coming," she panted. "I can feel them coming."

"Dammit," spat Taylor.

He pushed the cart past the exit station.

"Official police business," he snarled at the girl whose job it was to check tickets. Millman came waddling up like an asthmatic rhino.

"You can't just take that stuff!" he wheezed.

Taylor turned and glared and Millman withered before he could say anything else.

Damn, I wish I could do that. I'm just not intimidating. At all. I glare at someone and they ask if I'm constipated. But I wasn't going to go without getting at least one parting shot off.

"You have a nice day, then!" I gushed. "Okay, buh-bye!"

I couldn't think of anything fittingly snarky to add, so it would have to do.

We cleared the door into the frigid night air and were, in an instant, drenched from the falling snow. I shrugged it off while I fought to keep my mind on anything but how cold I was, and how likely it was that we were going to get torn apart. Each piece of what I laughingly called a "plan" played back in my head while I tried to work out the details as if I were trying to get through a level on a video game.

A howl echoed through the darkness. They were still a little ways away, but not far enough. As fast as they moved, even in the snow, we'd have to hurry.

The looks on the faces of the two boys who were helping us with the salt were priceless when Taylor opened the trunk. I guess they'd never seen a car full of assault rifles and grenades and weapons of mass destruction before.

"Shit," muttered Taylor. "Not enough room. Back seat."

The workers laid two bags across each seat before hurrying back inside.

"Lock the doors!" I called after them. "Get everyone inside and lock the doors!"

We crammed into the car, Andrea and I in the back seat, cramped onto the bags of salt, our heads pushed against the ceiling. Maggie sat with the net gun in her lap while Taylor drove.

"Explain to me again how this is going to work," said Taylor as his car fishtailed around a corner.

"We have to get him into a circle of salt," I said. "We find his house, lure him out, and trap him in a circle. Easy."

"And why are you volunteering to be bait?" The worry in Maggie's voice was evident. It bordered on hysterical.

"Because I need you two to spring the trap when I get him out. Andi's my wheel-girl. He's got the guns, and you've got the raw power. It fits."

Taylor sputtered for a moment before glaring at me in the rear-view mirror.

"And what are we supposed to be setting up, genius?"

"Rube Goldberg," I grinned.

Taylor's car handled about like I expected it would... like a barge. Nothing like my Chrysler, which was safely tucked in some body-shop bay, thanks to my insurance company. Where my car could corner on a dime, Taylor's made a slow wide creep around corners, and God forbid anyone be in the way. Once it got moving, it took all kinds of power to get it stopped. But it was fast. The engine dwarfed mine in horse-power, and while it sucked down gas, it could run at frightening speeds. Still, I missed the heated seats in my car.

"I don't think I can do this." Andrea's voice wavered as she spoke. The kid was terrified, and I didn't blame her one bit. Hell, I was scared too.

"Jake Steele could do it," I muttered under my breath.

"Who?"

"Nevermind."

We pulled up to the park and I stopped the car.

"You have to drive," I said. "I can't look for them and drive at the same time."

She nodded and slid over in the seat while I got out and went around. It wasn't snowing as hard, but the steady fall piled on my shoulders, dusted and slicked my hair. The dirty tire tracks we left in the snow were already fading, like they were being erased. Small drifts built up around the tree trunks. Even though it was dark, even though I knew what was waiting for us, and I knew there were a couple hundred rat-demon possessed people who wanted to kill us, I still saw it as beautiful.

I got back into the car and noticed for the first time just how small Andrea was. Sure, I knew she was shorter than me and was very thin, but it didn't really hit me until I saw her sitting behind Taylor's massive wheel just how tiny she was. She wasn't much more than a child, and I regretted letting her be a part of this whole thing.

I sat in the seat and closed my eyes, lowered the walls of my perception and opened the doorways in my mind. When I opened my eyes again, the whole landscape was different. Parts of the park still blazed in vibrant greens and golds, but there was a swath cut through the middle where the rats traveled, a bleeding gash of black that led from the city and up into the neighborhood.

"That way," I said.

Andrea put the car in drive and hit the gas. The great land-yacht lurched as it made its way through the snow. Of course, the vermin couldn't have taken the main road. That would've been too easy. Their black trail cut through yards and houses to make a more-or-less straight line south. We had to drive until we found the right streets, then figure out where to go from there. It took us almost an hour of driving up and down every street, during which the mouse-men were conspicuous in their absence, until we found the hole in the neighborhood. The empty streets and noiseless air made me nervous.

The house was immense, fitting for a full professor, honored time and time again by the university. The darkened windows that looked out above the snow gave me the shivers, as if the house were staring at me. But that part was just my imagination. What really gave me the creepy-crawlies was the house itself. With my perception shifted, the absence of light stood out stark as a dark rip in the fabric of the neighborhood. The homes around it were losing their life, those that hadn't already lost it. Its darkness spread like oil across the ground, seeped into the other yards and climbed up the sides of the homes.

"It's this one," I said.

"You sure?"

I nodded, and sat for a moment, staring, dread churning in my stomach.

"So now what?" she stared at me. "Go ring the bell?"

I turned to Andrea and blinked.

"Don't tell me you haven't thought this part through."

I pulled a large bag from the floorboard and opened the door.

"You stay here," I said. "Keep the motor running. Wait until you're sure I'm inside the house, then haul ass back to Maggie and Taylor."

"But what about..?"

I was out of the car before she finished whatever she was going to say. Any questions she raised would raise questions in me too, and at that moment, I couldn't afford to doubt anything. Even a plan as stupid as this one.

I opened the pillow-case, reached inside and pulled out a hand full of road salt. Taylor had his net gun and an assault rifle, Andrea had another net gun and a pistol, Maggie had her magick, and what did I have? A pocket full of light-sticks and salt. When

I was coming up with the plan, I figured a gun would be useless to me. In hindsight, I found myself wishing for the reassuring weight of a gun to calm my nerves.

"I hope you're right, Maggie," I said as I began pouring a circle around the car. Whatever happened to me, Andrea would be safe as long as she stayed in the car. The rats couldn't get past the line. It took the whole bag to surround the car enough that I felt like Andrea was adequately protected.

As I poured the last little bit, a noise behind me made my stomach flip. A high screech echoed through the night, followed by the crunching of snow. I looked up to see one of the vermin, his eyes blazing with hatred, the energy around him like a black inferno, leaping at me from behind a bush. I let out a yelp and ran for the door in the desperate hope I could get inside before he caught me. Andrea screamed, but I couldn't look back. It was right behind me, and there were more coming. So many more. They came teeming out from behind the houses and trees like... well... rats. Most of them surrounded the car until I couldn't see it anymore.

I spun and ducked as one of the monsters leaped and sent him smashing into a bush, but my little maneuver opened me up to an attack from two more. They tore at my coat and my hair, and when they knocked me to the ground, I thought I was as good as shredded. One bore down on me with snapping jaws. I raised my arm to my face and...

The possessed man flew backward with a yelp after a bright flash of burning light, like a camera flash. It clutched and clawed at its face while another made its way toward me at break-neck speed. I looked down at my arm, where the flash came from. The tattoo burned and glowed and itched like crazy. I felt a smile wrap itself around my face as I raised my arm and scrambled to my feet.

"'That's right!" I screamed. "Andi! Get out of here!"

I couldn't see the car, but the engine bellowed as Andrea hit the gas. The car shot off into the darkness, fishtailing around the corner and leaving broken bodies in its wake. I turned and ran to the front door of the house and tried the door.

Imagine my surprise when it came open. I rushed through and slammed it behind me and put all my weight against it. I fully expected for all of them to come pushing it down upon me. My heart beat in my ears and every muscle tensed against the solid wood of the door.

But it was quiet. Silence greeted me where I knew there should've been screaming and claws ripping at the frame. But there was nothing. I listened for any sound, any scrape, any whisper, but it was quiet. The voice in my head, on the other hand, started screaming in earnest.

They led you here! It's a trap! You're going to die Maggie's going to die Taylor's going to die Andrea's going to die...

The silence was broken by slow clapping from up above. I turned in the darkened foyer to see Plumb at the top of the stairs.

"Bravo," he said. "So glad you could make it tonight."

Shit. He knew I was coming. It was a trap, but I was the mouse. I should really learn to listen to that little voice in my head sometimes. I just hoped mine was the better mousetrap.

"Don't bother trying to run," he said. "Step out that door and my children will rip you to pieces. They're heading to finish your friends off now. Probably the best thing for you to do is come inside and talk."

"What do you want to talk about?" I took a few tenuous steps away from the door.

"Your future, dear boy," he said. "And mine."

He came down the stairs like a movie villain, still dressed in khaki pants and a sweater-vest, still looking like the very image of the crazy old college professor. But now that I knew what he was, there was something much more menacing to his movements, something much more frightening about the way he moved.

"You're not Plumb," I said.

"Figured that out all on your own, did you?" he laughed. "No, I'm not Jason Plumb, though his has been a good look for me lately, don't you think?"

"Did you kill him?"

"I did nothing of the sort," he snorted. "He was half dead already when he found me. He offered his body to me. And I'm so glad he did."

He reached the bottom of the stairs and crossed the cavernous living room. I was glad that I'd shut off my sight, but I could still imagine his cancerous black energy wrapping around mine as it tried to suck my life away. I backed up a step for each one he took forward until I was against the door. A loud bang on the other side made me jump as one of the creatures outside slammed into it.

"They can still smell you, you know," he said. "They can smell the life pouring off of you and your friends. They're hungry for it, and all I have to do is let them have you. Do you know what they'll do to you, if I let them? They'll peel the flesh from your bones and chew your body to paste."

"So why haven't they?" I didn't really want to know, but I figured, the longer I kept him talking, the longer I'd stay alive.

"Because I don't want them to," he smiled. "Not yet. You and I have things to discuss."

My flesh tried to crawl off my spine as he spoke. It wasn't so much what he said, or even how he said it. I'd encountered demons that spoke like Vaudevillian bad-guys before. It was that, even as he threatened to rip me to pieces, he was so damned friendly about it. Likeable, even.

"Like what?"

"Come with me. I want to show you something."

I followed him across the room toward the back of the house to the basement door.

"It's a beautiful house, don't you think?" he said. "Much smaller than what I'm used to, but running water and air conditioning... well... it's a fair trade-off."

From the doorway, the stench of feces and sweat drifted up. He gestured for me to follow him down.

The basement was immense, much larger than the footprint of the house. The bare floor was covered in shredded paper, piled high in corners and nested around the room.

"I like you, Mister Cooper," he said. "You don't have any idea the potential you have, but I do. Someone of your talents can be very useful. I'd like to offer you a place. With me. I can offer you more than you'd ever imagined."

He led me around to a side chamber and opened the door. Inside were piles of stolen items. Jewelry, silver, other baubles that had no other value than that they were really shiny lay glinting in the pale light of the bare bulb.

"Take what you like. You like gold? It's yours. Trinkets? Yours."

"Why me?"

"Why not you?" He spread his arms wide. "Who else in this city deserves what I'm offering? They're all sheep! They can't fathom what lies beyond. But you... you've been there, haven't you? Yes, I can tell. You, above all others, can appreciate what it's like to feel the void and come back. You know what it's like to be abandoned, don't you? We're kindred souls, you and I."

My stomach rolled at the implication.

"What's the catch?"

"Ah. The witch has to die," he said. "The others can live. I'll even throw in that little tart as your own personal fuck toy. But the witch has to go."

My blood boiled, but I tried to keep a cool demeanor. My poker face was awful, but I was determined to keep it together.

"Why her?" I already knew the answer. Power. She had it, he wanted it. It was a simple as that.

"My own reasons," he smiled.

I turned and walked back into the main room. On the way, I took a quick glance at all the walls. Every single one had a hole bored into it which lead to tunnels in every direction.

"What's in it for you?"

"Do you know what it's like to be forgotten?" He smiled. "To be abandoned? Of course you do. But think of it on a larger scale. To be adored by thousands one day and left to ruin the next? Once people sacrificed their children to me. Their children! Then they were gone. I only want to continue living. I want to pick up where I left off."

"What, so your group of demon-worshiping freaks died out and you're *bored*? Is that it?"

Plumb's face twisted in rage as he cut the distance between us in the space of a heartbeat. His old weathered hand felt like a steel clamp around my throat as he slammed me against one of the support beams.

"*Demon?*" he bellowed. "I'm no lowly demon. I am a *GOD!*"

Just what I needed. A monster with an ego the size of South America. His grip tightened for a moment before he composed himself and released me.

"I don't expect you to understand," he said. "But I do expect you to choose. I don't have much in the way of patience anymore, so make your choice. "

I turned away from him and slid my hand into the pocket of my coat until I found the handle there.

"Everything I want," I said. "In exchange for what?"

"Your service," he beamed. "Not like these others. I have no intention of making you like them. You can go on living comfortably..."

"While you tear the city apart."

"For starters, yes."

"I don't know," I said. "That sounds pretty good."

Plumb smiled and let his guard down, which was what I was waiting for. I pulled the switchblade from Taylor's dealer out of my pocket, pushed the button for the blade, and swung at him. The blade dragged a neat line across his cheek and scraped the bone underneath. Plumb howled in fury as he tumbled backward.

"How 'bout not," I sneered. "You fucking rodent!"

The sound that came from Plumb's mouth didn't seem physically possible. A horrible chorus of voices screamed at once from his throat, along with what sounded like twisting, rending metal, he reeled as he clutched his face, and I turned back toward the openings in the walls and dove through what I hoped would be the right one.

"I'll tear you apart myself!" came the otherworldly voice behind me.

19

That little voice inside my head screamed again, this time to let me know how badly screwed I was. Diving through an open tunnel dug by a rat demon (oh, excuse me... rat *god*) seemed like a good idea at the time, and I wanted him to follow me, but for some reason it never occurred to me how pissed off he'd have to be to follow me, so I never figured his rage into the plan. I considered all too well what he'd do to me if he caught me, however. As I threw handfuls of road salt behind me while I ran, I couldn't help but think that somewhere in all of this, the plan went south.

I had to get him out of the house somehow, trap him and pull the demon out of Plumb's carcass. Rather than knock on the door and politely ask him to come out, we went with plan "B." Same basic idea, only this time, I was the marble in the Rube Goldberg machine.

In hindsight, there were a lot of details I hadn't considered, like how an overweight, out of shape guy was supposed to outrun the crazed maniac, and how I was supposed to keep him from peeling my skin off with a dull butter knife. An action hero, I wasn't. Fear, however, gave me quick feet.

It was too late to go back and rethink it when Andrea

and I pulled up in front of the house, and even more so when the rats surrounded the car and left her without a choice. Now, with my luck, I had the entire legion of Mickey Mouse Club rejects chasing me down while King Rat came and made a meal out of my life force. Some days, I just couldn't win.

I ran as fast as my out-of-shape, stubby legs could move, sucking air through my mouth and flailing my arms in front of me in the darkness. His footsteps landed hard behind me, followed by the skittering noises of more of them as they joined the pursuit. And while I would rather have left through the front door, it wasn't an option, so I picked a tunnel that looked like it might lead the right direction and hoped there wouldn't be any nasty surprises in the darkness. I'm kind of dumb that way.

The rough rock gave way to smooth concrete as the tunnel opened up into one of the city's storm drains. It was a taller ceiling, but there were no marks to tell me which way to go. My lungs already burned when I gasped for breath, and my legs felt like quivering noodles.

A squeal from beside me made me jump as one of Plumb's minions leaped out of the darkness, claws and teeth raised. I spun and raised my tattoo shield over my face. The tattoo blazed a cold blue as the light struck my attacker in the face and sent him scrambling backward. I took it as a sign and fled down the dark corridor he'd leaped out of, snapped a light-stick and threw it ahead of me as I ran.

Further down the path, the corridor narrowed enough to feel the walls and ceiling scrape against my hunched-over form as I shuffled through. The little voice in my head stopped screaming. In its place was a whispered prayer that the passage would open up soon. I could hear them, smell them. They were coming and I was running out of steam.

At the next intersection, I hesitated. There were four

openings, including the one I'd just come out of, which left three for me to choose from. My breath caught in my throat, leaving me a hacking mess for only a couple of seconds, but they cost me. A hand clamped around my damaged ankle and dragged me off my feet. I fell hard and my face slapped the concrete with a dull crunch. Warmth spread over the side of my face in a sticky river that I figured was blood. Seeing as we were in a sewer, the alternative to blood was not something I wanted to consider.

I flipped over to see Plumb's hate-filled face staring from out of the darkness, pulling me back in. Behind him glowed a hundred sets of eyes. I went cold and kicked my feet as I tried to crab-walk away from him.

"I'll tear your soul out," he growled. "But I'll leave just enough for you to feel what I'm doing to you!"

More out of desperation than any plan, I grabbed a handful of muck from beneath me and threw it into his eyes. He let go, but only for a second. I scrambled back to my feet and ran again, praying I could find my way in the darkness.

I triggered my sight in hopes there would be some path to lead me, and was immediately struck blind. There was no color to pick up on, no energies to follow, not even the swath of black to trail, because the entire tunnel was black. It was like some giant clogged artery, choked off with evil and hatred, that fed the city. I was lost and I knew it.

"I'm sorry, Shannon," I breathed. "I gave it my best shot."

She appeared in front of me, weak and blinking in and out, her movements jerking like some of the frames of her life were missing. She stood in front of one of the tunnels, her face twisted in fear.

This way, I heard inside my head before she blinked and was gone. I didn't take the time to question it. I just hurtled into the tunnel and moved as fast as my exhausted body would carry me. But even so, then what? There had to be miles of tunnels, even assuming I was in the right one. I began to doubt I was going to make it out alive. What I wouldn't have given for just an ounce of Maggie's power, or even just to see her face again one more time.

My legs screamed, my lungs burned, and my heart beat like a Buddy Rich solo, but I wasn't ready to give up. Maggie wouldn't have given up. Taylor had gone through more in the past three days, and he still hung in. Even Andrea, as scared and naive as she was, wasn't turning tail against these bastards. I'd be damned if I was going to let a bunch of over-grown sewer rats get the best of me. Shannon was counting on me. Hell, the way I looked at it, the entire city of Pittsburgh was counting on me. Maggie might have been better equipped to deal with raging demons, but she wasn't down here. I was. And I wasn't going to let them down.

My lungs felt like they were falling apart and my limbs ached from running and fear, but I pushed myself forward, forcing a laugh as I ran.

"Come get me," I wheezed, "You fucking wannabe! M-I-C-K-E-Y...Why? Because you're an asshole! M-O-U-S-E!"

From behind came Plumb's disturbingly unlabored by heavy breathing.

"You insignificant worm! I'm going to kill your friends while you watch! I'm going to make you bear witness while they commit unspeakable acts in my name! They will worship me as their new God!"

"You're a joke!" I panted as I ran. "You're just a rat! You're not worth shit!"

Plumb howled again, this time closer, and I hurried until I came to another intersection. To my left was a steel ladder that led, I hoped, to the street. To my right, more tunnels. I climbed and reached the manhole cover as Plumb and his brood came through the entrance. I pushed the cover against my shoulders and forced myself through, rolling onto the empty street.

The snow stopped falling a while ago. Above was a clear night sky. Below, the snow reflected the stars.

It's strange, the things a person notices when he thinks he's about to die.

The street-lamps weren't lit, and they didn't need to be. The white around reflected enough of the moon and stars to make the night bright enough to see. I forced myself up off the wet pavement and spun to try to figure out where I was. There were no cars, no people, not even a stray opossum or deer moving in the night. The buildings around me looked like every other neighborhood this side of the river, but without people. My spine crept upward as I allowed the thought to form in my head.

Where the hell is everyone?

As if in answer, the doors of the houses flew open to reveal hungry faces and hateful eyes. I recognized the street at last as one of the places hardest hit by poverty, where hope and pride were at an all-time low. It was the perfect place for something like Plumb to prey on new followers.

"Oh, come on," I cried. "Give me a break!"

"You're not going to escape," said Plumb from behind me.

I turned as he emerged from the manhole cover, rising up like his minions were lifting him out. It was quite dramatic, and I might have laughed if I'd seen it in a movie. But seeing it live and in person scared the hell out of me. I had to piss him off even more, make him follow me. And to do that, I had an ace up my sleeve.

"I'm going to..."

"Blah blah blah," I shouted. "You're going to do this or

233

you're going to do that. You sure are stupid for a 'god.'"

His face twisted even more, but I wasn't finished.

"You think this wasn't part of the plan?" I panted. "You think I didn't want to get you and all your little Mouskateers out here with me? I just needed to give my friends time," I said, nodding with my chin.

Plumb followed my gaze toward the Pittsburgh skyline until he saw a bright orange glow on the horizon.

"Your house is really pretty when it burns, isn't it?"

"No!" he bellowed, then he squealed and the majority of his followers took off running down the street in the direction of the blaze. Andrea must've followed the plan, waited until everyone was out of the house and chasing me before she doused the thing with gasoline and lit it up. It was crude, but effective.

While his back was turned, I made a suicide dive for the storm drain. I figured, the storm drain might have been an enclosed space where I couldn't see, but at least I knew what direction the rats were coming from. Besides, I managed to get my bearings, and knew which way I had to go. With any luck, Andrea was long gone from Plumb's house, and while the other rats were trying to save his hoard, I'd beat a hasty retreat.

It sounded good in my head, anyway.

Plumb screamed, no longer bothering to form words, but settling for guttural growls and shrieks of anger. I guess burning his nest made him more angry than I thought.

Good.

20

To anyone outside my plan, I'm sure I seemed like a thundering moron, or at least suicidal. Going out of my way to make a super-powerful monster angry enough to chase me isn't exactly on my list of most intelligent things to do. In fact, most of the time, I try really hard not to make anyone angry. It's just not in my nature. Oh sure, I'll go out of my way to aggravate my friends or annoy telephone sales people, but for the most part I try to stay on everyone's good side. Particularly if those people could suck out my life force and tear the appendages from my body. Call it a rule.

The smooth concrete walls were testaments to the engineering of the city. Large enough for men to walk through, large enough to sweep away even the worst rain and snow, but not entirely utilitarian. I couldn't help but think that there was some artistry at work when the planners laid out the under-street passages. I remember when I was a kid, my father used to tell all sorts of tall tales about homeless people actually living in the sewers, along with pet alligators that had been flushed down toilets and then grown to mammoth proportions on a steady diet of garbage. Those stories always terrified me as a kid and kept me away from the storm drains with the fear that I'd meet one of those monster-gators or an entire society of underground dwellers and never be heard from again. I grew up and found out there were far worse things under the city streets. Things that scared me more than any urban legend could've ever scared a little boy.

But as I ran down that narrow tunnel, I couldn't help but smile to myself. He was following. He was closing in, but he was still following, and angry enough to just keep following until it was too late. I just prayed that everything else was going to plan.

Guided by my sight, I followed the trail of darkness past places that were just grazed by it and plummeted straight down the darkest paths. I knew full well that no matter how fast I ran, no matter how little time I tried to stay in that pitch, every second shaved a little more off my life energy. It was sucking me dry, and as tired as I was, I could feel it. It couldn't be too much farther.

I dropped another light-stick as I rounded another corner and found more rough-hewn walls. I had to be under an older part of town, built before too many modern conveniences. It was a good sign, but it also presented a problem. The older the section of town, the smaller the tunnels. I had to get through, but it was getting harder to walk upright.

I ducked into a short passage and paused for a moment. I strained to listen for Plumb, but I was met with silence, save for the sound of my own heartbeat and raspy breath.

Fear shocked its way through my body.

"You still back there, rat?" I called.

Silence. Oh shit. He gave up.

"What's the matter, rat?" I yelled as I broke another light-stick and held it up so I could see. "Puny little worm like me get the best of you?"

"Not exactly," came a voice from right in front of me. I spun to see Plumb squatting in the corridor, a wicked smile crossing his green-lit face. "Come on, now. You really think I don't know these tunnels better than anyone?"

Before I could stammer out a witty reply, or even just cough out a strangled yelp, Plumb was on me, his thin frail body pinned me to the muck-covered floor with impossible strength. He tore at my jacket with clawed fingers and leered so close to my face that I could smell the last thing he ate. It smelled like garbage.

"You're more trouble than you're worth," he shrieked. "You could've had everything you wanted, but now I think I want to see you suffer! You're going to watch as I kill that cop. And when I'm done, your women will bear my children!"

The thought of Maggie and Andrea being forced to submit to that abomination broke something loose in me. Maggie was my friend, and it was my fault Andrea was involved. Maybe they didn't need a man to protect them, but part of my father's old-fashioned upbringing sparked to life inside me. I had his desire to protect folk. And dad also had one hell of a temper.

I twisted under him and managed to get my left arm up between us and pushed my tattoo against his forehead. When it erupted in light, he screamed in agony and fell back. Not much, but just enough for me to push his body off me and to roll on top of him. I straddled his body and punched him in the face, all the while screaming back at him.

"You dirty motherfucker! Die! Die! Die!"

It didn't occur to me until he launched my body off of his that he still had plenty of power, and all hitting him would do was piss him off even more. He roared as I scrambled to my feet and fled down the tunnel. Despite myself, I snickered as I ran. Sure, I wanted him mad enough to follow me, but now he was insane with rage. If he caught me again, I was as good as dead. Or worse. And judging from the sounds that pushed me along the corridor like the hot air from a cannon, he was mad enough to follow me to the ends of the earth.

I came to another intersection. Right, left or forward. The dark trails spread through all directions which left me without any clear choice. I was about to play a quick game of "eenie-meenie-miney-moe" when I caught a flicker out of the corner of my eye. I didn't have question what it was. Shannon was there again, pointing the way.

I dropped another light-stick and dove for the left passage and was relieved to see it opened up a bit. Not so much that I would call it comfortable, but enough that I could stand up straight and stretch my legs at a dead run, if they weren't already threatening mutiny. My feet were cold and wet from the melted snow and garbage in the drain, and I'd already lost the feeling in my toes, but I couldn't stop. Missing toes, I could learn to walk again. Missing head would be much more inconvenient.

Plumb was still behind me, following either my scent or the trail of green chemical light as he skittered along through the tunnels. He screamed himself hoarse as he ran. At least, I kept hoping his voice would give out, but it never did. It just continued that sound of metal on metal, a chorus of train whistles that echoed through the concrete tunnels. The sounds pummeled me, struck me from all over and made my insides jiggle and my ears ring. And through the din, I lost the sense of pain in my legs, the burning in my lungs. My world no longer had that sensation, but was only purposed to pump my legs faster and to get me to the end of that tunnel.

There's nothing quite like abject terror to push a person farther than he thought was possible.

By all rights, I should've collapsed in a heaving wreck, but I kept going, ignoring the pain in my ankles, the burning in my muscles, and even that little voice in my head that kept screaming at me that I wasn't going to make it.

Icy filth splashed around my feet as I ran down the black

corridor. My breath came in ragged gasps until, around another bend, I saw light. If I'd been looking through my normal eyes, it might have looked like a dim, flickering glow from another hole in the wall. But with my perception altered, it shone brighter than a magnesium flare in the darkness, so white and hot it almost hurt to look at it. It was the beacon I was looking for.

I felt a surge as my heart leaped in my chest and I found the strength to run, straight into the light. The white light at the end of the long dark corridor was what many people said they saw when they died. If what I saw was even similar, I understood why they said it was beautiful.

Plumb howled and snarled as he closed the distance, but I didn't dare look. Bad enough I knew he was back there, I didn't need to see his hate-filled eyes. Besides, I'm pretty sure that if I chanced a glance, I'd turn into that movie stereotype and trip and fall and I'd become the monster's victim instead of a... what? Hero? I didn't feel much like a hero. More like a frightened rabbit running for his life.

I dove for the opening and prayed I hadn't misjudged it. If I had, I'd wind up splayed on the wall like a bug. But as luck had it, I managed to just clip the edge on my way through, which sent me into an ungraceful crash that ended with me crumpled in the center of the room. I didn't stop to get my bearings, but scrambled forward and looked up to see severe expressions on faces all around me. Before I could say a word, hands reached out and grabbed me by the arms and lifted me to my feet.

21

"Move your ass!"

Taylor's strong arms hauled me up and threw me toward the opposite side of the room.

"Get ready!" another voice warned.

I chanced a backward glance. Plumb shot through the hole and landed in a feral crouch in the center of the room.

"NOW!" someone said.

A loud pop echoed through the air as Taylor fired his net gun and snared the rat. The net wrapped around him, then Taylor pulled the attached line and tried to drag the rat forward.

"A little help here!" he called. A second popping noise came from the net gun Andrea held. The second net wrapped around the first, and together they pulled Plumb into the center of the room.

A tall man that I was certain I'd seen before stood by the hole in the wall. At the command, he completed the circle by dumping a bag of salt in front of the hole. Fast as snakes, Maggie and several others touched the ring and charged it with their life energy. It snap into place like a glowing egg and held Plumb's darkness inside. .

He thrashed against the nets, wedged his fingers into

their steel webs and tore them as if they were spider webs. Then he threw himself toward me but rebounded off the wall of energy. He slammed against the edges of his invisible prison, fought hard to gain a handhold outside or even to get hold of one of the figures standing around. When I was sure he wasn't going to break through, I felt my body go slack, then it shook. Not just a minor tremor, but a full shake-the-coffee-out-of-the-cup quake. I gasped for air and lay on the ground, unable to make myself even sit up.

"Good job," said Taylor as he brought a blanket to put over my shoulders. I didn't have the strength to tell him it wouldn't do any good. I was already soaked to the skin from my hair to my toes. But it was a nice gesture.

Maggie knelt in front of the circle with her fingers pressed to the outer edge. With my perception shifted, I could see the energy flowing from the others in the room to her, then out her fingers and into the circle of salt. She was the power source keeping the "magick force field" intact. Andrea knelt beside her, hands on Maggie's arms, letting her own energy flow into the witch.

Around the room stood a half-dozen people, only a few of whom I recognized right away. The six were dressed strangely, all wearing some type of ceremonial robe. One wore the traditional garb of a Catholic priest, purple stole around his neck and brandishing a crucifix. Another stood wearing saffron robes that I took to mean he was a Buddhist. A third stood pointing a long, double-edged sword at Plumb with unabashed anger blazing in his aura. Him, I recognized. As I did two of the others, who wore long cloaks with pentacle clasps.

"We got him," said Brea of the Evergreen Group. "Are you okay?"

"I'll live," I said. "I think."

"I can't hold this for long!" Maggie's voice was strained.

To Taylor, or anyone else for that matter, the scene must've been a strange one. A ring of people wearing robes from every religion I could think of standing around a battered old man who looked like he'd gone insane, writhing and snarling, in a circle of salt. But I saw the real battle taking place. Every person in the room glowed with energy so brilliant that when they stood together it looked like an arclight. They stood with their own energy, their own faith, pulsing together, a living entity unto itself, surrounding an orb of pitch black that tore pieces off the bubble and digested them. It was the single most terrifying thing I had ever seen.

"Together!" shouted Bill of the Evergreen Group.

They began a low chant, each to his own faith, each building their own power. The auras swelled, fed by... what? God? Nature? Each other? I didn't know. But the effect was remarkable. The light swelled and combined with the others in the room until thing in the circle flinched. Over the din of their murmured prayers and Plumb's screams, I could make out only snatches of what they were saying.

Oh Lord, bless thy servants... There can be no light without darkness... Merciful Allah... Mighty Cern... Mother Hecate...

It was at once so chaotic, but also beautiful. The voices rose in fever and pitch as the light grew brighter, and I watched as the darkness in the circle shrank and splintered. Pieces of darkness split and dissipated while Plumb's body twisted and convulsed. He screamed in some language I didn't recognize.

"It's working!" shouted Bill.

Then another sound caught my attention. Sounds like metal grinding in high squeals erupted from the hole in the wall.

"The Mousketeers are coming!" I screamed.

Taylor didn't hesitate, but raised his assault rifle and

moved around the edge of the circle, the gun trained on the opening in the wall. I couldn't tell exactly how many of them there were, but from the amount of noise they were making, their numbers were frightening.

The chant grew to a fever pitch as the light grew so bright that all I could see was white. It was like being inside a blank canvas, or being blind, except I knew there were shapes around me, people I cared about, monsters on the other side of the wall. Everyone in the room pushed their abilities to the limits, and all I could do was lay curled up in the corner of the room like a beaten puppy? Not likely.

I dragged myself over to the circle, unsure of what I could possibly do, but determined to do something, anything, to help.

When Maggie and I were trapped in that bathroom stall, she drew on my energy to protect us, just as she drew on Andrea's now. But as I got closer, I saw her features go slack, her eyes glass over, and I saw her body begin to topple.

"Maggie!" I shouted. Andrea didn't look any better. Her cheeks were paler than I'd seen, and she looked like she couldn't have been more than a few seconds away from keeling over as well. If either of them broke contact with the circle, whatever this ceremony was would be over in a heartbeat, and in the span of another everyone in the room would be dead.

I slid up next to Maggie, put one hand on the circle of salt, and pushed her back with my other hand, and willed all my remaining energy into the protective barrier.

It flickered and faded, but stayed up. I guess I didn't have as much in the reserve tanks as I thought. The others were deep in concentration and couldn't help me, Maggie and Andrea were down, and the only thing keeping this room full of spiritual fighters from becoming tomorrow's rat droppings was me. I needed to think of something, and fast.

When I first developed this strange ability of mine, I had no idea what was happening to me. Dead people appeared every day, and most of them scared the hell out of me. But somewhere along the way, thanks in large part to Maggie, I learned a few things about communicating with the dead. It was a two-way street, for starters. They could contact me, but I can also contact them. Some folks did it with an Ouija board, others through séances. But for people like me, who were more or less jacked into their wavelength, sometimes calling a restless spirit was as easy as saying her name.

"Shannon!" I cried. "All you dead people! Help me get this miserable piece of shit out of here!"

Okay, so it wasn't an exorcism rite or a formal summoning, but it got the job done.

At once I felt a surge as hundreds of disembodied souls flooded the room. They took positions behind the Evergreen Group and what was left of their energies flowed into the priests of many faiths. I didn't know how many came to me, but I thought I saw Shannon's face, smiling, as she poured what was left of herself into me.

The power that raced down my arms was phenomenal. Too much, in fact. My hands got hot just below the wrists as raw energy flowed out my palms and fingertips. The heat intensified, became more than a pleasant warmth and moved into a painful burning sensation. It felt like my hands were going to blow off at the wrists, and I couldn't let go. The salt was like a live electrical wire and I was the dumbass who'd grabbed it. Nothing left to do but enjoy the ride. If I woke up without hands, it would be a small price to pay.

"If you're going to do something," I screamed, "Do it now!"

Together, the Evergreen Group joined their voices into a

symphonic wail, punctuated by those that had staffs and swords striking them on the floor in rhythm. When they reached what had to be the highest point, Bill pointed a small dagger into the circle. The others did the same with the talismans of their faiths. As if someone pulled a trigger, the blinding white energy that they'd built rushed out of their bodies and struck the wriggling form of Plumb. The sound was as deafening as the light was blinding, but I still couldn't let go. Even the tattoo on my arm smoked with the energy flowing through it, but I didn't dare turn my head away. I had to know, had to see what the end looked like for God of Rats.

The energy coursed through him, chased the black from every corner, bathed him in the purest, whitest light I'd ever seen. His body convulsed and fell to the floor as the darkness wrenched up through the pores of his skin and left the body an empty husk.

"Contain it!" shouted Bill.

One by one, the members of the Evergreen group moved around the circle until they were on all sides of the floating black orb of energy. They wrinkled their brows and pushed, compressing the darkness into an orb the size of a bowling ball. Then one of them kicked what appeared to be ceramic kitchen jar into the circle. They guided the orb into the jar, then closed and latched the lid.

The heat in my arms finally stopped and I fell back, my vision a strange mix of energy patterns and dancing lights that blurred and went dark before I could even ask what happened.

22

The sinking feeling in my stomach was all too familiar, and I knew what was coming. A long fall with a short stop. Only this time, something was different. I didn't scream. I didn't feel the same sense of panic, even though I knew that the long black nothing was about to open up for me again. Somehow I was at peace with Death coming to grab me by the collar and drag me off. I belonged there. I'd managed to avoid her cruel embrace for five long years, but no one outruns the Reaper. I felt my descent slow and looked around to see faces around me, smiling faces, and hands holding my body, slowing my fall, and I knew them. Shannon was one of them, no longer torn and bloody, but whole, like she was the day I met her. The others were the faces of the others killed or enslaved by Plumb. The anthropology students, the shop owners, all of them. I looked down and saw hundreds of shining faces with arms outstretched, guiding me to the ground without a sound. When my feet touched the cement below the building, they vanished, and I was left with the strangest sense of peace.

My eyes fluttered open, and all I could see was white. Speckled white ceiling tiles banded by white metal strips ran the length of the room, with only an emergency sprinkler to break up their pattern. I heard beeps and hushed voices, smelled disinfectant in the air. I hurt all over, but hurt was my body's way of telling me that it was healing.

"Am I dead?" I croaked.

Maggie shot up out of an oversized easy chair beside my bed like someone bit her on the keister.

"I should say not," said a short middle-eastern man in a long white coat. "But you've been out for a while."

"Get me out of here." I tried to sit up, but the room spun under me and my stomach flipped. I decided sitting up wasn't the brightest idea in the world. "Last time I was in one of these places, I woke up with a toe-tag on."

"I see that," said the doctor as he closed the chart. "But not this time. Those burns will take some time to heal, but I think you'll make a full recovery."

I looked down at my hands. From the elbows down, I looked like a mummy. An I.V. tube disappeared under the gauze, pumping a clear liquid into my veins.

He turned to walk out of the room. "Not too long," he called back over his shoulder. "He needs rest."

When the door closed behind him, Maggie leaned down and kissed me, hugging me tight. Despite the fact that I felt like I might break under her embrace, it felt good to have her again.

"I thought I died," I said.

"You almost did," said Maggie. "I've never seen anything like that. It was like you were on fire."

I waved one of my mummified arms at her.

"D'ya think?"

"How?"

"It was the girl," I said. "Shannon. And the others. I used their energies, what was left of them, to power the circle. All I wanted to do was give the others enough time to do... whatever they did. Did they destroy it?"

She shook her head.

"Something like that can't be destroyed," she said. "Only contained. It's one of the first rules of energy."

"Einstein's law," I nodded. "So where is it now?"

"The Evergreens took it somewhere. I don't know where. I really don't want to know. But I know they'll keep it safe."

"Where's Taylor? And Andrea?"

"Andrea is at my place, taking care of Bitsy," she said. "Turns out the kid has a real thirst for knowledge. And Bitsy seems to like her."

"That cat's a good judge of character," I said. "Taylor?"

"I don't know," she said. "Once it was over, he hustled everyone out and said he needed to clean it up before the police got there. He's trying to keep us out of it, but I don't see how he can. He'll be lucky if losing his job is all that happens to him."

I nodded. Taylor walked into the situation with his eyes only half open. When they got opened the rest of the way, most of what he thought he knew crumbled in front of him. He came through when it got tough, though. I hated to think of him going through hard times because of it. Especially because what we did was right. My opinion of people didn't always count for much, but for what it was worth, I thought of him as a genuinely good man. And a friend.

As if on cue, the door to my room opened and in walked Taylor, wearing a fresh cheap suit. He looked like he'd shaved and gotten cleaned up, but I could tell by the red rims of his eyes that he hadn't slept much.

"You're awake," he said as he closed the door behind him. "Good. I wanted you to be the first to hear. They're letting me keep my job."

"How?"

"Best you don't ask," he said.

"What about us?" Maggie sank back down in the chair. "We'll need to give statements..."

"Why?" said Taylor. "You were never there. Outside of Stanley helping me with some forensics work, you two had nothing to do with it."

"Well I'm asking anyway," I said. There was no way I was letting him fall for this, not by himself. Granted, my playing the noble-guy card might've made my life even more difficult than it already was, but Taylor had been through too much, had fought alongside us, and letting him fall just wasn't something I was prepared to do.

He took a deep breath and closed his eyes. When he opened them again, there was a look of surrender there. He knew I wasn't going to stop asking, and that it would only be a matter of time before I browbeat him until he told me.

"The security cameras," he began. "They didn't catch you two, just me."

"How's that possible?" Maggie and I exchanged confused looks.

"Maybe something with your hocus-pocus messed with the electronics," he said. "Or maybe they were so badly damaged in the attack that nothing was salvageable." Then he grinned. "Or maybe I have a friend who owed me a favor."

Maggie and I looked from each other back to Taylor, who seemed pleased with himself.

"That's still a lot of heat on you," I said. "How're you going to explain Plumb? An old guy in an occult shop basement isn't something the police are likely to forget.

"Officially, I followed a hunch back to the scene of the crime. When I got there, Plumb was already dead from his little doper buddies. I cleaned up a few of the more interesting pieces, wiped the place, and called it in. They showed up believing that they'd killed him in a drug-induced haze, then they dropped when their bodies couldn't handle the withdrawals. The department is calling this new drug 'Sparkle.'"

"What new drug?"

"Well, that's just it," he smiled. "It's really hard to trace because no one's seen it before, and there aren't any tests for it. Just symptoms."

"But what about..?"

"Look," he said. "We did a good thing. No matter how we got there, we did a good thing. When they found Plumb's body, they went to his house and found a lot of the stolen stuff. It's neat and tidy, and the case is officially closed."

"Is that going to work?"

"Better than the truth," he shrugged.

"About what happened..." I began.

"I'm not sure what I saw," he said with a wave of his hand. "And, honestly, I'm not sure I want to know what really happened in there. It just looked like a bunch of people in goofy robes chanting, then the old fucker dropped dead. There were thirty bodies in the storm drains, half dead and the other half... well... not exactly alive. There are more of them all over the city. So far, the body count is over two hundred, but I know it'll get higher. I can't explain it so a judge would buy it, and I don't think you could either. The official story is that the professor was using his classroom and South American trips to traffic and deal some kind of South American drug that fried 'em all out."

He sat down on the edge of the bed.

"I came by to let you know that things are working out for me. I'm not out from under the microscope yet, but at least they're not pressing charges. And they're letting me keep my pension. I came by to say thank you. For everything."

He got up and opened the door.

"Be seeing you, Cooper," he called, then nodded to Maggie. "Ma'am."

"See you, Detective." He disappeared through the door.

"Those are some burns," said Maggie, after he'd gone. "Do they hurt much?"

"They feel like burns," I said. "Of course they hurt."

"Calling the victims like that... you know, there is a word for that. Necromancy."

"I'm no neck-row... whatever you called it," I said. "I just wanted to help."

"You did," she said as she leaned down and kissed my forehead. Her neck smelled sweet and her lips were soft against my battered skin. "You're a good man, Stanley Cooper."

She crossed the room and turned out the light. For a while I drifted in and out of sleep. Whatever drug they put in the I.V. was good stuff. It gave me just the right amount of pain relief and "don't care if it hurts." It didn't matter. Somehow I knew I wouldn't see Shannon again. I glanced beside the bed and watched as scats shot across the room, doing whatever it was they did, and smiled. As my eyes closed against the drug-induced haze, I knew I wouldn't be dreaming of falling again.

About the Author

© Lily Coy Johnson

Scott A. Johnson is the author of nine novels, three true ghost story guides, a chapbook and a short story collection. He currently lives somewhere near Austin, Texas, with his wife, daughter, four cats and a pug.

For more information, look to his website at
http://www.creepylittlebastard.com

Other books by Scott A. Johnson

An American Haunting

Deadlands

Cane River: A Ghost Story

The Journal of Edwin Grey

City of Demons

Deadlands: The definitive edition

Shy Grove: A Ghost Story

The Mayor's Guide: The Stately Ghosts of Augusta

The Ghosts of San Antonio

Haunted Austin, Texas

Droplets: A Short Story Collection

The Stanley Cooper Chronicles:
    Book One - **Vermin**
    Book Two - **Pages**
    Book Three - **Ectostorm**